Cinched

Imagination Unbound

Cinched

Imagination Unbound

Edited by John G. Hartness

Falstaff Media

Cinched
Imagination Unbound
Copyright © 2015 Falstaff Books

All stories within are copyright their individual authors

This is a work of fiction. All characters and events portrayed in the contained works are fictitious or used fictitiously. All rights reserved, including the right to reproduce this book, or portions thereof, in any form.

ISBN-13: 978-1523739561
ISBN-10: 1523739568

Published by Falstaff Media
Charlotte, North Carolina

Printed in U.S.A

Table of Contents

Basque of the Red Death

Eden Royce

She looked like death, but the harsh Carolina sunshine made her look more attractive than she really was.

Helen's gait faltered as she looked up at the woman peering down on her with appraisal and undisguised distaste. Old…so old. Deep lines whittled themselves into her face, causing the chalky powder to rise to the surface of her sandpaper skin. But the woman's gaze was sharp, even weighty, and it caused Helen to stumble.

Her mother seized her arm in a mousetrap grip. "Remember what I tol' you," she growled close to the girl's ear. Her breath was loaded sour with the potent smells of dry peanut shells and day-old coffee.

"Yas'm."

The sun beat down on both of them during the walk to Miss Maggie's and sweat gathered in the girl's armpits and between her heavy thighs. It coursed down her back under the worn muslin of her dress like teasing fingers. Gnats taunted them, flying in their soaked faces, then deftly avoiding their clumsy fingers as the pair trudged along the hard-packed dirt.

After that journey, the shaded porch was almost cool. No sun reached it through the dense overhang of ancient oaks. But there was plenty enough light for Miss Maggie to pass her judgment on the trembling girl.

"Gal ain't nowhere near pretty," she said, tilting her head left then right like a bird considering a crust of bread. "No figure. And this here—" Miss Maggie leaned over the porch railing and ran a finger over the angry, inflamed pustules covering the girl's doughy white cheek. Helen flinched. Partly from the pain as several of the imbedded pimples pressed deeper into her skin and partly from the way the soft, cool fingers seemed to slide around in their thin casings of flesh. Her mother grabbed a wedge of skin at her sow-like waist and twisted it. Hot fire shot through her side, eclipsing the pain in her face, and she froze.

"Not a sound." This she muttered through compressed lips, but the dusty smell of sun baked peanuts and battery acid coffee hung in the sticky air.

Helen sank her teeth into her lower lip.

"Bumps, bad skin is a problem," Maggie continued, pressing in Helen's forehead and chin. "They're deep."

"How much?" the mother asked.

Maggie wiped her hands on a starched handkerchief and tossed the soiled fabric on the rocking chair behind her. A frail-looking girl, no more than eight or ten, dashed out of nowhere to provide a new cloth and remove the old one. "Not much."

Helen watched the girl scurry away, as silent as she had come.

"She might not help you with no mens, but she can do just as good at cleanin' and such. Better than that lil' darky, I bet. Oh…" Her mother's jaw went slack as though she remembered she'd left washing on the line. "Um…'scuse me, Miss."

If she was offended, Miss Maggie didn't show it. "I already got two for cleaning and tidying and such. Twins, in fact. Enough trouble."

"I don' need a lot. Just need to put food on the table for the young ones. We hardly got nothin' no more."

Maggie sniffed. Helen wondered if she was smelling the raw grain alcohol scent that clung to her mama. It leaked from her pores, mixing with nervous perspiration to make a rank cocktail. She'd heard the jokes about her mama when people thought she was too stupid to understand. People said Henrietta Davis would spread her legs for the right amount of moonshine, but all the still owners had ridden her bike long ago. They chuckled. Now she had to open her purse, just like everyone else wanting a taste.

"This your oldest?"

Henrietta nodded and shoved her big toe in and out of the hole in her shoe. "Oldest girl. Got a boy — most sixteen."

"Where's the boy?"

She didn't meet the older woman's eyes. "Been gone."

"Mmph." Maggie turned and opened the screened door to the house. "Bring her back with all her things tomorrow."

"How much you givin' me for her?"

"You'll find out tomorrow."

"I need the money now." Her voice rose and a wildness entered her gaze.

Unaffected, Maggie held her stare. Henrietta mumbled something and wiped her hands on her own threadbare dress. "I'll see you tomorrow, then." To her daughter, she growled, "Come on, now."

"No, you leave her with me."

Henrietta's doughy mouth opened around worn, ragged teeth like leaning tombstones. "She goin' home with me."

"Mama, I—"

The ringing slap made the girl's eyes water. The tang of blood was in her mouth like she'd sucked on a new penny.

"You want your money, she will stay with me overnight."

Maggie chuckled. "Don't tell me you can't find something to do with yourself for one night?" She lifted a silver pendant shaped like an old style corset, complete with tiny hook and eye closures, from where it rested against her bosom. The bodice popped open and she glanced inside. "Ten to six. Skeet's Hardware closes soon. See what he might have for you."

To Helen's surprise, her mother trudged away without another word, presumably to talk with Mister Skeet. Miss Maggie looked down at her where she stood on the dry hard-packed earth, sweating and stinging and terrified. The black woman's eyes betrayed nothing when she spoke.

"What's your name, gal?"

"Helen, ma'am."

"Well, one day we're gonna have to change that."

He was tall, dark, and an imbecile. But he had money inherited from parents that had long ago established their importance to Charleston society, so everyone ignored his lack of sense. His flagrant disregard of the law and his cruelty they also overlooked.

"Jenkins!" His voice bordered on shrill as it rang through the historic house, reaching the third level where his house servant remade beds, replacing torn and bloodied linens as needed. "Get down here right now."

Despite his advanced years, Jenkins made it to the first floor library before his name could be called again. "Yes, Mister Darlington, sir?"

Darlington held out his half empty glass, his feet never moving from their elevated position on the ottoman, and Jenkins refilled it with brandy.

"Have you contacted that woman to arrange for the party?"

"Yes, sir. I've been in contact with her on your behalf. But she still needs to know more to make your…selections." The servant's heavy-lidded rheumy eyes were impassive and his speech was slow, carefully precise, as though he rarely spoke so eloquently.

Darlington frowned. He hated having to prompt his staff. They should know his wishes, even anticipate them, and have them fulfilled before he thought to ask. And Jenkins had been with the Darlington family since before he was born. His father had purchased the slave from a cotton merchant in the upstate. Ungrateful shit. He'd be damned if he would let some foolhardy Yankee calling himself President tell him how to handle his property.

Reason reared its well-coiffed head. *Jenkins knows about your preferences, keep him close. He was loyal to this family and that isn't going to stop unless you make a mugger of it. Take good care.*

Bryce Darlington had never listened to reason. "Don't be stupid, man. Young, untouched, narrow waist, long hair. It's the same every time." He gulped the brandy down in one swallow. "And nothing darker than an octoroon. I can't stand that scent the full Negresses have."

"Yes, sir."

He nudged at the trembling, naked girl crouched on the floor with his foot and she wailed, a sound full of raw pain. "And get rid of this. I'm done."

"Yes, sir."

The girl pleaded with him as he dragged her out of the house, but he tried to close his ears to her. He was old now, tired—so tired—of this mess. Tired of spiriting away these girls—little more than children anyways—through the night like they were headed for the Underground Railroad.

"Don't! No…no…help me."

"Too late for that now, innit girl? Already messed up now." As he looked at her by the wobbly light of the small gas lantern, the bruises on her body covered by an old sheet, he saw that she had been pretty. Too bad they never left Master Darlington that way. He felt no other sympathy. Women had to bear the weight of men's lusts or stay away from them.

"I didn't do anything wrong." Her cries were now whimpers. "Where are you taking me?"

"Back home. Leave you outside the door."

"I can't go home. My — my mama won't have me back."

They rarely did. Only if they were stolen from their beds in the middle of the night would they be welcomed back. Once they left home, or more likely, were sold for a few dollars, the door to their childhood was closed forever. "Then there's only one other place for you."

Old habit made Jenkins knock on the door to the slave entrance of the big house. Although the plantation house now belonged to Miss Maggie, he never felt right walking up the front steps. The ghost of Massa was still too fresh. He knew deep down it always would be.

In the rooms, on the steps of the plantation house, in the yard by the oak tree. Although the only ropes hanging on the ancient oak held a handmade wooden seat swing. In the fragmented light of the lantern, he saw the child's plaything move, swinging back and forth in an aching creak that made his knees like water and his heart flutter like a bird's. *Remember, this is for Mass — Mister Darlington.* He turned away.

Rapping his large, age-swollen knuckles on the hard wood made him wince. Winter would be here soon. Quick yet methodic steps sounded inside and a set of smooth-skinned twins appeared at the opening of the door. They glanced at each other and before Jenkins could speak, one of them took the broken girl by the hand and whispered to her. The girl nodded, sagging with relief or exhaustion, Jenkins couldn't tell which, and they padded off silently down a darkened hallway.

The other twin motioned for him to follow and led Jenkins through the recessed servant entrance to the main rooms of the plantation house. Gone were the oil paintings depicting the austere faces of former masters; their disapproving gazes had given Jenkins a reminder of his place each time he had come here for errands when Mister Darlington Senior was a younger man. Instead, colorful fabrics adorned the walls, framed as though they were masterful artworks.

The twin led him to a richly carpeted sitting room where Maggie sat, smoking a long thin pipe. She was surrounded by headless mannequin bodies, their middles all draped with bright corsets in various states of completion. Her fingers pulled a thick needle through the embroidered fabric, each stitch leaving a worrisome pop in the air as it pierced. He had for a brief moment the need to defer to her, but he quelled it. She was no better than he was despite her money.

"Maggie." He addressed her by her given name and forced away the tendril of fear that it brought to him.

She didn't react to the flagrant disrespect but responded with a formality that made his rudeness seem almost as violent as an attack. "Mister Jenkins, what can I do for you?" Her hair was twisted into an elaborate network of braids that she seemed to be duplicating on the scarlet material. He pulled his gaze away. It would not be good if he got himself caught in one of Miss Maggie's designs. Not good at all.

"Massa—I mean, Mister Darlington wanna throw a party." His former practiced eloquence was gone, replaced by a Pidgin English that chose only essential words to convey meaning. "He sen' me here to—"

"Another one? I told him I was not supplying him any longer. He does not know how to take care of things that do not belong to him."

Jenkins couldn't have agreed more. No Darlington cared about the property of anyone else, unless it was when they were working on a plan to take it away from the owner. Then once they'd gotten it—the land, the business, the woman—they had to destroy it. He'd seen it happen to slaves and free men alike. "I'm jus' to make arrangements, is all."

"Here in the dead of night?" Maggie snorted. "But how else would it be done? I know you can't read—not well, anyway—and even if you could, your *Master*," she coughed and spat sputum into a handkerchief, "would never allow any written communication about such a delicate subject. Nothing that could show up somewhere embarrassing."

Jenkins didn't reply.

"People say that boy is an idiot, but to me his doings is sly, too plotted for a fool to carry out. No… he wears the fool's cap only when it suits." She took a breath. "No more arrangements. No more parties. No more girls."

An owl called in the woods outside, its cry shattering the cricket song. Jenkins's voice was surprisingly gentle as he replied. "You know what he gon' do to you if you refuse." Fabric rustled, but the sound seemed far away to him now. "And what he gon' do to me for bringin' the message."

The tender hum of the night returned slowly, accompanied by the pop and drag of the needle and thread through the fabric.

"I know, Thomas. I know."

He hadn't heard his given name, the one his mama used to whisper to him as she rocked him in her arms, in too long. Tears pricked at his eyes, but he straightened his back and held on, silent.

A few more stitches and she asked, "How is the girl?"

"Messed up. Inside and out this time."

The needle sank into the age-softened flesh of her finger and a drop of ruby blood pooled on the skin. She touched it to the fabric and it disappeared into the cloth. Maggie nodded. "How many?"

"'Bout six or seven. He got some really high up men plannin' on comin'."

"Seven then. What day?"

"Two weeks from Saturday."

"Fine." He looked up and one of the twins had returned to hold the door open for his departure. "This will be the last time, Thomas."

"Yes, ma'am." He turned and rushed from the plantation house, fleeing to the harsh, unreliable protection of his master.

Maggie watched as Jenkins, then his shadow, disappeared down the hall. "Get Helen up." The twin scurried off.

With measured slowness, Maggie crossed the room, her hands caressing each of the dress forms in turn. Each corset handmade for the girl that would wear it. A little something extra stitched into the lining of each creation. Laces and silks and heavy brocaded fabrics and hours of back breaking work. Darlington's other sources for girls must have dried up, as he had not come to her in over a year. She picked up one bolt of coutil, tested its strength, then chose another, stronger fabric.

Helen appeared in the doorway, eyes heavy and mouth

hanging open. Her thick waistline stretched the seams of the brushed cotton nightdress she wore, making it too short to cover her completely. "Come here gal, looks like I finally might have a use for you."

"But I can't sew a'tall, Miss Maggie."

The older woman tore off a length of the tightly woven cloth and wrapped it around the girl, measuring her girth. She nodded then took a piece of coal from the bin next to the fireplace and scraped it against the material, sketching out five long, bent rectangles. Then she gave the impromptu pattern to the slack-jawed girl. "Cut this out for me. See here? Can you do that?"

Helen stared, confused.

"Can you do it?" she repeated. "It's important that you have your hand in this."

"Yes'm," she whispered.

"Good. Sit here now." Helen sat in a corner of the sitting room, legs splayed, to concentrate on her task. Maggie nudged her legs closed with the tip of her heeled boot. "You don't open your legs until everything's just about said and done. Might as well learn that now."

When Helen finished, she held up five bent rectangle strips of plain cotton material. "Excellent work," the older woman nodded as her fingers traced over the pattern pieces.

The girl smiled, her pleasure making her face more homely than before. Without thinking, she put a hand to her face to press and pick at the inflamed red and white pimples. Miss Maggie's treatment of wiping her face daily with warm urine had lessened the angry redness, but the swollen pustules returned whenever she stopped the ritual.

"No, none of that now. We don't have much time and we need you to be perfect."

"Perfect for what?"

Maggie smiled.

Hours later, Miss Maggie looked up from where she knelt sorting through silks and linens in her sitting room, surrounded by the headless, armless dress forms and Helen's heart stuttered. She didn't know why, but she felt something move, outside her, circling her, sniffing. Miss Maggie pulled out a roll of black satin, slick as spilled ink. The fabric seemed to absorb the light in the room, feeding on it and growing more beautiful. "This corset will be yours, gal. You will wear it, but we will make it together."

Helen crawled over and touched the silky blackness where it lay shimmering on the older woman's lap. "Mine?" Any thought of fear was gone.

"Yes, you'll be going to a party and you'll have to dress up. Will you wear it?"

"Like a real lady?" She'd seen Miss Maggie's girls leave the plantation in carriages, dressed in their finery and had craved being that beautiful, that wanted...useful. The girl's hand traveled to her face again and this time, Maggie didn't stop her. "Yes'm — I mean — yes, ma'am."

"Good. Now here, take this." The needle was brutally sharp and drew blood the instant Helen touched it. "No matter. Just press it on the coutil." When the girl hesitated, Miss Maggie pushed on. "This will go under the black fabric, no one will see it."

Helen pressed the blood from her finger to the cloth, leaving tiny red dots. Then she pressed the strip of fabric to her cheek, enjoying the way the textured cloth felt against her skin. It scraped gently, taking away a little of the constant needling itch of her face. The coutil came away with scarlet smears that quickly darkened into rust brown.

"Now we begin," Maggie said.

For twelve days they worked on the corset after the house had gone to bed. The inner lining of coutil had become stiff and hard with dried blood, but the black satin, now edged with black velvet darker than a crow's eye covered it perfectly. Helen's fingers were sore and painful, but she hadn't stopped the basic backstitch Maggie had shown her that first night. When she washed dishes, each fingertip stung like fire ant bites, but she didn't care. She was going to be a lady. Ladies wore beautiful things. They were useful.

The next day after dinner, Maggie called her into the sitting room. "Time to try it on, gal." Helen hesitated in taking off her dress in front of Maggie and the twins, who had spoken little to her since her arrival almost six months before. But now they delicately lifted the heavy basque corset from the dress form and held it for her to step into. Maggie watched silently.

As the twin girls molded the corset to her body, a weightiness covered her. It was heavy…so heavy and she could barely keep herself upright. Then the twins laced the velvet-covered cord through the eyelet rings and she almost giggled at the brushing tickle it left on her skin. Then they pulled. Each girl took a cord in both of their small, strong hands and tightened. Helen gasped and without thinking clasped the edge of the mantelpiece to keep her balance. The steel stays pressed in against her ribcage, their cold metal forming to her body. Her breasts, forced into the basque's formed cups, felt caged. Inside, she felt hot, burning, her organs crushed into grotesque, unnatural shapes. She moaned, but the sound came out as a breathy gasp, her lungs unable to expand further.

"It's perfect."

Helen looked around the room trying to verify Maggie's declaration, but there was no mirror. Finally, in the polished glass of the window, she caught a glimpse of herself. She seemed to float in the corset, black surrounding her in its elegance. Her skin, once fish belly colored, now glowed with moon-like paleness. In the watery reflection of the darkened window, even her face held smoothness. Was this what it felt like to be beautiful? Was this the power it had?

Then it was whisked away as the twins moved to loosen the stays and remove the garment. Her breath and belly came back with a grunt and she felt back to herself — and strangely bereft of…something.

"A little more work to do, then it will be ready. Go on back to your room now. I'll bring it to you when I'm done."

Helen stood there, still in her cotton drawers, flat breasts now lying against her belly. Slowly, she slipped back into her nightdress and padded down the hallway. She passed the rooms of the other girls that would be going to the party on Saturday night. Their corsets were already completed and draped over a dress form in each of their rooms. Navy blue hung in Esther's room, and purple in Deborah's. Ashley's red hair likely got her the forest green, but Helen didn't care for the orange creation — it was too bright and sparkly, more like a circus performer than a lady. White was assigned to the new girl, who hadn't spoken since she arrived, and violet stood in Camellia's room.

Camellia had fought not to go to the party. She wanted nothing to do with clothes or dances. Helen couldn't understand why she wouldn't want to wear the things Miss Maggie made for the other girls. They got to ride in carriages and sleep late the next day after. Despite Camellia's scratching and spitting, she was going to the party. Miss Maggie had slapped her while the twins held her arms—they were so strong, stronger than they looked at their tender age of nine—and then leaned down to whisper something in her ear. After that, Camellia had slumped forward, drained of all energy. The corset and its matching organza skirt, in a violet exactly like fresh lavender, now resided in her bedroom. As Helen walked tentatively by, she saw the limp form crumpled on the narrow bed.

"Ain't you happy to go out?"

"What are you, stupid?" Camellia snapped from under the bedspread. When she saw Helen there, she softened. "Oh. No, I'm not. If I had any other way to live, I would."

"But you get nice things. Clothes and your hair did."

"Do you know why?"

Helen shook her head.

"Never mind. You wouldn't understand anyway." She shrugged off Helen's bumbling attempt at a comforting touch. "Just…just be glad you aren't…" She threw the limp goose feather pillow, flat from sweat and hair preparations, on the floor. "Be glad you don't have to go. I'd rather die than bear that again. Know what the funny thing is?"

"No." Fingers to the face. Picking. Camellia turned away.

"The funny thing is I'm too yellow to do it myself. Know what yellow means?"

This she did know. "Means scared."

"Yeah. Scared. One thing you should never be is scared. Makes you a little dead inside, you know? And dead is something you either want all of or none of. A little bit is no good."

Helen stood in the hall staring at the door long after Camellia ushered her out with the excuse that she had to get ready for bed. When her feet started to get cold, she shuffled back to her room.

The next evening, Miss Maggie brought the finished corset

to Helen's room. There was no dress form; she walked into the room with her creation draped over her outstretched arms. She lay it on the single bed and closed the door. A long, black silk skirt, reaching to the floor attached to the ornate basque. Helen touched it reverently, unable to believe that it was hers.

"This is…mine?"

Maggie inhaled. "Yes, if you choose to take it on."

"Put it on?"

"Both, child." Her voice was weary, but resolute. "If you choose to wear this, and it is your choice — to go to this party — you must know that you will be unlike any other girl there."

Helen reached for the garment again, but Maggie took her hand. "This is important. Wearing this corset will change you as I've added…something old to it." She felt Maggie's hand again, the soft, cool fingers sliding around in their thin casings of flesh. Her look seemed desperate, pleading for her agreement. "You need to understand why — "

"Do you want me to wear it?"

Startled by the interruption, she answered honestly. "Yes, I do. You're a good girl, Helen, I never — "

Helen felt a surge within her. Determination, resolve, it didn't matter. It made her feel like she knew what to do. How to help. She smiled and it was almost lovely. "Will it make me useful to you?"

"Very," Maggie whispered.

"I'll wear it."

The needles sank into her breasts and stomach when Maggie pulled the cord tight, piercing and sending their ancient magic deep into her muscles, her bones, changing her. Helen did not scream.

Midnight. The grandfather clock chimed in the front hall of the palatial home on the Battery, Charleston's elite locale. Facing the water, the house looked out onto Charleston Harbour and all her glory.

The carriage came and went and Helen stepped onto the walkway, up the stairs and into the Darlington house. Black satin swept the floor with swishes like a paintbrush. Sweep, scrape. Sweep, scrape.

Walk in, Miss Maggie had said. *Walk in and speak to no one. Look at no one. Keep walking 'til you can't walk anymore.*

The door opened as she raised her hand. The heavy oak doors swung wide, allowing her to enter. Inside the party was in full force. Gas lamps lit the interior down the paneled hallways. Laughter and music clashed with the clinking of glasses. The sound flowed around and over her now, not penetrating her cloak of purpose. Heavy, gilt-edged mirrors reflected a face—pale, china white, run through with dark veins like expensive cheese—and a wine stain gaze that left its mark on the flocked walls.

From a side door, a servant appeared. An older Negro man, his features at first looked exasperated: one of the girls had not joined the party on time and he marched toward her. As he got closer, his purposeful step faltered. "I—I—uh..." His words failed him as she drew near, her steps never varying. She watched as the servant drew himself back, curling inward like a dying bloom, to hide from this beautiful monstrosity before him. Another part, one fashioned from years of beatings and neck under shoe heel grinding, surfaced under her gaze like a new seedling. The need to run. Run and tell Massa...'bout this...this thing.

Stop.

The word shook him roughly. No movement on her face, save for the veins as they lifted and lowered the pustule-covered skin, but he knew it was she that spoke. From the bottom of the garment, waves of lush fabric rolled to the floor. But as the sea air blew around the grounds and through the windows of the house, the skirt shifted and billowed, revealing nothing under the bound torso.

"Jesus…at your feet, Jesus." The rest of the words petered out, nonsensical gibberish, as Jenkins let his bladder and bowels and his tears go.

The guest in the black corset continued up the stairs and into the house.

Merriment rang in the halls as Darlington's friends enjoyed their party, weighted with drink and lust. The girls were beautiful, frightened butterflies, pressing themselves against the windows seeking freedom in vain.

"Green!" Darlington's voice rang out over the revelers' excitement. "Who is the lucky winner? Whose ticket is green?"

"Mine!" Shouts swelled around the reply and shuffling of the guests, all men in formal dress, began.

Impatient, the host asked again. "Who is it?"

A portly man maneuvered his way through the throng of guests in the ballroom, waving the winning ticket. His suit was impeccably tailored, but it did little to conceal the ropes of sweat ringing the armpits and crotch. "She's mine," he announced, reaching for the girl dressed in forest green silk.

"The young lady is mine for the evening, in fact." Another green card popped up above the crowd much to the awe of the guests. Whispers started, rumors grew. Was this on purpose or an accident? It had never happened before.

Darlington bit back his ire. Jenkins would get his for this mistake. Two of the same colored cards in round one? The night had just begun. He would have to address it, make it look intentional. Make it his triumph. "Fellows, I see my little twist has come to light early."

Murmurs swelled first, then receded, mirroring the tide outside the doors. "Tonight you are partners. Enjoy her together or in relay as you will." Darlington smiled what he hoped what a reassuring smile. "Off to the green room with you. Orange! Who is holding the ticket orange? Step up and take your girl."

One lay claim to the girl in orange, and as Darlington circled her waist with his hands to lift her away from the platform and into the winner's waiting grasp, a movement caught his eye from the long aisle running along the length of the top floor. Was it Jenkins? The old fool had not been up to check with him in far too long. But then he heard the swish of skirt, cloth dragged against the ground. Another girl? Possibly. He hadn't planned for that, but there were plenty of men that would enjoy a new…face.

He pushed the one in the orange corset, rough with embedded jewels, to its new owner and stepped away from his party. Forgetting to make his polite excuses, he heard the rumbling of his guests but ignored them. How dare anyone thwart him in his own house? A woman to boot, dressed in black like a new widow. He wanted color, liveliness, bright girlish blushes. He pushed past those milling about in the grand ballroom, examining his selections for the evening, pinching a bit décolleté here and squeezing a bit of bottom there.

He rounded the open double doors and turned in the direction the girl had gone. Was she so stupid that she couldn't find the party? Worse, had that woman given him a deaf girl? He wouldn't pay for a broken one. He refused to play with broken toys. There she was passing the second archway down the hall. He hadn't seen this one before. She seemed to glide along, head erect, not looking at all of the glorious things around her. Gilded paintings adorned the baroque style architecture, complete with marble columns and large scale ceiling frescoes.

"Stop!" Her pace didn't alter as she continued through the third archway. Graceful, elegant. He found himself wanting to know, wanting to see her face. Don't run. Not you. Even so, he quickened his pace to catch up with her. Later, he might show her what it meant to be a girl purchased for the night, but first his curiosity must be satisfied, then his loins. He'd have her, show her that she was playing a role — that of a beautiful ornament crafted for amusement and nothing more. A role that she could be stripped off as easily as he could rip her clothing.

His heart beat faster, anger firing in his chest, and he pursued the woman — he thought it must be a woman now, no young girl would have that much poise, that much insolence — through his home. Through the floor to ceiling windows, he caught reflected glimpses of her, a white arm, inky hair, then it was gone before his eyes could fully conceive of her.

He ran, against his earlier judgment, but even with his quickened pace, he could barely keep her in sight. Five, six arches, curving around the side of the house, passing several rooms of either side. He'd have her soon. His cock leapt at the thought. One more arch and she'd reach the end of the hall, where heavy wooden doors closed off the final room. There he'd corner her.

The guest in black glided through the door at the end of the hall, not disturbing it from its hinges. Inside, the room itself was cast in dark shadows from the moonlight washing in through the drawn curtains. With her touch, candles flared to life bringing into view quilted red velvet furniture, heavy and ornate, and a grandfather clock.

Helen sat on a red chaise longue and waited for him to join her. Her mind was clear, no thoughts. Not of the party, not of the crushing tightness of the corset. Of what he would do to her, she had no cares. She lay on the chaise, moonlight reverently falling on the black basque where it hugged her now shrunken waist.

When he reached the room and wrenched the massive door open, he was panting. Darlington's breath came hard, wheezing through his lungs, as his narrow silhouette entered the doorway. "You dirty muck wench," he huffed, gulping in lungfuls of stale air. "How did you even get in here? I had to—no matter." Breath returning, he grinned and entered the room, closing the door behind him. "You're here now. Can't wait to teach you some manners."

He inched closer to her and Helen could smell him, smell his disease. As the shifting light from the moon danced with the candles, she could almost see it. There. Flowing through him, imbedded below the flesh, in the muscle, into the bone. But he was right, it didn't matter.

Not now.

"But I have my priorities," Darlington continued, loosening the waist of his trousers. "Must fill up that little notch of yours first."

He stepped forward, eager for a taste of new flesh. Helen turned her face away, but he grasped it in one hand as he fished under the voluminous skirts with the other. The corset shuddered, squeezed, finally revealing to the sputtering candlelight the mottled splotches of blood decorating the fabric. The grisly pattern shone through the layers of satin, of velvet.

His grin of victory froze as he turned her to face him, the fine webbing of veins crossing her skin pulsing with another, deadlier disease. His hand under the skirt fished of its own accord, seeking even in the midst of what his eyes told him wasn't—couldn't— be possible. Darlington's feeble mind couldn't process, couldn't understand... nothing. There was nothing. Where her puss should have been, that soft, warm cavern, was emptiness.

A whimper escaped him as his cock deflated, shrinking back, hiding in a futile attempt to escape. The veins rose from Helen's face, reached out to him, searching for the best place to enter. They writhed in glee at the many, many possible orifices and finally chose them all.

What disease?

Helen didn't know, but it began to consume him from the inside. He made no sound—couldn't, as the veins had worked their way into his mouth first—but Helen could see the pain. She observed it from a mental distance, recording his agony, memorizing his gurgling fear.

Moment later, he fell to the floor, desiccated, a husk of dusty skin.

The clock struck midnight again and what was once Helen looked up, stood, and stepped over her host's carcass. Somewhere inside she hoped the girls in their beautifully colored corsets would survive her—those that wanted to, of course—but her own lacings tightened again, sucking, squeezing out every desire except the need to return to the party.

Cazadora

Andrea Judy

Flowers fill the cemetery for Anna-Leigh, and even after the mourners leave, the scent of fresh blossoms lingers in my nose as I sit on the ground and pick at the petals. A travelling merchant had dropped off most of the flowers before he'd hit the road to go further west.

"You shouldn't be dead," I say, the fourth time I've said that today. "You just shouldn't be."

The dirt doesn't offer a response.

"We were gonna get married and have kids all at the same time. How am I suppose to turn fourteen without you?" I ask the silent patch of dirt marking her grave, but it doesn't offer any answers.

Whatever haunts our deserts takes too much. Not even the men who wrangle up the cattle go out alone at night. Anna-Leigh shouldn't have been out that night, not by herself, not for anything. A mistake because she wanted to get some flowers grown by the moonlight. She told me if you slept with them under your pillow, you'd see who you were going to marry.

I didn't believe her, and now she's dead.

I rub my eyes. Tears can't fall anymore; they were gone hours before the funeral even started. They dried up right after I heard those terrible words that the beast of the desert killed my friend.

Anna-Leigh's the third victim this month, and there doesn't seem to be an end in sight. The men go out hunting for it every night, but all they ever find are hints, noises in the brushes, footprints in the sand, and trails of blood that lead them to its latest prey. Sometimes it's just a poor cow, or buffalo, but sometimes it's people like Anna-Leigh.

"I'm gonna stop whatever this thing is," I promise my friend's gravestone, wiping my eyes even though there aren't any tears left to fall. "I'm gonna find it and-and..."

"And do what, child?" a woman's voice asks.

I turn around to see a woman standing at the edge of the cemetery. She is dressed in white and gray with breeches that hang along her long legs. A hat hides her face, but the thing that most draws my eyes is the corset around her waist.

It's the most beautiful thing I've ever seen: all lined in silver satin that glimmers in the setting sun's lingering light. The clasps on the front are an antique bronze with flecks of patina on them. The seams glimmer with a soft white-gold light that makes the entire garment sparkle. Panels of lace stitched into both sides of the corset hold two small guns.

I've never seen a corset before in my life, just heard stories about them from some of the vendors who pass through town from time to time. It looks like something otherworldly.

The woman clears her throat, and I look up at her. "I want to kill the thing that killed my friend," I finally say with as much force behind my voice as I can manage.

The woman tilts her head, and the shadows roll across her face. She has darkly tanned skin like mine.

"That is much for you to take on, my child." She walks over to my side and looks over the grave with me.

A flower appears in her hand, and she drops it on top of the fresh grave.

"I can do it," I say as I stand up and pull the hem of my dress down a bit.

"You have hunted before?" she asks me.

"Dad's taught me how to shoot. I can hit a bottle off the fence easy." I puff my chest up.

She laughs; it's a dark sound, like a storm starting to build across the desert.

"Shooting is not the same as hunting. A bottle does not bleed or scream when you hit it," she tells me simply, still facing ahead towards the gravestone we are both looking at now.

I swallow hard and try to imagine what hearing something die might sound like, but I can't. All I can think about is Anna-Leigh being killed. How loud must she have screamed?

I shake the image from my head. "I think I can do it."

"If you think you can, you have already lost," the woman tells me. "Thinking accomplishes nothing."

"Who are you?" I finally ask.

"My name is Maria. Who are you?" she asks.

"Aiva. Are you visiting Hopewell?"

Maria shifts her weight on her feet. "I came to hunt the creature."

I look up at her. "You? You're a hunter?"

She nods her head, hat still firmly in place, shadows still obscuring her face from my view.

"So you chase after bad things that come from somewhere else?" I ask.

The woman tilts her head then answers. "I do. I hunt down those things that have no place in this world, and I'm going to send them back to where they belong."

"And where is that?"

"Not here," she says.

"Do you know what it is?" I ask. "Is it a monster?"

Maria doesn't immediately answer my question, and instead just stands in silence for nearly a minute. Just as I'm about to give up, she answers. "That depends on what you think a monster is."

I frown. "Everyone knows what a monster is. Something bad that hurts people and does bad things."

"So does that mean that a man who comes to your home and shoots at your family is a monster too? Or just this thing that does not belong in your world?" she asks.

I shake my head. "I don't know if people are monsters. Monsters are...they're things that aren't people that do bad things and cause a lot of trouble for everyone."

The woman nods her head. "If that is how you define a monster, then yes, this creature would be considered a monster."

"What do you think a monster is?" I ask, looking up at her.

She takes another long few moments to answer. "I think a monster is anything that hurts people that do not deserve it," she finally answers. "Whether that creature be man, woman, child or beast. What face it wears does not make it a beast."

"So, is that why you're hunting down those things?" I ask. "Because they hurt Anna-Leigh?"

She nods.

"Can I help you?"

She shakes her head. "No, child, you should go home where it's safe."

"But I want to help you!" I protest.

Maria shakes her head again. "Go home, little one," she says, turning and walking towards a horse waiting at the edge of the cemetery.

When the horse spots Maria, the gray mare's ears perk up.

Maria climbs on, adjusts her weight on the saddle, and then turns back towards me. "Home, little one," she orders once more before she and her horse canter towards the town, moving slowly out of my sight.

"My papa runs the inn! It's got the yellow door!" I call after her.

I stare after them for several long seconds, watching the glint of her corset until it disappears fully from my view. Grabbing my shoes and throwing them back on, I race for home. My father's got to know about hunting monsters.

The bar and inn my family run stay empty. Ever since travelers started spreading the word about the monster in the desert, not even the lure of mining has helped bring people in.

Taking the short cut through the fields, instead of the winding trail into town, I make it back home in just a few minutes.

"Papa!" I yell as I run inside.

My father nearly drops the glass he's washing out. "Where have you been?"

"Papa, there is a woman here and she is going to kill the monster that killed Anna-Leigh!" I run over to him.

He sighs and puts the glass he's cleaning down. "Aiva."

"No, really, she's here! I told her to come see you and we could give her a place to stay!"

He looks up as the door opens and Maria steps inside. She bows her head. "A room for the night if you please."

My father stares at her and then to me. All I can do is beam. "I told you! She's going to kill the monster!" I tell him.

"One night?" he asks Maria.

She nods and walks up to the bar.

Papa goes over pricing with her while I sit on a bar stool and watch her. Her corset's beautiful even in the dull light of the bar. It still glimmers like it's made out of pieces of stars all stitched together. I want one like it, but I don't even know where to find a corset. There isn't anyone in town who even owns something like that.

I sigh softly as Maria hands over her money and walks up the stairs to her room. I look to Papa and smile. "I told you she was coming."

"Just because she's staying the night doesn't mean she's hunting anything," he tells me.

I shake my head. "You just don't want to say I was right."

He sighs. "Aiva, I need you to get in the kitchen and help your mother with dinner, all right?"

"Yes, sir."

He shoos me off, and I run around the bar and into the kitchen. Mama already is cooking, so I step in beside her to help get some potatoes peeled and tossed into a pot.

But my mind is on Maria and her corset. Something about it keeps singing to me, drawing itself back into my thoughts again and again. I nearly slice the palm of my hand because my thoughts are scattered and anywhere but with the peeling of the potatoes in front of me.

"If you can't pay attention in here then go do laundry, Aiva. You are slowing me down," my mother tells me.

"Yes ma'am," I tell her before I run off to gather up the laundry and head outside to wash it in the nearby creek.

I wonder if Maria is from a big city where all the women wear corsets like that or maybe if it's just something that has been passed down by her family. Maybe someone gave it to her as payment for hunting down some other monsters. I glance up towards Maria's room and am surprised to see she is looking out the window towards the creek and me. I'm almost positive that she's watching me, so I turn back to the laundry, carefully getting everything wet and washing it clean.

The currents are a little rough, but I don't fall in and I even manage to not get myself completely soaked. Next I hang everything on the lines set up in the back, and by the time I'm finishing up, Mama's yelling for me to get back inside and collect the guest.

I approach Maria's door and smooth out my dress before I knock on the door. "Ma'am?" I call. "It's supper time. If you're hungry, we have some stew ready."

I step back as the door opens and Maria looks out at me. "Thank you," she says after a moment. "You were out in that water earlier?"

I nod. "Just doing laundry. Did the noise bother you?"

She shakes her head. "You should be careful out there."

"I'm always careful, ma'am. Don't worry, it doesn't have much of a current."

"A current isn't the only thing that can drown a child in the water," she says before shutting the door and stepping into the hallway beside me.

I glance at her and realize that her corset isn't on. Instead, a loose blouse, still in a soft white, hides her mid-section. I swallow hard and smile as I guide Maria down to the dining room table where Mama already has everything laid out.

Papa sits at the head of the table and bows his head to say prayer; Maria doesn't bow her head or even close her eyes for prayer.

"Amen," Papa says, opening his eyes and digging into his food.

Maria eats a few bites, and then Papa starts questioning her about where she's from and what she's doing here. Papa doesn't like women traveling on their own.

As they continue talking, I slide out of my chair, murmuring something about cleaning some dishes. Once I'm out of sight, I rush back up the stairs so quickly I nearly trip over my own feet in getting back to Maria's room. I've already got a skeleton key on me so I can help Mama keep the inn clean, so opening the door is easy.

One small black bag sits on the floor of the otherwise empty room. My heart's hammering in my chest, but I step inside and shut the door behind me before rushing over to the bag and starting to riffle through it.

As I'm carefully pulling out another white blouse from her bag, I catch a glimmer of light and put the bag down. Sitting on the corner of the bed is the corset. The fabric looks so light that the only thing I can imagine it's made of is the mist that rolls off of the water in the early morning.

Shaking hands reach out and touch the shimmering gray fabric. The warmth, like a living thing's skin, hits my fingertips and I jerk back. My heart roars in my ears, and I take a sharp, shuddering gasp for air. Fabric that's been off of a body shouldn't be this warm.

"It is quite rude to break into someone's room and go through her things."

I look up to Maria standing in the doorway, leaning against the frame with her arms crossed over her chest.

"I-I-I'm sorry!" I blurt out, taking several quick steps back, tripping over the bag of clothes and hitting the ground.

Maria walks into the room and over to my side, looking down at me. "I didn't take you for this rude of a child."

I swallow hard. "I'm not. I just—" I motion helplessly to the shimmering fabric on the edge of the bed. "I've never seen a corset before."

Maria tilts her head, then nods. "You like the corset then?"

She walks over to bed, picks it up, and wraps it back around her waist. The clasps click back into place. Then she turns to me. "Would you like to help me tighten it?"

"Y-Yes ma'am!" I say, quickly getting back to my feet, brushing myself off.

She turns her back to me. "See those strings? Take them and pull."

My heart's still racing as I grab the strings and carefully start pulling, gently at first then I give a tug with all my might.

The corset knits together and then is still; it looks flush against her waist like it's part of her skin and bone.

"Now tie it," she tells me.

It takes a few attempts for me to get the thin strings to stay together, and my knot looks like a piece of garbage that somehow got caught against her back, but she doesn't mind or tell me to redo it.

"Thank you. Now get on out of here and go help your parents."

I nod and scramble out of the room, pulling the door shut behind me. I lean against the wall, gasping for air. If she tells my parents that I was in her room without her permission, I'm in trouble. But it didn't seem like my being in there had upset her too much, so I'll have to hope she won't tell my parents she caught me in her room.

Back downstairs, I silently go to help Mama clean the dishes and then go to my room for bed. I just change into my roughhousing clothes, some jeans and a shirt that's too stained to be worn out in public again, and then hide under my covers.

Mama comes and tucks me in, kissing my forehead then blowing out the candle beside my bed. I wait until the house goes quiet and no more light creeps in from under my door then I creep out of bed.

I carefully collect my papa's gun from behind the bar and strap it around my back. The weight presses into my spine, slightly painful, but I can ignore it as long as I focus on going out and hunting down the thing that killed my friend.

Sitting on the edge of the porch, I wait in the total darkness. Not even the stars are out to give me any kind of light; instead, clouds roll around overhead, blotting out any bit of light the moon tries to give me. The door behind me opens and I hear the soft scrape of boots against wood.

Standing up, I turn around to find Maria staring at me, one hand on the gun in her corset. "What are you doing out here child?" she asks.

"I want to help," I insist. "I've got my own gun. I can help, I promise, just let me go with you."

"Child, this is not a fight for you," she tells me, shaking her head again as she walks past me and out to her waiting horse.

"But I—"

"A gun does not make one ready for war," she answers before I can finish talking. "You should stay here with your family. The darkness does not take kindly to those who wander out of their homes this late."

"But I have to help!"

She doesn't let me get any closer before she's already mounting her horse and steering the large mare onto the path. "Goodnight, child. May your sweet dreams keep the monsters away."

Her horse snorts softly and then she's down the path and quickly out of my sight.

Heart hammering in my chest, I shift on my feet, and hesitate just for a moment. I swallow hard, curling my fingers into my fists. I don't care what she says. I have to find what killed my friend. I adjust the strap of the gun over my back and head after her. I know the path well enough that the lack of light doesn't stop me, just makes me stumble over a few sand dunes.

The first howl echoes across the desert, low and distant enough that it doesn't set my heart into immediate panic. Instead, I just walk a little faster towards where I think she's gone. The path is a little less sure now, and doubt makes my feet heavy against the sand, but I keep walking. The light of home is behind me now, and I am not turning back.

I take a deep breath, pull the gun from my back holster, and keep my finger ready on the trigger. I don't know how much good a gun will be against something that isn't supposed to even be real. I just hope when I do find it I'll be ready for it.

I hope.

Another howling screech rolls around the air and feels like a breeze cutting against my skin, too cold to be natural this time of year. I wrap my arms across my chest and walk a little faster. I hear a horse up ahead. I've got to be close by now.

The next screech snaps right against my ear, and I don't even look before I run.

I might have left my heart standing behind me as I run because I certainly can't feel it beating in my chest even as I sprint towards what I hope is safety. The city is lost behind me, all lights burnt out against the blackness of the night sky that twists around me like a blanket drawn to suffocate, not soothe.

Something burns against the back of my leg, white-hot daggers cutting into skin, flesh and bone. Without looking, I kick and feel my leg hit something solid that grunts and then flies backwards. The pain vanishes as I sprint across the sand, burning a path of glass in my wake before I crash into a tall, gray horse that turns its head towards me and snorts. The hot breath ruffles my hair as I wrap my arms around the horse's neck and hold tight as I pant for air.

My heart finally catches up with my body and drums through my chest on a rampage back to its proper spot. I slump to the ground, gasping for air at the horse's feet. It dances in place then neighs. I stay where I am. Better to be crushed by a horse than face whatever was out there again.

I'm sure it's only a few hour-long seconds before footsteps crunch across the sand and a pair of dark boots appears in front of me. Looking up I see a pure white dress and a beautiful corset. I sigh with relief. "Maria."

She kneels down to my side. "What happened?"

At first I can't get the words out of my mouth. The story tangles between my brain and tongue, but then it finally all bursts free. "I don't know. There was screaming and then something grabbed my leg. I kicked it."

Maria seems amused. "You kicked it?"

"It bit me. Or something," I say with a wince as pain burns up my leg and through my blood.

The amusement drains out of Maria's voice as she looks over my leg. "You are bleeding." Her voice is calm, and that makes me nervous.

"What?"

Maria doesn't answer, just gets back up and goes over to her horse's saddlebag. She pulls out a small kit then sits down beside me. Blood spreads across her clothing. My blood.

"You're staining your clothes," I say, not sure what else to do right now. My head spins.

I look around and try to keep the world still, but all around me the stars swirl like we've been caught in a water eddy spiraling towards the bottom.

Maria doesn't respond, just presses a thick rag against my leg.

I grimace and try to curl away, but Maria holds me still as she opens a bottle of alcohol and pours it over the wound. Grunting with pain, I finally drop down flat on the ground.

"You will be fine," Maria tells me, pressing her hands firmly against the wound. Instead of the warmth of the rag, I feel her skin against my leg, so cold that my flesh goose pimples under her touch. Everything flares across my skin, like feeling the whole wound in reverse, numbness, pain, then nothing but anticipation.

Maria pulls her hands away, but not before I see the blood on them.

"What did you do?" I ask. The sting is entirely gone from my leg, and I'm having trouble remembering even where on my leg the wound even was.

Maria shakes her head. "You should get back home," she tells me.

"No. I can help. I know how to shoot a gun."

"There's a difference between aiming at cans and bottles and aiming at something not from this world that is coming to kill you. Ride Viento back home." She motions to her horse.

"No, you need her," I say. "I can't take her."

"Just ride her back, but do not barn her for the night. She will find her way to me," Maria says, standing back and taking a few steps away.

Viento dances from side to side as I reach out to touch her flank. Maria puts the aid kit back into the saddlebag, though there's a faint glimmering from the bag.

I nod and get onto the horse's back. A horse will help me find this thing faster anyways. Maria hands me the reins, and I turn Viento back towards town. The mare moves steadily through the desert, ears swiveling around, listening to everything.

"Shhh..." I try to soothe the horse as I pull her to a stop and dismount once Maria is out of sight.

Viento dances but holds steady as I reach around to the saddlebag. What was glimmering there?

Digging past the general first aid supplies, my fingers touch something warm and lighter than air. I tug on the fabric, and see the edge of a corset made with a golden fabric.

A screech rips through the air, and Viento rears back before bolting. She nearly knocks me to the ground, but I manage to catch myself as the horse speeds by me and out of sight.

The howling noise starts circling closer, but this time, I'm ready.

In the distance I make out a pair of burning red eyes. The monster is finally here and this time I'm ready!

I pull my gun free and aim. The eyes circle closer, and I see a flash of teeth, white and sharp, lunge towards me as my finger squeezes the trigger. The recoil of the shot slams into my shoulder and topples me to the ground. I thud into the sand.

Rolling to my feet, I grab my gun back and try to reload it. The barrel's clogged and all but useless until I can take the time to properly clean it out. Wrapping both of my hands around it, I hold it like a club, ready to smash anything that comes too close.

I peer towards the red eyes I'd shot and head that way. The world is silent around me, and something about the total stillness intimidates me more than any howling red-eyed creature. The deserts are never totally still and silent.

Ignoring the pounding of my heart, I peer forward and notice a spot in the sand. Something's been hit and is on the run now. A trail of blood leads through the sand, leaving a thick wet trail against the darkness of the night. Holding my gun tight in my hands, I start down the trail. The pools of blood get thicker as I gain on the wounded beast.

In the distance I hear Viento neigh, but she doesn't sound

close or like she's in distress so I keep moving. The trail continues forward through the sand and off of the main path that all of the townspeople and travelers take. I hesitate but keep after it, still glancing over my shoulder every few steps to keep myself oriented. As long as I can see the light from my house, I can find my way back from just about anywhere in the desert.

Blood splatters in thicker splotches in a wild stumbling trail before it ends and there's a disturbance in the sand, like some kind of fight took place. I look around but I can't see anyone else around. "Maria?" I call.

I wait for a moment, and then hear something that might be an answer but could just be the wind.

"Maria?" I try again.

"Here."

This time the voice calls clearly, and I follow it to another large pool of blood. Maria sits on the ground with dark red staining through her corset as her hands press against her wound.

At her feet is a large coyote-like creature made of mist that seems to be fading into the ground by the second. Its sharp red eyes track me, and a faint growl rumbles through the air before it falls silent.

"Maria!" I rush over to her side, whistling and trying to call for her horse, and after just a few seconds, Viento is galloping into sight. "What happened?"

She shook her head. "It was hurt. I did not hear it."

I try to put my hands over the wound to help the flow of blood, but Maria shakes her head. Instead she reaches down and begins to unfasten the clasps of her corset.

"Maria, you shouldn't be moving."

"You must mend this," she tells me as she unbuckles the last clasp and the corset slips off her body. Pressing it into my hands, she takes several long, deep breaths and runs her fingers along the long split in one of the seams where the blood has soaked through. "Mend it, and I will wait here."

"You're bleeding! What's a corset matter right now?" I shake my head.

"There is a kit of supplies in the saddle bag," Maria tells me.

I frown, but go over to Viento's saddle bag and pull out her first aid kit. The small golden corset brushes against my fingers, but I ignore it and set the kit down by Maria. She riffles through it and finds a small sewing kit. She pushes it into my hands and takes the first aid kit.

I glare at her. "You're going to die because you care more about this corset than your life! You've got another one in your bag, just replace it!" I throw down the sewing kit.

Maria stares at me before she says, "You saw it?"

I nod. "Yeah, the golden one in there. Stop talking and do something about the blood!"

Maria takes a deep breath. "I will tend to my own wound, child," she says stiffly, and I watch her take out the supplies and press some clean fabric to her side to wipe away the blood.

"Why do you care so much about this corset getting fixed up anyways?" I ask.

"It's my life," she says simply.

I wrinkle my nose, looking at her, and then to corset I threw to the ground. It's shimmer fades slowly as red grows across the fabric. "The corset is bleeding?" I whisper.

Maria looks at me again then nods. "You need to mend it, child. Please. I cannot."

I look between Maria and the corset before I sit down on the ground across from her, running my hands over the corset. This time the fabric is cold and coarse in my hands. "I don't even know how to fix something like this. It's got boning and I've never fixed a bleeding piece of fabric before," I say.

"It's just like fixing a tear in a shirt. Sew."

There's only one needle and one spool of gray thread. I thread the needle and start trying to stitch the ripped seam together. Maria watches me as she presses a rag to her stomach where she's wounded. "Tighter stitches. It does not have to be pretty," she tells me.

"It might not even get done. I never paid much attention to the sewing lessons my mother gave me."

"What better time to learn then?" Maria asks.

"Why's your corset bleed?" I ask her.

"So that monsters don't hurt me," she answers.

"This helps you kill those things?" I look up at her.

She nods.

I keep stitching the corset together. It's only when the tear is nearly fixed that I notice the blood has faded from the corset and the warmth is returning to the fabric. Again it feels silk smooth under my touch.

My stitches are messy but effective at pulling the ripped fabric back together. The corset itself pulses beneath my touch. I can't help but trace my fingers across it, letting the warmth run through my body, so different than the chill night air all around us that nips me nearly to the bone.

"How'd you get it?" I ask.

"It was a gift," she answers. "One hopefully never to be given again."

"Why do you have two of them?"

She shakes her head. "Just finish sewing, child."

"Are you going to be okay?" I ask Maria who still sits with the first aid kit, working over her wounds out of my sight.

"I will be fine. Just finish that, all right?"

I put the last crooked stitch in place and tie off the end of the string, biting the excess off with my teeth before standing back up. "That's the best I can do. I've never been too good at sewing."

Maria pulls it from my hands and runs her fingers over the bumpy stitches. "It is perfect," she tells me before pulling it back on, looping everything into place before turning back towards me. She stands tall. "Thank you, little Aiva, but you should go home now."

"The monster is dead!" I tell her.

She shakes her head. "A monster is dead. Take Viento home," she tells me as she adjusts her corset one more time before walking away from me. "You only get three chances, and this is your last chance, child. Go."

A howling screech pierces the sky again. I look to the ground where only a puddle of blood remains from the monster that lay there just moments before. I clutch the gun close to my chest and try to start cleaning it out as the howling grows louder and closer.

Viento dances from side to side, her tail flicking around her like a whip. She's nervous, scared even, and I bet that not much would scare Maria's horse. But I try not to think about how scared I am, and instead I just focus on the motions of reloading the gun just like Papa taught me. Everything is a process, and if I focus on that, I'm okay.

The gun cleaned and reloaded, I tuck it over my shoulder and take a deep breath before I step out after Maria. I don't see anything that looks like her trail. As the howling gets louder, I start to worry that maybe I've lost her or maybe she's just vanished.

I take a deep breath and let my hand rest on the gun on my back. Well, even if she won't kill whatever's out there, I will. I'm going to stop these monsters right now. There's not going to be a single more night where anyone goes to bed with a hatchet under their pillow because they're afraid those beasts are going to break in and try to hurt them. Never again.

The howling gets louder, and I can see something red glinting like two eyes against the darkness around me. Whatever is out there is getting closer. It knows I'm here and it's coming for me. I stop walking and aim the gun, carefully balancing it on my shoulder.

My heart stops for the moment, and I don't even take a breath as time turns itself inside out around me and nothing moves for several long seconds that seem to stretch on for years. Then a shadow steps forward moving separately from the night. I fire the gun and blast into the darkness, but the creature howls and then lunges forward.

Somewhere there's pain that ruptures across the stillness of desert, and then I'm falling towards the ground, dropping to the sand. Looking up, I see the darkness starting to close in towards me, blotting out even the stars.

Then there's a gold light that cuts through and a screaming noise that ruptures through the pain and the darkness. The thing that eats the stars disappears in a spray of white and gold light that streaks across the air and twirls before it rushes towards Maria and dives into her corset. Shimmering gold sparks across the fabric before diving into the seams and vanishing. I stare at her, trying to form words as she comes over to me, kneeling at my side.

"Oh, little one, I told you to go home."

"Did you get it?" I ask.

"Yes, my child, the monsters are gone." She brushes the hair from my face and her skin is so very cold against mine.

I stare up at her and see her face for the first time. Her hair frames a thin face with the cheekbones sticking out against her dark skin. She has a pained smile on her face.

"What happened?"

She shakes her head. "Nothing, my child. Close your eyes and go to sleep."

"I don't want to go to sleep," I tell her.

She shakes her head, and then steps from my side. I try to reach for her, but my fingertips just miss. Weights press onto my eyelids, and I can feel myself starting to drift away into darkness. As my eyes start to close, I catch a glint of Maria kneeling by my side, and then something golden in her hands.

I can't keep my eyes open anymore now that Maria is here. She starts to hum to me. It's a lullaby that I don't recognize. A warm weight wraps around my sides like a hug, and I let the embrace wash me away.

There's a tightness around my waist when I wake up. Even with my eyes open, I can't see anything ahead of me but pitch-black. Reaching out to touch the space in front, I can feel a smooth wooden surface acting as my sky. I'm boxed in with wood all around me.

Starting to struggle, I try to find any gap in the trap, but I can't. I open my mouth to scream just as I hear a thud on top of the box and then the lid opens. At first I wince, expecting the sharp light of day, but instead I squint up at Maria standing in front of the night sky.

She offers her hand to me and I take it, letting her pull me up and out of the box. I look around. "We're in the graveyard."

Maria nods.

I look behind at the fresh dirt grave and the coffin I just stepped out of. I swallow hard and try to piece together anything.

My memories are jagged pieces of a torn up painting: pain, gold, warmth, darkness, then nothing. I press my hands over my chest and feel nothing but a hollow stillness.

"Am I dead?" I whisper.

"You are, my child," she tells me, stroking my cheek again.

I pull away from her touch and walk straight over to the creek near the graveyard and look down into the still water. I don't look like a monster; I still look like me except...

I run my hands along my side and feel the smooth warmth of the corset now around my waist. It's the soft gold one from her saddlebag.

Maria comes to stand beside me. "You are not a monster."

"Then what am I?" I ask her.

"You are just like me now," she tells me, tucking my hair behind my ear. "You will stop the things that do not belong in this world."

"But if I'm dead, I don't belong here either," I say, shaking my head and sitting down on the damp ground by Anna-Leigh's grave.

"That is why you hunt," Maria tells me. "Now come, we must go."

"Go where?" I ask, looking up at her.

She sighs. "To find the next creature."

"How do you find them?"

Maria leans over me to press a hand to my corset. "This will guide you. It feeds on those creatures that hurt the innocents. It will make you strong; it will keep you alive."

"But what is it?" I run my hands over the corset. It feels like a part of my skin, a part of my bones holding me together.

"It is a promise to spend your afterlife hunting."

"Why...how do I have it?"

"I told you to go home, but you kept hunting. You found it and the corset chose you, my child." Maria offers her hand. "Come, it is time to go."

I take her hand and let her pull me to my feet. Waiting for us outside of the cemetery are two gray and white horses. I recognize Viento, but there's a smaller mare beside her. "For me?" I ask.

Maria smiles and nods. "We ride, Aiva."

I hop on the horse, and smooth my hands across the horse's neck before tracing along the corset on my body. Its warmth wraps around me, and I am ready to hunt.

Snake Bite

Misty Massey

"The serpent never seeks revenge."

Desi smoothed her hands down the front of her corset, turning before the mirror. Silk stitches twined along the boning, red satin gleaming in the late afternoon light from the curtained window. It fit her like a glove, with no hint of the danger lurking just under the seams.

"And it certainly doesn't wear a garment like that."

"I'm not a serpent," she murmured. "Just because you trained me doesn't make me a shaman, Manteu."

"I didn't teach you the ways of the Chawan so you could murder white men."

"I only hunt the guilty, old ghost."

Footsteps thudded in the hallway. Desi looked up just in time to see the bar owner appear. "On the floor, woman! You ain't any prettier than the rest, no matter how long you stare in the glass."

She slid past the portly man into the heat and noise. Men sat at tables, stood at the bar and danced with some of the other girls while the piano player banged out jaunty tunes on the upright against the far wall. At the large round table in the middle of the room, several well-dressed men played a high-stakes game of cards. Behind the largest pile of chips, looking as satisfied as a well-fed cat, sat a handsome fellow with a cheroot dangling from his lip. Charles Westerfield. Fifteen years back, he ran the Brown Hill Boys, a nasty crew of bandits known far and wide. Now the richest cattle baron in the state, he owned most of the land for miles around. Most of the people, too.

She hadn't seen him in person since the day he killed her family.

"Just one more," she whispered, before the old ghost could try and talk her out of it.

She tugged at the bottom of her corset, steeling herself. She created the corset while working for a seamstress in Kansas City. Several tiny pockets sewn along the length of the boning, inserted in a way that hid them from the casual glance. In each pocket, she placed fangs shed by wild rattlers. Each fang was fitted with a tiny bulb made of snakeskin and filled with snake venom, distilled to dangerous purity. The corset was lined with strips of bamboo wrapped in the shed skins of diamondbacks, to keep the venom stored in the collected fangs from accidentally seeping through to her own skin. Unlike ordinary assassins, who relied on thrown blades or garrotes in the darkness, Desi preferred a close kill. Most of the time her needle-sharp fangs were deeply imbedded in the neck or arm of her target and she was lost in the shadows before anyone thought to pull a gun.

Two of the bar girls stood by Westerfield's side, fawning over every hand of cards, bringing him drinks when he ran low and occasionally letting him tuck chips deep into their cleavages. Getting close enough to slide a poisoned fang into his neck wouldn't be easy.

Strolling over to the bar, she leaned backward on it with her elbows, pushing her chest forward. As she expected, men near her began to take notice, staring at her chest while asking her to dance. She accepted the occasional dance, each time making sure to laugh coquettishly and smile with as much brilliance as she could manage. Now and then she glanced toward her target, only to see him pretending not to look her way.

Walk away, Desdemona.

She wished Manteu's ghost would remember not to talk to her in front of people. He tried so many times during his last days to convince her vengeance solved nothing. Now that he was dead, he spoke of nothing else. The only time he shut up about it were the days after she'd successfully killed a target. Desi sometimes wondered if he'd be resting in the arms of his people now if she'd let him put her on an eastbound train all those years ago. She felt guilty if she gave it too much thought. He'd been kind to her, kinder than he needed to be. But Westerfield was the last. Once she killed him, she and the old ghost would both be free to move on.

Westerfield looked healthier. Certainly cleaner. Seeing him like this, his wavy brown hair neatly oiled and arranged, and his nails so clean they gleamed, sent her mind wandering to the day he and his Brown Hill Boys stopped her father's wagon on the trail west, demanding money. She'd whispered to her brother to stay quiet, but in an instant shots rang out, and their parents were lying dead in the trail dust. Ben grabbed their father's rifle and launched himself out the back of the wagon, only to be cut down without firing a shot of his own, leaving Desi cowering behind her grandmother's rocking chair. She didn't know how to fight, and she didn't have anywhere to run. After an eternity, the flap opened, revealing a dark-haired man with a predator's eyes. "Well, hello there. Why don't you climb on out?"

She obeyed, not knowing what else to do. The men had her

surrounded, some of them grinning in a way that made her feel like a trapped animal. She backed up against the wagon until she could retreat no further. Two of the men pushed past her, climbed into the wagon and started to throw her mother's possessions around haphazardly. She heard the crack of wood as her grandmother's rocking chair broke under their hard use.

"Come on over here, missy. Let's have us some fun."

She shook her head, but the man yanked at her arm, pulling her against his body. He stunk of horse sweat and trail dirt. She struck him, pounding with her fists, as the others laughed and jeered.

"Let her go." Their leader hadn't moved, but at his words, the rest of the men stopped laughing. The man who'd grabbed her didn't let go.

"Come on, Charles, we ain't had any sport in weeks."

"No, and since it doesn't look like we'll be getting any real cash off this wagon, she's likely to be the only thing worth selling." He hunkered down in front of her, took her chin in his hand and forced her to look at him. "You a virgin, girl? Some farm boy had a poke at you yet?"

The fear drained away, replaced by indignation. She'd never been asked such a rude question before by a stranger. Even her mother had never said such things, and she'd had the right. Desi tightened her jaw and jerked free of his hand. "That ain't your business."

He smiled humorlessly. "That's what I thought. We keep her intact, boys. Sell her to Miss Penny in Landsdown. Fetch us enough to eat on for a month, at least."

She looked around. The wagon stood in the shadow of a few low hills, boulders scattered beneath the scrub trees. If she could lose herself in that mess of rocks, maybe she could evade the men long enough for them to give up and move on.

"What's your name, pretty thing?" The man didn't grab for her, just waited with his arms crossed

"Desdemona."

"I'm Charles Westerfield, pretty Desdemona. You'll ride with me."

She walked slowly toward the waiting horses, stopped and looked back. The bandits had unhitched the mules. Her father's body lay half-undressed in the dirt of the trail, his shirt, belt and boots missing and his pockets turned inside out. She couldn't see her mother or Ben. Flame suddenly leaped over the canvas of her ruined wagon, snapping in the light breeze. The bandits threw her father's body into the fire, and Desi turned away, blinking back tears.

Westerfield waited for her. "Time to get moving," he said as he lifted her onto the horse.

Before he could mount, she snatched the reins from his hands and kicked the horse's side as hard as she could. "Hee yah!" she cried, and the horse launched forward. Desi gripped the horse's mane and squeezed her legs tight. Air rushed past, whipping her hair into her eyes. She heard angry cries from behind her, but she didn't dare look. With one hand, she whipped the loose reins against the horse's neck, urging it to go faster, to reach the rocks, and salvation.

The world dropped out from underneath her with a sickening crack, the horse screaming as it fell. Desi let go of its mane and rolled away into the grass, then scrambled to her feet to run the rest of the way. She reached the first of the boulders and threw herself at them, scrabbling for a handhold. Reaching the top, she looked back at the men pursuing her. They'd caught up to the horse, writhing on the ground, one leg bent horribly. Westerfield took out his gun and knelt by the animal's head. An instant later, there was a loud pop. The horse jerked and lay still. Westerfield rose to his feet and looked at Desi.

She climbed down the back side of the rock and rushed toward the next. The back side was smoother than she expected, and she lost control, sliding down to land hard on hands and knees in the rocky dirt. Her hands ached from scraping on the rocks. She looked up and noticed a hollow under the boulder. Dark as a cave, but just big enough for her to hide in. If she kept silent, they might never find her. She crawled to the opening and thrust both legs into the darkness.

Too late she heard the warning rattles. Pain lanced through her calves. Sharp pain, like tiny knives slicing into her skin. And after the slice, burning, so much burning. She flailed down into the darkness, trying to push the snakes away, but only succeeded in being bitten on her hands and arms. It took all her energy to drag herself back onto the open ground. Her legs and hands were throbbing. She'd been bitten in several places that she could see from the bloody marks. Her head spun, and she collapsed against a rock. Her chest stiffened as if bands of iron closed around it.

"Damn girl, you cost me a horse."

Desi squinted up at the man, Westerfield, standing on the boulder above her. The need to escape him had faded away. All she wanted now was to go with him, to get to a doctor and make the pain stop.

"Help...me..." she whispered, but he shook his head.

"Too far to town." He sighed, turning away. "Bye, pretty thing."

She didn't hear him leave. No sound but her own sobs and the angry rattles all around. Her throat tightened, choking off her air. She was damaged goods, not even worth punishing over the loss of the horse.

"Desdemona, pay attention."

Desi jerked at the sound of the old ghost's voice in her mind. She'd let herself wander into the past. Not a place she wanted to visit. And soon, when she left Westerfield dying on the floor of this cheap saloon, she never would again.

"You awake, little lady?" A cowhand snapped his fingers in her face.

She smiled, hoping to salvage his good will. "I am, now. Buy me a drink and we can have a dance."

He took hold of her arm, squeezing just hard enough to make her wince. "I'm thinking maybe you and me need to have a little private talk instead." He yanked her forward, toward the stairs that led up to the rented rooms.

Desi set her feet hard, resisting his pull. The man turned around to get a better grip, and she slapped him as hard as she could.

The cowhand raised his arm to strike her, but someone grabbed him. Westerfield. The cowhand paled, letting his arm drop as Westerfield released him. He also let go of Desi. She took a step back, rubbing her aching elbow.

"Randolph, isn't it?" Westerfield said, his tone pleasant but his eyes hard as steel. "You work for Anderson?"

The cowhand nodded, all his bluster fading.

"I think you've had enough entertainment for tonight. Head back to your bunk, now."

The cowhand ducked his head in deference. "Yes, sir, Mr Westerfield. Sorry sir," he muttered before vanishing out the swinging doors into the night. Westerfield watched him leave, then waved to one of his own men. "Follow him, and make sure he goes home. Then tell Anderson I'll need a word tomorrow."

He returned his attention to Desi.

Desi fluttered her hand before her face. "Oh, my sir, thank you for that. That man was such a brute."

"Think nothing of it," he said, holding out his hand. She placed hers in it, and he bent to kiss it. He stopped just short of touching her skin, his warm breath causing gooseflesh to rise in spite of her true feelings. He looked up from his inclined position, catching her eye and smiling. He brushed a finger along her cheek. "What's your name, pretty thing?"

She suppressed a shiver. Pretty thing. That's what he called her the day he killed her family. Probably the same thing he called every woman he met. "Dora," she said. "Just arrived in town yesterday."

"I can see why Herman snapped you up. I'm Charles Westerfield. Why don't you help me win at cards, Dora?"

"Delighted, sir." She let him lead her across the room to his table. He waved the two girls waiting for him to move aside and sat down in his chair, Desi leaned against his shoulder, allowing her breast to press against him. He didn't react, but she saw his eye flick toward her, and knew he noticed. Good.

"Nothing worth having is achieved easily, Desdemona. You're letting him get too close to you."

Quiet, old man, she thought. She needed to concentrate on watching Westerfield. She only had one chance to slip a fang or two under his skin and press the venom bulb. She laid her hand on his shoulder, watching the dealer pass cards around the table. Westerfield had a decent enough hand – two, five and six of clubs, ten of hearts and jack of diamonds. Very possibly a flush if his luck held. She squeezed his shoulder gently, then slipped a finger under the edge of his hairline, stroking his neck. Westerfield threw away the jack and ten, and took the two cards the dealer offered him – the three and king of clubs. She felt his shoulders relax even as her heart raced. He'd never be further off his guard than when he won a hand.

Desi dropped her free hand to one of the concealed pockets on her corset. Pressing the top, she felt the fang hidden within slip out. She caught it as it fell, careful not to depress the fragile bulb. She turned it in her fingers and raised her hand to strike at the man's vulnerable neck. Suddenly he turned and grabbed her wrist, his cards forgotten. "What's this, Dora?" he snarled. He squeezed until the pain forced her hand open.

The fang tumbled to the floor, and he stomped it. Reddish liquid stained a small spot on the boards when he moved his boot away. "Poison was to be my timeless end, as the bard said?"

Manteu, help me, she thought, but the old ghost was silent for once. The whole room had gone still, everyone staring at her. Herman stepped forward, hesitation in his step as well as his voice. "Mr. Westerfield, sir, she came with references," he began, but choked to a stop when Westerfield shot him an angry glare. He dropped his head and slowly walked behind the bar again.

Westerfield yanked her hand up before her face, forcing her to look at the back of her hand. There, faded over time, was a scar. In the distinctive pattern. Two fangs. Snakebite. Such scars were all over her limbs, had been for so long she hardly paid attention to them any longer. Manteu tried to warn her, but she hadn't listened. She changed her name, colored her hair, taught herself to dance and play cards, every skill she needed to get close to bad men. She forgot what her scars meant.

But Westerfield hadn't. He left her to die, but he didn't forget her.

Cold swept through her body, setting her shivering in spite of herself. He smiled, a predatory smile that almost paralyzed her.

"You owe me a horse."

As the crowd watched, silent and still, Westerfield shoved her toward another one of his men. "Take her out to the house," he said. "Tie her up. And keep an eye on her – she's a venomous little thing."

The men pulled her arms behind her back, tied her hands together with a length of twine and dragged her outside. Westerfield followed them to the swinging doors. "I'll be along shortly. Still have a hand of cards to play."

Hours...days. She couldn't tell how long since the men tied her to the wall. Her hands were secured with rope to a chain hanging above her head, and her arms and shoulders ached from the strain. Westerfield's men didn't hurt her, or even make an attempt at defiling her. They stripped her of her jewelry, her corset, skirts and shoes, stacking almost everything on top of a hay manger, leaving her shivering in her shift. They nailed her corset to the wall opposite her, and they made a game of shooting it with pellets from slingshots. The pebbles ripped the silk, leaving it tattered and stained with the venom from the broken fang bulbs in the many hidden pockets. She could no longer feel her hands, and her feet were ice cold.

Worst of all, the old ghost said not a single word. She didn't blame him. He'd been so careful with her, teaching her the ways of the serpent shaman. She used the weapons without the wisdom. She wished he'd chastise her once more, just so she could know he was listening when she told him how sorry she was.

Twelve years ago, she woke up in the dark, listening to the soft singing of words in an alien language. Her body was heavy, her thoughts slow. Noticing she was awake, the old man stopped his singing and moved to where she lay. He raised her head and offered her water, and she drank it without argument. In surprisingly fluid English, he told her his name was Manteu, and that she was safe.

She didn't remember Manteu finding her among the rocks. He told her the snakes called him to come for her. According to him, the snakes felt she was sent to wear the mantle of serpent shaman when Manteu died. It surprised him as much as it did her because she wasn't Chawan. He was the last of his people, as far as he knew, the rest killed by white raiders encroaching west. If any of his kin survived, they were absorbed into other tribes and lost to him. He was certainly the last shaman. The snakes told him that truth.

At first, Desi hadn't believed all the nonsense about snakes talking. It was the sort of silliness savage people thought before they were brought into the fold of Jesus and his church. But the longer she stayed with the old man, the more she came to realize that he was neither savage nor silly. The day of her twelfth birthday, the snakes talked to her for the first time, not in words, but in visions behind her eyes that communicated exactly what they wanted. A few summers later, while Manteu was coughing his life into a bowl she kept near his sleeping pad, the snakes warned her that she should prepare to take over for the old man, but she didn't want to believe them. After he died and started haunting her, she went to live in the city, where the only snakes she saw were the ones she found to milk for their venom. Manteu assured her that someday they would welcome her back, but what could they do for her now?

Westerfield walked into the room. He discarded his fine coat and rolled up the sleeves of his linen shirt. In one hand, he held a single-tail whip. Desi swallowed hard against the lump that clogged her throat.

Westerfield jerked his head at the two men. "Out," he said. "Don't disturb me for any reason." He followed them to the door, swinging it closed and dropping the inner bar behind them.

She was alone with him.

"I've been working the sums in my head, pretty Desdemona," he said, with the casual tone of a man who had all the money he could ever need. "That horse you killed, probably worth at least twenty dollars."

"I didn't kill it," she said, her voice dry with fatigue.

In a flash, he swung at her. Sharp pain exploded across her chest, so hot and sudden she could do nothing but gasp. Blood oozed from the cut, staining the white cotton.

"You stole it, and it snapped a leg under your care," he snarled. "That makes you responsible."

She dropped her head. The abrasion on her chest stung, and she took slow, deep breaths to try and calm her pounding heart.

"So back to our accounting," Westerfield said, as if this was all a dull financial transaction between business people. "Taking into consideration the trouble you caused me having to ride those mules of yours back to town, I'd say you owe me a total of forty dollars. Can you pay that?"

Desi sobbed, against her will.

"What's that?"

She looked into his handsome, hateful eyes. "You killed my family!" she cried.

He struck her again, this time across her belly. Blood trickled down her legs, dripping into the dust at her feet. Tears rolled down her cheeks. She wanted to argue, to cry out, to fight, but he had all the advantages. Just the same way he had on that day so long ago.

He looped the whip over and over in his hand. She couldn't tell if he was about to strike again. Her body was tense with the fear of the pain he could inflict. He paced back and forth in front of her for what seemed an eternity, then stopped. She winced and turned her face away.

"I could be convinced to let you pay me for the horse. It would only take a few years on your back to cover the loss."

"No," she whispered.

"No?" Another strike, this time across her legs. She couldn't help a cry, but it seemed to drive him on. He lashed her again and a third time, until she was sobbing.

"That's just as well," he said. "I'll probably enjoy killing you more. You should have come for me first. Maybe then I wouldn't have known you were gunning for me."

She raised her tear-streaked face, but didn't make a sound.

"That first man you killed, Harrison Bell? My cousin." His voice tightened, and he leaned in close to her face to spit the words at her. "My mother wrote me about the strange way he died. As if he was snake bit, but in the middle of a saloon. Once I read that letter, I started keeping tabs on all the rest of the boys I used to run with. To be safe, of course. By the time you murdered Jim Flynn, I knew someone was after us. Just didn't know precisely who."

"Manteu!" she moaned. "I'm sorry."

"Who're you calling out for? Your lover? He can't help you now," Westerfield said. "I'm going to cut you until every drop of your blood has made mud of my barn floor. No one, least of all some slip of a girl, comes at me and lives to tell of it."

Call to your kin, Desdemona.

Manteu, she thought. You're still here.

As I swore I would be, until you accepted your life. Call them.

Westerfield raised the whip again, bringing it down across her raised left arm. She drew a ragged breath and started chanting the old words Manteu had taught her. If she was going to die, she'd do it honoring the man who saved her life. Westerfield lashed at her, harder and faster, raising wounds on every inch of her skin. After a time she couldn't tell one cut from another. She shrieked the chants with all the energy she could muster. She was no longer a woman, but a being of burning pain and holy words.

Suddenly Westerfield stopped. He was panting, tired from his exertions. Desi stopped as well, dragging breath into her ruined body. And in the momentary quiet, another sound intruded. A soft rattle. Joined by another. And another. The barn began to echo with the rattles of snakes announcing their presence.

Her kin...the snakes. It was time for her to come home. Desi began the chant again, softly, her throat dry but the words strong nonetheless.

"Stop saying that, woman!" Westerfield snapped his whip toward the sounds, sending bits of straw and dirt flying through the air. He spun, looking desperately right and left for the snakes he could hear. "The hell with this!" he cried at last, dropping the whip and striding to the barred door. He reached under the bar to lift it, but hissed and jerked his hand back. A snake fell from the bar, slithering across the floor and out of sight. Westerfield held his hand out in front of him. Blood dripped down his fingers.

"I'm bit!" he said. Running back to where Desi was chained, he grabbed a handful of her bloodied hair. "Call off your pets!"

Desi smiled up at him and chanted louder. From every corner of the barn, the rattles sounded louder, and snakes of all types began slithering toward Westerfield, backing him against the wall next to Desi.

"Release my hands," she said. "Otherwise, we'll both die here."

Westerfield dug in his pocket with his uninjured hand, pulling out a folding knife. Keeping one eye on the gathered mass of snakes hissing and slithering at him, he reached up and sawed at the ropes until they fell away. Desi's arms were cold from lack of circulation, and her legs had no strength. She collapsed to the floor. Dirt stuck to the open cuts, and her joints ached, but she was free.

The man was clearly frightened. His face was pale. His wounded hand was beginning to puff up. "I'll forgive the debt, just call them off!"

"Speaking of debts—" she cocked her head curiously, "you owe me a family."

The snakes struck simultaneously. Some bit his legs through the linen of his pants, while others wound round his body to reach the soft flesh of his face and neck. He screamed, flailing his hands to knock the attacking snakes away. He fell to the floor, writhing and crying out. Desi dragged herself away, watching as the venom worked its damage on him. His cries became gasps as his throat closed, and soon, he made no sound at all. His eyes were open, but the skin of his face was swelling them shut. If he was aware of her, he no longer showed it. She watched him for an eternity, to be certain he was dead, although it somehow didn't matter to her anymore. All she felt, at that moment, was a kinship beyond any human family she'd ever known. She reached out to the closest snake, letting it slide over her hand. Its skin was smooth and warm.

I go to my people now, Desdemona. Live well.

Desi struggled to her feet. "Manteu?" she called, but there was no answer. The snakes wound around her feet, as playful as children at the foot of their mother. She walked over to where her ruined corset hung on the wall. It hardly resembled the beautiful weapon it had been. It had cost so much, not only in cash but in effort, and in the end, she hadn't even needed it. Much like the vengeance she thought she could not live without. She reached out and stroked the tattered silk with one finger. A drop of the spilled venom stuck to her finger, but instead of wiping her hand on her clothing, she licked it thoughtfully. It wouldn't harm her now. Nothing would.

<u>Escape</u>

Kimberly Richardson

DAY ONE

It is dark. I am in pain. I have only a little light for writing but soon that will go away. I wish I could sit comfortably but that is denied to me. I can, at least, lie down or walk around to a certain point before the chain in the wall pulls me back. For the first time since I woke up here, I turn my head to look at the chain that limits my movement. It is a standard chain with normal (ha!) sized links, secured with thick bolts against one of the stone walls in this room. The chain gives me two feet in all directions as it ends in a steel ring that is linked through a bolt in the corset that I wear. Standard black leather with blunt metal claws on the top and bottom that dig into my skin, thereby limiting my movements even more. My room, or rather, cell: stone walls and a small window behind me allowing air from outside. The door is thick and wooden. No sounds except for very faint ones from the window. I have several coarse woolen blankets, a very small pillow filled with straw, and food two times a day. Aside from the corset, I wear nothing else. I don't mind. Anything else would hurt my skin, given my conditions.

I don't remember coming here or how I arrived. All I know is that I woke up in this…place with a woman standing over me.

Once she saw that I was awake, she removed my clothing then placed the corset on me and left with my clothes in tow without a word. I yanked on the chain several times in a futile gesture of trying to escape. I sat down and cried, wondering just how I got here. Was I drugged? Was I kidnapped? As other questions entered my mind, the door opened, revealing a man dressed in a white shirt and pants carrying a tray. He walked into the room, avoiding my feral gaze at him, and placed the tray next to me.

"Please," I moaned, "tell me how I got here! PLEASE! What did I do wrong? What's going on here?" The man said nothing but closed the door behind him, cutting off my screams. I screamed until I went hoarse then fell quiet. I then looked at the tray and noticed several dishes of food on it. Not caring if it was poisoned or not, I wolfed down all of it then licked my dirty fingers. Suddenly, the door opened again, this time revealing a tall bald man dressed in all black with a silver hoop earring in his right ear. As he walked in, I noticed that he had a whip with cords made of heavy rope that dragged on the floor. My eyes went wide as he walked toward me with a serene smile on his face.

"W-What are you going to do?" I whispered in pure fear as he yanked me to my feet then turned me away from him with my hands against the cool stone wall.

"One." I heard the noise only seconds after I felt the sting against my legs and buttocks. I whimpered and wanted to crumple on the floor, but the man pulled me up again then removed the corset from my body, revealing my vulnerable skin. I cried in silence as the whip now cracked against my back.

"Two."

When I came to, I felt hands placing a cool cream on my back. It smelled of mint. I did not care who it was or what it was. It felt good. I closed my eyes again. When I awoke again, I noticed several pieces of paper lying next to me with a small pencil. I looked down and noticed that I wore the corset again and nothing else. I looked up at the window and saw the beginnings of evening. *How long have I been here,* I wondered then slid up to a sitting position and took the pieces of paper and pencil and began to write.

I am scared.

DAY TWO

Morning came with the same man from before with the tray, replacing the one from yesterday with a new one. I smelled eggs, sausage, and even saw buttered toast. When he placed the tray next to me, I began to eat without care. He closed the door in silence just as before. As I ate, I looked around at my surroundings again and noticed that I now had more blankets and a pillow that looked to be larger and not filled with straw but rather—I reached over to squeeze it and sighed. It felt heavenly. I resumed eating. When I finished my breakfast, I wiped my hands on the napkin on the tray then noticed a small pitcher with a sponge behind the pillow. I grabbed the pitcher and began to cry; it was filled with cool water. I took a long drink then dipped the sponge into the rest of it and bathed my arms and legs, face and neck. The corset with its dulled claws dug into my skin, yet I did not care. I had cool water. As I washed myself, I looked at the back of my legs covered in bright pink welts, yet they did not hurt when I touched them with the sponge. I wanted to remove the corset so I could touch my back, but I could not. I soaked up the remainder of the water and squeezed it over my head, shivering at the cool water flowing through my long hair. I then crawled over to the blankets and wrapped myself in one then placed the pillow under my head and fell asleep.

I awoke to the sound of the door opening. I opened my eyes and saw the young man in black from yesterday, only now he had…I screamed as he pulled me up to a standing position, ripped off my corset, and placed my palms against the wall with my face pressed against the dirty stones. I heard him shift from foot to foot then SLAP!

"One." I felt the tears running down my face and onto the wall. Dear God.

"Two." SLAP

"Three." SLAP

I whimpered, "No more, please."

"Four." SLAP

I wanted to fall to the floor, but I knew that it would result in more of this.

"Five." SLAP

I closed my eyes and prayed.

When I awoke, I felt hands placing the same mint-scented cream on my back as before. I closed my eyes thinking that the hands were very caring. Almost loving. Yes. I almost felt love.

DAY THREE

After I woke up, I wrote down everything I could remember

of yesterday. It took me a while to find a comfortable sitting position. The corset hurt against my back. I looked down at it and touched it. It felt cold. Cold and leather. The claws were made of some sort of metal and each ended in a dull tip that merely pressed against my skin. The corset covered my breasts and ended at my hips. I touched it again then sighed. Why was I here? What did I do? Just then, the door opened, revealing the man with the tray. I crawled over to my blankets and watched him with wary eyes as he placed the tray next to me then left. *He never said anything to me*, I thought as I dug into the food. This time it was cut fruit, pieces of chicken that looked to be grilled, and a thick loaf of bread. I tore into the bread and moaned when I swallowed the warm chunks. The door opened again as I lifted a piece of bread to my mouth as the same man brought in a pitcher of water with a sponge to replace the one I used yesterday (was it YESTERDAY!?) then left again. I quickly finished eating then cleaned myself with the sponge and water. I wanted to be clean. Clean, clean, clean. I got the corset wet again yet I did not care. Once finished, I slowly turned to face the chain that held me in place then began yanking on it with as much force as I could muster.

"Damn it," I yelled. "Give, you motherfu —" The door opened, revealing the man that made me cry. I released the chain and whimpered as he walked toward me. As he reached for me, I twisted and squirmed yet he grabbed my arm and hoisted me to my feet. I crumpled to the floor. He pulled me up again then slammed me against the wall as he ripped off my corset. I cried.

"One. Two. Three. Four. Five." I no longer cared about how the whip cracked against my back. I wanted to die. I closed my eyes. "Six. Seven. Eight. Nine. Ten." He sped up, I thought in my half dream state. Over and over, the whip fell against my back.

Over and over, over and over.

When I came to, I made sure to roll over to see who placed the mint cream on my back. It was the man who had savagely beaten me. I looked into his eyes, twisting my body and the welts. I lay in his lap.

"W-who are you?" I croaked. He did not answer, but his blue eyes now focused on my own pleading ones. "Who are you? Why am I here?" He said nothing but gently rolled me back so he could apply more of the mint cream against my back. It did not sting. It felt good. I touched one of his knees and tenderly rubbed it. That was my thanks for the cream. Did he care? After applying the cream, he then reached for the corset and placed it on me then moved me over to my blankets. I rolled to my side and watched him pack up his "tools" then left my room without a word. I closed my eyes and fell asleep.

I woke to the sound of the door being opened. I braced myself for anything to happen, only to whimper as a young woman dressed in white walked in. She carried a white robe.

"No, no!" I screamed. I knew what she represented. This would be the end. She was worse than the man with the whip. She was cruel. I screamed over and over as she walked toward me. I felt her remove my corset and then she lifted me to my feet. I wanted to protest and yank away from her, but I knew that it would not do me any good. I felt the robe placed on my body then she smiled sadly as she led me out of the stone room. I wanted to die.

"Well, Miss Lanier, how did you enjoy your stay?"

"Very much, thank you." Gloria glanced around the entrance room then at the others who waited for their escort to take them to their place as reserved. Some of them wore expressions of happiness, while others had their eyes closed as if in anticipation of what was the come.

"Miss Lanier, I see that…yes, you ordered the Black Corset Treatment, is that correct?"

"Yes, correct."

"Well, please sign this invoice and you'll be on your way!" Gloria signed the document, wincing only a bit from the dull pain that throbbed from her back and down her left arm.

"Ooo, would you like something for the pain?"

"No, no, I'm good. Thanks, Julie." She then checked the invoice, making sure that she received everything that came in that particular vacation package, then smiled as she handed it back to the receptionist.

"All righty then, thank you for visiting ESCAPE again, Miss Lanier! And a BIG thank you for being one of our regular customers!"

"Thank you as always, dear. You know, I wasn't sure if I was going to like the Black Corset Treatment or not, seeing as how you guys just released it last month."

"You wouldn't believe how many of our Level One Customers have requested that treatment!" said Julie with a smile on her face. "Although, and I'm not supposed to tell any of our customers this," she said as she leaned closer to Gloria, "but we're supposed to be revealing a new level in the next three months for our Level One Customers only." Gloria's eyes lit with excitement.

"What's it called?"

"*Violet* Corset. That's all I can say," said Julie as she held up her hands in mock submission. Gloria laughed then asked when would she receive the program book, to which Julie stated that it would be next week. Gloria winked then waved goodbye as the bellboy ran up to get her belongings to take them to the taxi. Gloria followed the bellboy outside to the taxi station and to the rest of the world. As she carefully got into the taxi, she smiled as she rubbed her back against the faux leather seat. Violet Corset. The best that money could buy. She closed her eyes and dreamt of the man in black as the taxi drove off.

The Circus

Emily Lavin Leverett

He was handsome and so, so young, like the heroes we have come to expect in stories like this. Tall, too. Blond. Gray eyes. Under his arm he carried a beat up black leather bag covered in dust and wear. He scanned the yard, eyes never stopping on anything. He shifted his weight, rolling from heel to toe and back.

They were always nervous.

We stepped out from behind our wagon, our tuxedo jacket over one arm, top hat in hand. He saw us, and his eyes lit up. Uncertainty fluttered in them, too, but by the time we got to him, he'd shifted his bag to his opposite side, clutching the battered handle, and held out his other hand.

We shook it. Up close, he was more lovely. His face was familiar. Had he been at the show last night? Maybe. They usually started there.

"I'm…"

"No." We released his hand and cut him off. "Thank you for your interest, but we are not hiring at this time." We pulled loose the knot in the tie at our throat.

He shoved a hand through his hair and his smile turned to a frown. Even frowning, his face was smooth. We'd seen so many faces, passing through from town to city, with lines turned to creases by the sun, the fear. His weren't.

"Please," he said.

We shook our head. "We don't take in strays. It's too hard. You're running from something." We held up a hand before he asked. "You always are. You're not the first. You won't be the last. You're always trouble. We do not want trouble."

We turned and walked away. In the distance, the tent puffed out its sides and floated down. Strongman and Lion Tamers would be done soon. We'd move tonight.

"I'm Peter," he said as we retreated. His footsteps were muffled by the dirt, but we could hear him, not running, trotting. Catching up. He fell into step next to us. "I'm not in any trouble."

"You must be," we said. "Only people in trouble run away to join the circus." We cast a sideways glance at him and thrust a hand into our pocket.

"I'm not in any trouble with the law," he insisted.

"A girl, then?" we asked.

He snorted, like a horse, and we stopped.

"Please," he said. "No law will come after me." He grinned. "No angry father with a shotgun either."

"And your people? Have you any people? Will they miss you? Seek you?" Indecision rose in us. Some of us wanted to give him a chance. Those eyes, that build, lean and long and powerful up close. The rest of us, no, not so much. Those eyes, that build, fierce and dangerous up close.

He saw our confusion. "No family."

We did not expect him to elaborate.

A loud clang broke the silence of our stares. Acrobat cried out.

We turned from him and sprinted toward the cry, top hat and jacket dumped on the ground. He followed, outpaced, (not difficult, we work together well on some things, sprinting is not one of them), reached the tent. A pole had fallen the wrong way. Acrobat's leg caught.

The elephant curled his trunk around the pole, lifted. Acrobat cried out again.

Peter darted to him, dropped his bag on the ground.

"Don't touch him!" Strongman loomed.

Peter yanked open the bag, ignoring the massive Strongman, but a tremble in Peter's hands revealed his fear. He grabbed scissors and cut away the material. He drew a sharp breath. "Broken," he said, looking at Acrobat's face. "Can I touch you?" He added hastily, "I was a medic in the war."

We were next to them now. We crouched next to Acrobat, eased him up, and leaned him against us. "Let him," we said.

Gritting his teeth, the small man nodded. "My acrobatics," he whispered.

"Shush." We nodded at Peter.

"I'm sorry," he said. "This will hurt."

Acrobat shrieked at the pop of the bone as Peter set it. We clutched Acrobat tighter and whispered in his ear.

"There," Peter said. "Can someone get me a splint? It should heal fine. I'll wrap it." He pulled a clear bottle of liquid out of his bag. "To ward off infection," he said. "It will sting."

Acrobat grunted.

A half an hour later, Acrobat was propped up in his bed, Strongman hovering over him. Peter had given Acrobat something for the pain. It seemed to be working.

Strongman looked at the boy. "War medic?"

"Yes." Peter did not turn away from his patient. "I'll check on you later."

With Strongman, we followed the young doctor out the door where a group had gathered. They all looked to us.

"He'll be fine," we said. "Rest, recuperation."

"Is he staying?" Strongman asked.

"If you'll have me," Peter answered before we could speak.

We shrugged. "Useful."

"I am Elephant Tamer." Huge to the point of fat, with gentle eyes, Elephant Tamer smiled at Peter and held out his hand.

"Lion Tamers," said one of twins. His dirty blond hair matched his sister's. They were compact, lean, and in their tamer costumes.

"Mermaid," the woman next to them said. Lanky red hair, damp from her time in the tank, she sat in a wheelchair, legs covered with a blanket.

"Strongman," he said, holding out a hand almost the size of Peter's head.

To his credit, Peter shook it. "I'm Peter," he said. "Thank you for taking me in."

"We haven't yet," we said. "Until Acrobat is well, you can stay. Then we will see."

The rest murmured assent and wandered off, leaving us with him. "Sounds fair," he said. "Where do I stay?"

"Do you have things? Or just your medical bag?"

"Just the bag," he said.

We caught our growl before it escaped. "No trouble?" we asked. "You swear?"

"I always carry my bag with me," he said. "There's a change of clothes in the bottom." He set it on the dirty ground and opened it again. He handed us his wallet. "I came to the show. I had to stay."

We flipped it open. Cards, papers, words that Acrobat would understand. One had a picture of Peter on it. We pawed through. Another picture. Peter, young, with two older boys, almost men.

"These are?"

"Brothers," he said, voice distant.

"Gone," we said.

He did not respond.

"Come," we said. "There is one empty wagon. You may have it." We led the way and he followed. "Emcee left us not too long ago. For a man who loved horses, who loved him, who would give him a home. We could not—would not—keep him from that." We moved up the stairs and opened the door. "We do not keep it locked, in case he comes back." We pointed at the vanity at one end of the small room. "The key is there." We turned. "The bed is made. There are clothes in the closet. We do not know if they will fit." We moved past him back to the door.

"Thank you." He sat on the bed. "We leave tomorrow?"

"Yes." We frowned at him. "If you are able, help them pack up and link the wagons. Do you know how to drive a motorized vehicle?"

"Yes," he said. "I drove an ambulance or two in the War."

"You may be useful. Good evening." We stepped out the door.

"Wait!" he called.

We paused, but did not turn.

"What's your name," he said.

"We are called Enchanter," we said and walked into the darkness.

When Acrobat knocked the next day, we were ready.

"I'll be ready by tomorrow night," he said, opening the curtains and letting in the bright sun. "It's noon," he added. "Have you eaten yet?"

We wanted to know how Peter was doing, if he had helped

this morning, if he was fitting in. The wagon jerked slightly, its wheels lurching into motion. We hadn't heard the start of the engine.

"He fixed it," Acrobat said without our asking. "Quieter now." He stared at us, waiting for us to ask about Peter. We did not. We slipped into the corset, its red and black brocade held stiff and upright by the ancient whalebone inside it. We poured ourselves in and drew a breath.

Deft fingers—fast, but gentle, too—tugged and tightened the heavy black laces. As one, we breathed out as he pulled us in. In the mirror, our eyes settled to brown today. Our hands trembled as we pulled on our slacks, brushed our hair. "We need a day off." Our voice was hoarse.

"We have one. Today." He stepped from behind us, standing next to us, our reflections staring back. Without his fancy costume, jester's diamonds and sequins, he was merely a man. We traced our fingers down the stiff braces on our corset, shrinking our body from chest to hip. Our clothes were threadbare, but for our corset, and we'd need better clothes soon.

"A day off with no traveling. In the city." We swayed along with the rumbling and rocking of the wagon. "Where is he?"

"With Strongman and Tamers," he said. "He helped a lot today. He's not nearly as strong as they are, but he's willing to work."

"He won't stay," we said.

"Of course not." In the mirror his eyes twinkled, with their large black pupils. "They never do, love." He kissed our cheek and squeezed us in a hug. It was meant to be comforting, friendly, but it made us daydream about Peter's soft fingers.

"We should leave him at the next stop," we whispered.

"He saved my leg." Acrobat bent and stood a few times. "By

tonight I shall do flips."

"Careful," we cautioned. "And you would have healed anyway."

"Not so fast and not so well," he admonished us. He sat on the edge of the bed, his own narrow corset that let him twist and fly. "Do magic for me, Enchanter"

"No," we said. "Our magic isn't right today."

"Will you practice?" He leaned back against the window. Outside, scenery sped by. The town had been small. We didn't note the name. The money had been passable, we thought. But we didn't do the counting. The green scenery gave way to city outskirts. But even here, spring had started. Small shoots of green worked their way out of the twisted ground. In the distance, a farmer rolled across the field on a great engine.

"We always practice, don't we?" We shook our head. Voices echoed again. We were unstable today. The travel always made us nervous.

"Do you want me to go?"

We blinked. He sounded sad. If he stayed, he might touch us again. "Yes."

He stood. "See you at dinner?"

"Maybe. If we are stopped by then."

"We will be." He pushed open the door and the rumble of the wheels rolled in. He swung himself out the door and leapt to the wagon in front of ours. One deft kick and our door clicked shut. He didn't even slam it.

"Set us free," we said, turning back to the mirror. Tousled black hair, a little too long, that needed to be styled for the evening. Cheeks and lips pale, in need of color and definition. They could wait. "Please."

From under the bed our rat crept out, white fur bristling

and pink eyes twitching. We turned away from the mirror as he climbed up the vanity. We let out a tight held breath when he loosened the knot and pulled the strings free.

The next stop was a field outside the town. Lights sparkled in the distance, and we wondered about them, but we wouldn't go closer today. The bell rang for supper, but we didn't go. We shook our head, but even without the magic, we were we. Strongman tapped on our window, waved, kept walking. So much more comfortable walking than we were.

A knock at the wagon door. We sniffed the air. Peter. He tried the handle. Locked.

"Enchanter's resting." A voice. Acrobat? "Preparing for the show."

"Oh." Disappointment? We tried not to preen.

The tent was up, lamps lit and sparkling. Acrobat did flips across the center floor. The audience applauded. He bowed.

Strongman lifted bars that men could not, should not.

Acrobat pointed to a man in the audience, burly, strong. Tamer led him down, her steps light as dancing. He strained as he tried to lift what Strongman had held in one hand, aloft, with a grin. The man laughed and shook his head. Strongman tossed the dumbbell in the air, flipping it end over end, tumbling down. He caught it and bowed low as the light on his ring dimmed.

The lights in a different ring blazed. Mermaid, in her tank. Her tail thrust back and forth and she rose, in a sea of bubbles to the top, held herself at the edge, sang in a language no one understood. She splashed, sending water across the audience.

"She will be available for pictures after the show," Acrobat said.

She would? We were not amused. We had not done that before.

The lion, the gorilla, the elephant, all paraded around.

The spotlight dimmed on them, blazed on my ring. "Our Enchanter!"

We stepped into the light and fought the urge to sprint away. We shuffled ourselves. We curtsied, and when we rose, doves flew from our fingertips. A rabbit came next. In the audience, the children giggled. And then, when the doves and rabbits were put away, we sang with our nightingale voice.

We can never see the faces in the crowd. The spotlight is too bright. But we hear well, and there are tears. We sing for the lost lands. We sing for the lost loves. We sing for the wounded from war. We sing for those that have no voice, whose bodies are lost in fields, buried in unmarked graves, or brought home. When we stop, we wait. Applause. We leave.

"That was incredible." Peter waited at the edge of tent.

"Thank you." We were tired. We are always tired afterwards. Edgy. Our voice projected something we were not. Something human. His eyes human, too human. *Only* human. "Excuse us." We tried to step around, and he let us, but followed.

"I helped with the tent this morning," he said.

"We know." We are trembling.

He must have known, because he reached for our elbow, steadying us on the uneven ground. "You are beautiful," he said, his voice soft. "You shimmer in the ring."

"A trick of light and makeup." Our wagon was closer now, and the corset constricted us more than usual. Behind us the people poured from the tent, show over. Their chatter rang in our ears, confusing. The photographic bulbs shocked the darkness in a bolt of illumination. Our steps faltered. He caught us.

"Easy," he said, and helped us to the steps of our wagon, eased us down. "Are you okay? Do you want me to get one of the others?" He turned to go.

"No!" we said. "We're fine, but do not like the flashing."

He frowned. "That was my idea. There is press here. Pictures will bring more customers. We had to turn away a few tonight. The Acrobat—"

"Acrobat is his name." We cut him off.

"Sorry. Acrobat said there will be a show tomorrow, too. Maybe we'll even stay longer. Maybe even go to London."

"No." We almost shouted the word. "We must keep moving. We must not attract too much attention!"

He laughed. "You're a circus. What else to do you want but attention?"

Our hearts fluttered and we gasped for air. The corset was so tight. Too tight. We blinked, but the darkness edged out the light even more. Voices were confused, distant.

He caught our wrist. "Your pulse is out of control. I'm getting my bag."

We pulled our hand away. "Wait…"

But he was gone, to his wagon, Emcee's wagon. We reached behind us, clawing at the strings, trying to loosen them. He was back, kneeling in front of us. He drew out something, fixed two parts in his ears and leaned forward with the metal disk. We jerked away.

"I won't hurt you," he said, voice low, calm. "Settle down. This is just to listen to your heart."

We stilled. A human had done that before. Reached for us, with metal things, all of us. Panic rose again. We slapped him, nails clawing his face.

He reared back, hand darting to his jaw. "It isn't like that."

Like what? Thoughts raced through our mind, images of cages, from cages. It wasn't only us — those of us here — in cages. Other people, broken to bits, like us. We leaned away.

He pulled back. "You're afraid of me."

We nodded.

He put the tool back in his bag. "Someone hurt you."

Another nod. We pulled our knees up, wrapped our arms around them.

He frowned. Blond hair. Gray eyes. Not the only one to look like that.

He sat back on his knees and watched us. Our nose twitched. Our heartbeat thundered in our ears, unstable, a dozen beating on their own, not together. We hauled air into our lungs, shoved it out again.

"I am not going to hurt you." He never broke our gaze, never moved. He kept his hands on his thighs. "Do you want me to loosen the corset?"

Yes. But we shook our head. "No." Breathy still, but less so.

He rocked back and stood, offered us his hand. "Let's get you back to your wagon."

We let him help us to our feet. In the distance, lions roared.

"It is dangerous," we said, "to let people too close to Tamers."

He said nothing, only looking in the direction of the noise. "No shrieks of terror," he said finally.

"Goodnight, Peter." We turned from him and entered our wagon.

The weeks rolled by, though more slowly, and Peter had been

right. The press attention meant that there were crowds waiting at every town, and we when stopped, we stayed multiple days. People took more pictures. Peter collected newspaper clippings of us. All of us. Peter had made arrangements in London for our show, too.

We knocked softly on Mermaid's wagon.

She opened the door, rolled her chair down the ramp. She never let anyone in.

"Are you well?" we asked.

She shrugged. "Peter wants to examine me. He has almost everyone else." Her eyebrow shot up. "But not you."

We shook our heads. "His touch brings back too many memories."

"He's harmless," she cackled. She was old, oldest of us all, and her corset was frayed, ancient. She smoothed down the jagged, torn edges, resettled the blanket across her legs, folded her hands in her lap.

"I am, you know," he said from behind us.

We spun to face him, and he was smiling. Like always. He looked harmless, even smelled harmless.

"I came to check on you, Mermaid," he said, speaking past us. "Are you feeling all right?"

"Very," she smiled—flirted! "I'm going to leave you two alone." She rolled away.

He drove his fingers through his hair again. "She thinks I need someone, but I'm not interested." He looked at the ground, at her wagon, but not at us.

"We are not the right kind of someone." We wanted to walk away. All the others trusted him. He counted the money. He bought supplies. He talked to the mayors, the city men. All things that Emcee had done before he left us.

"You all wear corsets," he said. "You, Tamers, even Strongman and Mermaid."

"Hers is damaged," we said. We ran our fingers down our corset, settling them on our hips.

"No one will let me look at them with the corset off," he continued, a frown forming on his lips. "Why? They all said to ask you."

"No." We shook our head. "We told you that you could not join us."

"What?" He forced a smile. "I don't get a corset, too?"

Our turn to frown. "These are all we have. We don't know if there are more."

"Where do they come from?" he asked, and reached for ours.

We stepped back. "Who knows?"

"Who hurt you?" he asked, suddenly close again, but not touching us. Gray eyes so close we could see the specks of blue buried in them. He was taller than we were, but not by much, not when we were dressed for the ring.

We shrugged. "It does not matter," we said. "They are gone. We are away from them. We escaped during the War. From a city. From people with cages and—" We stopped.

He looked away from us then. Tightness gripped our chest. "Will you send me away? The others listen to you."

We pressed our lips to his, slipped our fingers through his hair and held him. He did not jerk away. When we stepped back, he stared at us. "Your heartbeat in your lips," he said, "it races like..." He shrugged. "Are you sure you are well?"

"Shouldn't our pulse race when we kiss you?" Tremors rushed through our flesh, raising goose bumps along our arms, our legs. "Go rest, Peter. We have a meeting, as we are sure Acrobat told you. A private meeting."

He nodded and darted in to press his lips to our cheek. We smiled. But watched him all the way back to his wagon, until the door closed and the latch caught behind him.

The tent waited for the show that evening. The rope barrier still up, the ticket booth ready for Peter. In the main ring, the rest waited for me.

"You will help us?" Lion Tamers asked.

We loosened the strings on their corsets, on Strongman, Elephant Tamer, and Acrobat. We whistled. Our rat scurried out and loosened our strings.

Our corset fell, and we tumbled away from each other, landing on top of each other, next to each other. The two cats leapt from the pile, landing delicately on the raised edge of the ring, tails swishing. Four mice scurried away. Three rabbits loped to chew on carrots left at the edge of the ring. A nightingale fluttered to a perch on the trapeze. I hopped up on the dais at the center, my head still spinning. My black fur sleek and shining, I stretched and barked.

Noises rose around us, the roars of the lion, the trumpet of the elephant. The gorilla beat his chest and hurled the dumbbell across the ring with a kick. The chimpanzee swung himself up to the trapeze.

I padded up to Mermaid, laid my head in her lap.

"Good boy," she murmured. Tears streamed from her eyes. The corset could not be loosened, could not be cut free. We had tried every sharp blade we had, but she was caught, trapped between human and dolphin.

My ears perked. From their perch, the cats hissed. Near the flap of the tent, a figure, tall. I charged, snarling, flung myself at it, knocked it to the ground.

Gray eyes, blond hair. He didn't fight. Others joined me,

surrounded him. His bag had been knocked from his arms, and his tools had scattered on the ground. I snuffled through them. His wallet tumbled from his bag, and I pawed at the cards that fell from it. The symbol on one, I knew it.

From the tent, Acrobat emerged, human again and tugging at the corset around his ribs and waist, our rat running along beside him. "Peter," he said, voice harsh and scratchy from the change. "We told you it was not a meeting for you."

I nudged the wallet toward Acrobat. He opened it and glanced down. "You were there," he said. His hand dropped to his side and I could see too. A badge. Like this, it was difficult for me to read — to make out the words. But I knew the symbol — we all did. It haunted all of us, fastened to every cage, to every man and woman who poked us, who mixed magic with science.

I growled.

"Wait!" Peter held up his hands, scooted away. "I wasn't a part of what happened to you. After the War, I joined." He pointed at the wallet. "Look at the picture in my wallet!"

Acrobat pulled out the picture he had shown us on his first day. Peter as a boy, and two young men.

"My brothers. They took them because they —" He flailed at the air. "They were different. Magical, like you —"

"We're not magic," Acrobat said. "We were made. We were human. Now…"

Peter shook his head. "I know what they did there. My brothers…" He dropped back to his knees. "I never found them. I knew some escaped during the London bombing. There were missing people posters — you." He looked toward me. "I hoped maybe you knew…"

I sat next to him, pressed my nose to his face. He slung an arm around me. Buried his face in my back, his tears wetting my fur. From the tent, the mice came, dragging the corset. My sister, the cats and rabbits, the nightingale. We crawled into the corset, our bodies joining, entwining. In my ears, my own heartbeat pounded in time with the others. I closed my eyes, the world was too blurry. Around our body, the fabric tightened, we stretched to our human size. We pulled on pants and a shirt, leaving it unbuttoned.

We wrapped an arm around him. "We're sorry, Peter."

He leaned in to us and let his tears fall. No loud sobs—just a continuous stream as his body shook.

We ran our fingers through his hair.

One by one, the rest of the troupe stepped away.

"They gave us animal form," we said. "We may have seen your brothers, but we don't remember. We fled when the bombs broke the building. We are sorry we cannot help you."

He reached for our face and we did not turn away. "You are yourself?"

We nodded. "They broke us—me—into pieces. Turned the others to their animals. We are always together, without all of us, the corset does not work. I lead. When we scatter, the black dog has the most of me."

He leaned in, his gaze piercing. His red rimmed eyes shaded a darker gray by grief. "Can I stay?"

Our companions had gathered at the tent doorway, human once more. "The world is changing," we said. "We don't understand the machines. But you do, yes?"

He nodded.

"We need Emcee. Someone to announce us, to bargain for us, to—"

"To watch over you." He wiped his tears away and pushed himself to his feet.

We let him help us up. "Yes but—"

"To love you?" He cut us off.

We froze. "Love is difficult," we said. A lie. It was easy, too easy, with him. The feelings rolled through us.

He shook his head. "Not for me."

We looked past him to the others, their eyes uncertain. "All of us?" we asked, our voice a whisper. "You'll love all of us?"

"Everyone in the Circus," he said and pressed his lips to ours. He trailed kisses down our cheek to our ear and whispered, "and you most of all."

We leaned our head on his shoulder. "Stay."

Homecoming

Dave Harlequin

There's nothing quite like the first real morning of a Carolina autumn. If you've ever properly experienced this, you know exactly what I mean. Sitting outside, looking up at the fog billowing from the mountains, the changing leaves hanging like curtains against the light of the rising sun, a crisp chill in the air, and the aromatic smell of late September mixing with that of nutmeg scented candles and freshly brewed coffee. Cliché as it may sound, there's certain magic in the air, and even if you can't really explain it, you just know that in this moment there's no place, in this world, or any other, that you'd rather be.

I wasn't born of these mountains, yet somehow it's the only place I've ever truly, honestly felt at home. In truth, I barely even remember much of my old life anymore, which, before I was embraced at least, was unremarkable on a good day. Even way back then I always knew I didn't belong in the so-called concrete jungle, which couldn't have been more apparent the first time I ever finally gave in to that overpowering gut feeling and took a vacation to hike the Appalachian trail like my forefathers did. Honestly, *gut feeling* just doesn't do it justice, as it's more like a screaming command. These silent screams of what I can only refer to as a pure, ancestral calling brought me here so many years ago, and it's that same calling that, no matter how far I travel, always brings me back.

They say home is where the heart is, and the same blood that pumps through mine is that of my kinsmen from centuries past, which forged and nurtured the very lands I've come to love, long before I drew my first breath, much less took my first taste of the sweet, deep red which has carried me far beyond my, shall we say, *originally-planned* years.

These old mountains, virtually untouched by the vast oceans of time, serve as a proud reminder of how these ancestors of mine came to call this land theirs, and a testament to my belief that they once shared the same look of awe at the majesty stretching all around me, and this feeling of unmitigated, untamed wonder that I still feel every single time I come back here. Every single time I come back...home.

You don't know me, but I've watched you from afar your entire life. Considering you are the only family I have left, I felt it was only right that I address these final words to you. My name is Gerald William Edwards IV, and by my count, I am your great, great, great granduncle. Of course, I tend to get confused sometimes at my age, so I could be wrong about that. Also, I am a vampire.

This will be my one hundred and forty-fourth year on this planet, a good even number. And though I don't expect you to believe me, I'd imagine that doesn't really matter anymore. There is so much fiction about my kind now, so many exaggerations and re-imaginings of late that I honestly don't remember which parts are even true anymore...at least, beyond the obvious few.

For example, I do often laugh at the trite, meaningless, and all too often utterly ridiculous stereotypes placed upon my kind by the so-called *normal* humans. Seriously? Who even came up with the garlic thing? It was one man, okay? One man, who just so happened to be allergic to garlic, *back when he was still human,* mind you, gets blindsided by one of those crazy Eurotrash vampire hunters who just so happens to get lucky and catch the one member of the order that the stuff hurts and writes a stupid book about it. Suddenly The Council says we all have to play along, I suppose because we have some legend to uphold or something. Hence this damned ridiculous attire they want me to wear to *"keep up appearances"* as they put it. But to hell with The Council, and to hell with their standards! These costumes — and yes they *are* costumes, it's the twenty-first century for God's sake — are little more than some trite, perverse fantasy the elders like to impose on the rest of us.

I know what you're probably thinking, *an imposed dress code?* Yeah. We are always expected to wear these bullshit, antiquated getups. Perhaps to look more like a gentleman of old, or maybe just to scare people, I honestly don't know. But they actually impose punishments on those of us that would just rather wear something comfortable as opposed to standing out when we're also supposed to remain hidden. Can you think of anything more illogical? Stay to the shadows, obey the code, don't ever tell anyone what we are, never let the existence of our kind become common knowledge, but oh — there is a certain standard to which you're expected to look for the family. I suppose that's fine for the ladies and the skinny pretty boys a lot of the hunters love to pick up as protégé pets and thralls, but what about those of us that turned in their mid-40s after the ale houses and good old-fashioned metabolism caught up with us? The old form-fitting Gay 90s (*that's 1890s to you*) slash Victorian look isn't so flattering anymore. Hence this god damned corset I have to strap and tie onto myself under my shirt! That's probably the worst part of it all.

Luckily the previous occupants of this lovely little rustic vacation home had some very comfortable clothes in the wardrobe...and plenty of firewood! The goddamned cold, it's always so goddamned cold. You never really get used to it.

The flames from the bonfire rage into the night sky with the fury of the old gods, and the smell of seared leather and hickory smoke fill the air around me. I always did have a way with words, didn't I? I have no apprehension about drawing attention to myself out here. Bonfires in these mountains are commonplace anyway, and besides, I don't really care if anyone does find me now. Cheap faux-velvet robe, belly hanging out over the piss-water brewery logo boxer shorts, a half a box of stale Cuban cigars, and a nice dark lager mixed with whoever the pretty blonde in bathtub was. If we had vampire beer commercials, there's a good one for you right here. Grab a cold one. It's killer time!

Alas, I often miss the mark on attempted humor, but I digress. If this is to be my last will and testament, or at the very least just something to write to kill time as I await my final hour, something that you won't even believe or care about, I'll just write whatever comes to mind, and everyone can kiss my cold dead ass, how's that? This drink seems to be having some effect now, so at least there's that.

Shit, I should've tried to work in something about a *Bloody Mary*—that would've been funny, but *cést la vie*. Sorry, I find myself rambling here, and I'm just making that Mary part up; I don't know if her name was Mary, as I don't typically stop to ask my prey for their names, no more than you ask the cows you eat theirs. They're just food. Didn't ask the pretty blonde, didn't ask her pretty boy husband, and didn't ask the guard at the gate to get into this fancy estate. None of them were even here when I first spotted this place two years ago, the night I made the decision to meet my true death here.

That reminds me, there is one thing I should probably address, as I know this must be a lot to take in. Feeding on others was never a problem for me, merely a necessity that was no more or less cruel than stuffing a bird, or plucking a garden. Death feeds life; it's as simple as that. But again, that doesn't really matter. I'm not writing to justify myself, least of all to you; I only wish to point out that my decision is not based on petty remorse spawned from one of your silly stories of the brooding vampire in search of love whilst lamenting his wicked ways. I'm not the slightest bit sorry for anything I've done — *well except following The Council's ridiculous customs, perhaps, but I've already said that —* just as I'm quite sure the happy little honeymooners that were kind enough to invite me in tonight and dumb enough to believe my half-baked bullshit of being the local country club manager weren't sorry for that greasy, deep-fried disaster that they ate earlier. Damn those two tasted awful. No, after a long, boring century I'm just frankly tired of all of this nonsense and as silly as it may sound, after a hundred years of darkness, I just want to experience that first autumn sunrise, my last sunrise, just one more time.

This place is really nice. One of those big modernized log cabin affairs, you know all the nice rustic architecture combined with all the luxury to make it all seem pretty fake. This is what rich people consider *roughing it,* I guess. Big massive windows overlooking the mountains, vaulted ceilings, bookshelves cut into the walls, a big stone fireplace, and of course, a really nice wraparound porch with some very nice lounge chairs and one of those hardware-store-special portable iron fire pits right outside the den. From the first moment I saw it, I knew that this was where I was heading. After I dealt with *Mr. and Mrs. Whoevertheshit* and got out of these ridiculous clothes, I gathered up all the firewood they had, built myself a fine little fire, and tossed them right the fuck in. It was really fulfilling to do it, too. My only regret was that those uppity pricks from The Council weren't here to see me roast their little *Count Fancypants* getup and receive their two-finger salute. But none of that matters much now, apart from turning what I had planned to be a lovely, well-crafted, literary award worthy goodbye into a bitter, half-drunk rant. Fuck it. At the very least, I made sure to gather up the charred remains of this corset along with a nice "*fuck you*" letter and package it all up for a very special delivery. I'll keep it beside me, so if you could add that to the outgoing mail for me, I'd really appreciate it.

When you manage to live for almost a century and a half, and you spend the last hundred years or so of that as a vampire who doesn't really pay for anything, one thing you do accumulate plenty of is wealth. I was always smart enough to loot everyone I ate—taking money, valuables, you name it. I also always had a thing for books, and at last count had over six thousand of them, in every genre there is, from the rare and obscure, to the commonly known classics, and everywhere in-between. I've also read them all, I'm proud to say. Every single one of them, usually more than once, even. They each have their own place on the many shelves in my library at home. I leave that money, that beautiful library, and the fairly nice plantation estate just outside Charleston, South Carolina, that houses it to you, my dear boy. It's no mountain retreat, but it's a lovely place all the same and should always stay in the family. You'll find the deed, keys, and a map on exactly how to get there in the trunk of your car. Do start remembering to lock it at night, by the way. Clearly anyone can just walk up and plunder through it.

Four nights from now, twin sisters named Valera and Eliza

will arrive at the house; they are two of my dearest friends and already have my permission to enter. They will be taking the two antique cars in the garage, the old film projector and its film reels in the attic room, and everything in the wine cellar. You will not have a key to the wine cellar, so don't even think of going in there before they arrive. After they've finished, they'll leave you the only key to it, and you may do with it as you wish. While I have specifically asked them to not harm you, I would still highly suggest staying out of their way. All I ask of you with all this money is just try to do something good with it; God knows I never did. Anyway, I should probably wrap this up.

There will be a nice fog today; I've chosen this spot well. Only about a half hour left of what they once called my endless night. As sappy as it may sound, I just hope the sunrise is as beautiful as I remember. I do apologize for my aforementioned rambling and bitterness. I once fancied myself quite the writer, but I digress, that was a lifetime or two ago. All I ask is that regardless of what you may think of me, that you please remember that life, no matter how long or short, is merely a collection of precious moments, and if you're ever fortunate enough to find the perfect one, pray to whatever god you believe in that you'll possess the wisdom to truly appreciate it. For it may very well be your last. Me, I was lucky enough to get to choose mine. And after a century of servitude, I'm just thankful to have this one moment of real freedom. Now if you'll excuse me, I'd like to take these fifteen minutes to relax. It's going to be a beautiful morning.

The Blue Lights

M.B. Weston

Never trust a coincidence. Looking back, I wish I had heeded that advice. I was an up-and-coming force in the banking industry; I knew what many often called coincidences almost always led to a trail of embezzlement. Why I couldn't apply that knowledge to regular life, I'll never know, just as I'll never know why I didn't sprint the other way the moment I saw *him*.

I first saw Captain Lawrence Wilson at Paddington Station in the crowd of people. He stood just over six feet tall, and his yellowed, pitted face drew him unwanted attention. I suspect, however, most people noticed his angry, pitiless eyes more than his complexion.

Seeing the captain brought back memories I had forced back into the recesses of my mind where only dark things lay. *He* resurrected visions of a face I intended to keep forgotten. Blue eyes, blond hair, soft curls. Her voice reminded me of wind chimes — especially when she said my name, John. Unfortunately, her pleasant memory no longer brought me joy. Instead, thinking of her only made my stomach feel twisted. I took a few deep breaths to steady myself and pushed her memory away yet again.

I noticed Wilson just as I purchased my ticket. *He should be dead*, I thought. *He would be dead, but for you*, I reminded myself. He would have stood trial for murder, if I possessed a shred of courage. Instead, I watched him board my train—alive.

Coincidence, I told myself.

I should have asked for a refund on my ticket. Instead, I lingered back, staying out of the captain's sight until he entered his railcar a few down from mine. I boarded my own car, hoping Wilson would disembark at a separate stop.

I took a seat next to the window soon forgot about the captain. An excited, anticipation-filled flutter filled my stomach. I pulled an ivory envelope out of my pocket and grazed my fingers over the Duke of Exeter's blue and red coat of arms prominently displayed on the envelope's flap. I opened the envelope and re-read the contents.

Mr. Blackburn,

The Duke of Exeter has heard of your fine work, and he would like to invite you to interview for the position of managing his assets and personal affairs. Please arrive at the Newton Abbot Train Station on Friday, October 12, 1883 at 2:00pm sharp. I will send my carriage for you.

Yours Sincerely,
Harold J. Meadows
Secretary to George Holland, Duke of Exeter

I felt the same shivers as I did when I first received the letter, excited that someone finally noticed my hard work and loyalty. While this position would take me away from the contacts and business partners I built in London, it promised a higher salary and the potential to return to London with even better prospects. I took every effort to ensure my interview ensemble looked perfect. I borrowed a friend's top hat, which would make a better impression than my bowler, and I spent more than I could afford on a pair of luxurious, black leather shoes. I wore my midnight-blue, silk waistcoat and my best coat. I considered wearing my warmer, second-hand jacket—especially considering the current October cold spell—but it sagged in the shoulders. I preferred the duke see me in fitted clothing, and I could handle the cold for a day. I intended to warm up later at the hotel, hopefully in celebration of a new job.

A quick flash of her face in my memory jostled away my elated fantasy. I forced it out of my mind and stared out the window as the train pulled away from the station. I rarely left London, and I relished the chance to see a world free of congestion and never-ending buildings. I yearned to breathe air uncontaminated by smoke and manure.

"Where are you headed?" asked the gentleman sitting next to me. I use *gentleman* loosely. His chapped lips covered his five remaining teeth, and multiple patches dotted his jacket and trousers. He probably bought them fourth-hand, I surmised.

I kept a straight face even though I wanted to wince from his unspeakably foul breath. "Devon," I replied, unsure of the duke's exact location. "Somewhere near Dartmoor."

"Ah! Beautiful territory. I've traveled there quite a few times myself. Planning on going out on the moors?"

"Not likely." I hoped my indifference might keep him quiet. I wanted to mentally run through my accomplishments and make sure I remembered everything that might help me secure the position with the duke.

"You be careful if you do decide to go exploring. The moors look innocent, but they're dangerous. I lost a pony in there once."

As much as I wanted to ignore the man, I couldn't help but give him a quizzical look. How did one lose a pony? Did it run off? *It probably feared the chap's breath,* I reasoned.

"It fell into one of the bogs," he explained. "Couldn't pull him out. Sank to its death. That's why they call the moors *the Dartmoor stables*. The final resting place for ponies that get trapped. And sometimes people."

The thought horrified me. I knew of bogs, the low-lying swampland on the moors filled with decayed peat and who knew what else, but I never thought about their dangers.

"Almost got stuck there myself once," he continued. "You get a foot caught in the quagmire, and it sucks you in. The harder you fight, the more it pulls."

"Then how did you escape?"

"First, you don't panic. Panic will kill a fellow. Use slow movements, and keep your body low to the ground." He bent over and illustrated an almost swimming position. "Try to get one foot free, even if your other sinks a bit. Crawl—or swim—out. Whatever you do, don't stand until you reach solid ground."

I nodded to placate him.

"Of course, it's best to keep away from bogs altogether. You'd best keep to the heather. That means dry ground. If you see too much moss, or the earth isn't stable, well, that's a sign you're nearing a bog."

"I appreciate your advice." I turned my gaze back to the window, hoping to avoid talk of drowning ponies and people. And what did he mean by unstable earth?

"Oh, and avoid the blue lights."

Once again, I involuntarily gave him my attention.

"Across the moors at night, sometimes you'll see a greenish-blue flash of light floating across the ground. Legends say they're the spirits of the poor souls who lost themselves in the moors and died. Their lights lure you in, and you never come out. You'd best stay away from them or risk becoming one yourself."

I kept my face serious, but I chuckled a bit inside. "I assure you, sir, that I have no intentions of venturing out on the moors — especially at night."

"That's what they all say." He sighed. "I'll never understand how such dreadful landscape can tempt so many reasonable chaps to their deaths." He leaned back against his seat and closed his eyes, leaving me to enjoy the rest of the train ride in peace.

The train finally stopped at Newton Abbot Train Station. I took my bag and stepped off the train. I inhaled. I could still smell the engine's burning coal, but I also caught a faint undertone of wet grass and soil. A light mist — clean, grey, and so unlike London's toxic yellow fog — hovered over the ground. I felt more confident in my decision to interview. The breeze picked up, blowing straight through my coat and waistcoat. I rubbed my arms, wishing I dared to wear my warmer jacket.

I picked up my luggage and headed to the station to wait for the duke's carriage. I leaned against a post and watched the other passengers disembark. My heart fell into my chest when I saw Captain Wilson leave his car as well.

Coincidence, I reminded myself, this time with a hint of doubt.

I turned my back to Wilson and instead faced the first class rail car. A diminutive, grey-haired gentleman wearing an impeccable suit and shoes caught my eye. His mustache hid his arrogant sneer. I took an involuntary step back. I feared this man, the Earl of Castleton, more than I feared Captain Wilson. Castleton inherited the title and the vast amount of land that came with it, but little cash to keep it up. In a matter of years, he turned his assets into ample cash flow and became one of the richest men in all of England, though not through purely honest means. The earl inspired fear among the commoners — normal folk without any titles trying to make life work. Castleton took what he needed from whoever crossed his path.

An unsettled feeling grew in my stomach. Castleton could make anyone do his bidding with the right motivation. I'm ashamed to say he once found my trigger point. She suffered for it. Her name was Mary. Mary Meadows—a name I vowed never to repeat.

I pondered the chances of Lord Castleton *and* Captain Wilson arriving at the Newton Abbot Train Station at the exact time as me. *Coincidence*, I told myself.

They glimpsed at each other, and each immediately looked the other way. Then, Captain Wilson saw me and his face took on a paler shade of sallow.

I should have marched up to the ticket booth and purchased a return ticket to London. Instead I opted to stay, refusing to let fear keep me from the interview. Soon, the rest of the passengers left the station, leaving Captain Wilson, Lord Castleton, and me— each of us refusing to acknowledge the other as we waited for our rides. Castleton stood as far as he could to the right, smoking a pipe while he waited. Wilson stood to the left, staring out at the landscape. He pulled out a pipe and filled it with tobacco. He felt around his pockets for a light, but found nothing. Instead of troubling either of us for one, he dumped the tobacco and put the pipe back in his pocket.

I took out the invitation once again and read the instructions. *Please arrive at the Newton Abbot Train Station on Friday, October 12, 1883 at 2:00pm sharp. I will send my carriage for you.* I craned my neck and read the sign above the depot: Newton Abbot Train Station. I checked my pocket watch and then the station's clock, which read 2:05pm. I re-pocketed the envelope and turned around, confident the carriage would arrive soon.

To my dismay, the captain took an envelope bearing the duke's coat of arms out of his pocket and double checked it as well. Though Lord Castleton never pulled out an envelope, I suspected he waited for the same carriage.

As minutes passed, I kept reliving memories I wanted to forget. Mary's blond hair. Her blue eyes. I thought at the time that I loved her. Lord Castleton had employed her as his governess, a prime but difficult position. His three children, while trained in all manners of etiquette, knew nothing of kindness or obedience.

The pit in my stomach grew. All three of us knew what happened, but none of us would ever talk about it. The sly captain knew enough to stay quiet. Lord Castleton's wealth and power cushioned him from worrying about the law. As for me, shame and fear kept my lips tight.

We waited for an hour-and-a-half. The wind turned icy, and I again wished I had brought my warmer coat. I checked my pocket watch. The captain looked visibly impatient. Lord Castleton showed little emotion. I pulled out the letter again to reconfirm the time and date.

Finally I caught a glimpse of an open-air cart bearing the duke's coat of arms pulling up by the station. I took hold of my luggage and stood up. So did the other two.

I should have run for it. Instead I waited.

The coachman, a young, slight man with black hair and focused, brown eyes, approached and introduced himself to the earl. "Lord Castleton, I presume."

Castleton nodded. "I expected the Duke of Exeter's *carriage* to arrive in a timelier manner." He eyed the cart with disdain.

"I apologize, my Lord. We were going to bring the landau, but one of the wheels gave us some trouble." The coachman opened the cart's door and ushered Castleton in. Castleton took a seat in the back on the left corner, facing forward. The coachman turned to the captain. "Captain Wilson?"

Wilson handed the coachman his bag and climbed onto the cart as well. He paused for a moment, looking as though sitting in such close proximity to Castleton might make him vomit, and finally took the seat across from Castleton facing backward.

Even in the cool weather, beads of sweat formed on my forehead. I wondered what strange chances caused Lord Castleton and Captain Wilson to board the same vehicle as me, and a chilling thought entered my mind. *What if the duke knew our secret?*

The coachman turned to me. "John Blackburn?"

I paused, unable to breathe. Should I pass off this encounter as coincidence or turn back to the station? After a deep breath and a long exhale, I nodded and handed the coachman my bag. I needed the job, and I refused to allow coincidence to interfere.

He took my bag and held the door open for me.

Even with my decision made, an involuntary shudder vibrated down my arms. I dreaded sharing a cart with either man. I finally stepped inside, convincing myself that neither would attempt conversation. I sat next to the captain, giving in to station and allowing the earl his own seat. Wilson scooted farther against his side of the cart, and I did the same. I never heard such loud silence.

The coachman hopped on the front and grabbed the reins. He turned around. "I apologize, Captain, but may I ask you to move to the right corner of the seat by Lord Castleton. For weight-distribution purposes."

The captain scowled at the coachman but obliged, leaving me the seat alone.

"We've got a two hour ride," said the coachman. "Let me

know if you need anything."

I honestly didn't know if I could survive looking into the eyes of both Castleton and Wilson for two hours. Fortunately, all of us avoided eye contact.

We wound through the country road, and I kept grabbing my hat to make sure it stayed on my head. The wind swirled around us, and I wished the coachman had brought the carriage instead. Soon I caught a glimpse of the moors. They looked like innocent rolling hills that produced their own unnatural fog. I found it hard to imagine that such territory contained the bogs the stranger on the train told me about. Crooked granite rocks formed at some of the hills' taller peaks. These were called tors, someone once told me. The barren, treeless countryside looked dreary. Not the London dreary, where rain and fog occurred daily in a bustling city, but the kind of dreary that settled around rural areas and seeped into the bones, making one feel alone on the rolling landscape. Maybe I liked city life, after all.

I kept my body twisted toward the front, staring ahead at the horses instead of at Castleton and Wilson. Each time I saw Castleton's eyes, I remembered back to the day it all started.

Back in my youth, I had worked as clerk in a bank in which Castleton sat on the board of directors. I still remember looking at a list of deposits, withdrawals, and interest for the earlier week and then noticing that the actual receipts differed from the books. The numbers differed only by a few hundred pounds dispersed here and there. I chalked it up to a mistake in bookkeeping and continued about my own business.

A week later, my curiosity overcame my complacency. I again recalculated actual receipts verses what the bank had recorded and realized that again, the numbers didn't match. I checked a few weeks later and found the same occurrence. I dug a deeper and discovered that each time, the discrepancies ended up in Castleton's personal account.

I kept the information to myself for a few weeks—long enough for Castleton to discover my newfound knowledge. I found myself staring at a huge promotion in return for my silence. I accepted. I still can't eat when I think about it.

I tried to think of something other than my past mishaps and wondered about Castleton's and Wilson's business with the duke. Maybe Castleton planned to visit with him over the weekend. Wilson's position as an army captain could indicate any number of potential business opportunities. Again I convinced myself that coincidence drove this unlikely meeting.

My thoughts left my conceived ideas pertaining to each of our visits and unfortunately settled on why I despised them. Mary, the governess. Her beauty grabbed more than my attention. It also grabbed Castleton's. Rumors said she spurned his advances. I suspect that spelled her doom—even before the whole thing started. Stubborn Mary always adhered to her principles.

"We'll take a shortcut to make up for lost time," the coachman announced. He turned off the main road. The cart bumped and jostled across the uneven terrain, and the seat cushions did little to shield us.

"I can't imagine why the other carriage's wheel needed fixing," Wilson mumbled.

Ahead, a line of fire and smoke rose into the sky. The coachman turned around. "Don't be alarmed. It's called swaling. We do it out on the moors every so often in order to keep the underbrush from becoming too much of a nuisance."

Soon thick, blinding smoke surrounded us. My eyes and windpipe stung from the fumes. I shut my eyes and covered my mouth and nose with a handkerchief.

Finally, the smoke began to clear.

"Confound it, man!" yelled Castleton. "Did you have to drive us directly into it? Is this even a road?"

The coachman ignored Castleton. I rubbed my eyes, waiting for the last of the smoke to leave. When I finally opened them, I saw Wilson staring wide-eyed down at the seat next to me.

I looked down as well. Horror filled my throat, constricting it more than the smoke. On the seat cushion—empty only a few moments ago—lay a pinkish-beige corset covered in dried blood.

I turned away, trying to breathe. Visions of blood on my hands, her dress, and those beautiful blond curls filled my memory.

"Is that some kind of joke?" demanded Castleton.

Wilson turned to me, rage filling his eyes. "Did you put this here, Blackburn?"

"What? Me? No!"

"You're sitting right by it," said Castleton.

"Where would I have hid it? Do you think I pulled it out of my waistcoat?"

"I say, you! Coachman!" yelled Castleton. "Did you put this here?"

The coachman turned around and glanced at the seat. He jumped in shock, yanking the horses' reins. The cart took a sharp turn to the left, throwing us to the side. The coachman pulled on the reins, bringing the horses to a stop.

"Was that absolutely necessary?" demanded the lord.

The coachman ignored him again, which surprised me. Few people ignore lords.

Castleton narrowed his eyes and his face turned a deep shade of pink. I suspected he planned to tell the duke of his servant's insubordination.

The coachman tied off the reins and hopped off. He walked

around to the back.

"What now?" asked Castleton.

"I'm checking the wheels, my Lord. We don't need any of them breaking off."

As he worked, I looked across the moors at the sun, which sank low toward the horizon. I checked my pocket watch. It was 6:03pm. I stared ahead and saw the duke's home, Holland Manor, in the distance. Relief filled me. I needed out of the vehicle, away from Castleton and Wilson and definitely far away from the corset.

I returned my gaze to the seat. The bloody corset still lay next to me.

"Which of you put this here?" demanded Castleton in a whisper.

I shook my head, as did the captain.

Castleton glared at both of us, but said nothing else in the coachman's hearing. Worry filled me. Which of them brought it, and why? I eyed Castleton, wondering if he had feigned his anger at the sight of the corset. Maybe he brought it as a warning, fearing I might talk if I left his watchful eye in London and took employment with the duke.

The coachman walked toward the front, jumped on, and took the reins. He pointed at the corset on the seat. "How did that get there?"

"We don't know," I answered. "It appeared in the smoke."

The coachman turned sober. "I've never heard of them materializing before."

"*Them?*" Castleton's arrogant tone started to sound comical.

"The spirits of those who've died on the moors." The coachman appeared distant. "They walk the moors at night, holding their blue lanterns, beckoning others inside to their doom. We call them Jack O' Lanterns here. But I've never heard of them doing something like this — especially in daylight." He looked genuinely scared. "We need to get to the Duke's residence. I've seen these Jack O' Lanterns before. I don't wish to see them again." He flicked the reins and threw his concentration into driving.

I looked carefully at the corset next to me. Was it hers? Did it truly materialize? My gaze fell on the dark maroon blotches. I wondered if they were truly blood stains, but repulsion overrode my desire to inspect the corset any closer.

No, it did not materialize in the smoke, I convinced myself. And Mary died in London, not here on the moors.

But she's from Devon, remember? I wondered why it took me so long to remember that detail. Did her soul return home to rest?

Rubbish. No Jack O' Lanterns with blue-green spirit lanterns dropped the corset on the bench. One of my companions did this to extract money, silence, or possibly a favor from the others. But which one of them would take the time to orchestrate such an odd gathering in such a random place?

While Castleton possessed the assets to arrange such a meeting, his wealth and power eliminated any need of the captain or me. My suspicions turned to Captain Wilson — a known gambler whose debt trapped him in Castleton's service to begin with. When Wilson grew low on funds, Castleton paid for his commission but at a price. The lord's generosity disguised his treachery and enslaved hundreds of people across London.

I broke away from my inner dissertation and noticed the other two eyeing each other and me with the same suspicion I felt. Two of us suspected the others, and one pretended to. I continued trying to ignore flashes of her face. I reminded myself of my innocence of her death, unlike the two who sat in front of me.

I decided to formulate an escape plan. Unfortunately, with the terrain and my lack of weapons, my strategy consisted mostly of running like a madman across the moors.

"Can someone at least remove this thing from the seat?" said Castleton, who probably had not picked something up for himself in years—if ever. He acted quite cavalier for someone facing such an accusatory item.

"*Don't touch it!*" said the coachman. "Who knows what magic it contains?"

"Magic." Castleton's voice held disdain. "You actually believe in these Jack O' Lanterns?"

I doubted that any magic actually resided in the corset, but the captain looked nervous. "I've seen the blue lights. They're real. I don't know what they are, but they're real."

"Do you think they're ghosts?" I asked.

"They're something. I didn't believe in ghosts until then." Wilson looked down at the corset. "This isn't a joke. Whichever of you put it here, fess up. You've made your point. I won't sleep for a month."

"I swear I didn't," I said.

"I wouldn't touch something like that," said Castleton.

I pretended to look out the side, but I kept half an eye on the captain. Was his excellent portrayal of fear an act?

But Castleton's just sitting there like nothing's wrong, I noted. Surely such a macabre reminder of misdeeds ought to stir some kind of emotion in him.

Castleton looked at Wilson. "Throw it out, then."

"I'm not touching it." Wilson's fear looked genuine. "If blue lights put it there, I don't want anything to do with it."

My suspicions settled back on the captain. I had trouble believing something like Jack O' Lanterns with blue lights would scare him this easily.

"You," Castleton said to me. "Throw it out."

"I'm with the captain," I said. While I didn't think the corset had anything to do with the blue lights or with a past soul who sank to her death on the moors, I enjoyed the opportunity to defy the earl.

Lord Castleton did nothing, and at that moment, I realized I had more power over him than I had led myself to believe. The freeing thought made me smile despite the current circumstances. I had grown tired of Castleton's bit in my mouth.

I studied the corset some more. Was it really hers? I stared carefully at the blood splatters. Did they match? I must admit that when I found her, I did not take time to look at the formation of blood on her dress.

I remembered her note to me: *Please come. I must speak with you.*

We met that night. I remember the feel of her embrace before she confided in me.

"Mr. Blackburn, you must help me," she had said. "I've discovered something I shouldn't have discovered." She proceeded to tell me of how she overheard Castleton and Wilson discussing their misdeeds. "I think Captain Wilson saw me," she ended.

I should have told her to send a telegraph immediately to Scotland Yard.

I didn't.

Instead I told her to keep it quiet. I wish I could say I encouraged her silence because I feared for her life, but I knew if she told anyone, the authorities might implicate me as well.

And now a corset—possibly her corset—lay next to me.

Across from me, Lord Castleton took the corset and flung it

over the side.

The moment the corset left his hand, we heard a loud bang near the rear left wheel. Before I could wonder why a wheel would make a noise like that, the cart lurched to the side as the wheel careened off and rolled away. The noise spooked the horses. They tore off, dragging the cart with only three wheels. I held tight to the front to keep from falling out and prayed the coachman could regain control of the horses. Lord Castleton tumbled out and landed on the ground. The captain rolled out as well, but he grabbed the side and hung on with his legs dragging across the ground. He finally let go and lay on the ground.

The cart hit a large rock. It bounced. I flew out, arms flailing. I landed flat on my face in heather and mud. I lay stunned, waiting for my ribs to stop throbbing. Soon, water seeped into my shirt and trousers. I turned my head and watched as the helpless coachman, the horses, and the cart disappeared into the fog.

I struggled to my knees before my clothes became too damp. I now sat alone, surrounded by mist that concealed Castleton and Wilson, one of whom might harbor intentions of eliminating the rest of us. Or, I realized, they might be conspiring against me. My peril increased without the coachman as a potential witness to discourage foul play.

Run like a madman, I told myself. I tried to stand, but my hard landing left me sore.

"*Blackburn!*" The captain's voice echoed over the hills.

Dare I answer?

"*Blackburn!*" Wilson sounded panicked. "Lord Castleton's hurt! Get over here."

The fog cleared a bit, and I could see their silhouettes. If I could see them, they could see me.

"*Coming!*" I yelled. I stood up and headed toward them. I

stepped into what looked like a soft patch of grass. It quaked under my foot, like a rug floating on water. My foot sank into the grass and dark-brown sludge rose up over my shoes and spilled inside. I tried to step back but felt my shoes sticking in the mud. With a good twist of each foot, I freed my feet and shoes and landed on solid ground. I thought back to the stranger on the train and understood what he meant when he said *the earth isn't stable.* A putrid smell floated out of the spot I vacated. I grimaced, not realizing decayed peat could smell so dreadful. Once I regained composure, I wiped my shoes on some of the heather while trying to quell my anger at ruining such an expensive purchase.

I headed toward the other two, ignoring the goo that slushed around my socks. I chose my footing with care. Most of the time, the ground felt steady, but the moss slipped and slid under me a few times. I found Wilson standing over Lord Castleton, who clutched his right arm to his chest. The captain seemed unharmed except for fresh tears in his jacket that flew about in the wind.

"It took you long enough," he muttered.

"The ground isn't exactly stable," I said. "It shakes…" I tried to find other words that would describe how it felt. "And slides."

Instead of mocking me, Wilson pointed in the direction I came from. "Over there?"

I nodded.

"Lovely. Out here, nothing is stable, Blackburn."

I wondered if Wilson just sent me a veiled threat.

Castleton tried to force himself to stand up. He groaned and fell back down. Without taking my eyes off Wilson, I bent down and helped the lord to his feet. He moaned a bit once he stood.

"Are you hurt, my lord?" I asked.

"He was thrown out of the cart," said Wilson. "Of course he's hurt, and probably more than just that arm." Wilson reached inside Castleton's coat pocket and yanked out a handkerchief. "Blackburn, hand me your handkerchief."

I hesitated.

"I'm not going to kill you with it, Blackburn. He needs a sling."

I tossed handkerchief to Wilson, who tied it to his and Castleton's, fashioning a makeshift sling. He tied it around Castleton's neck.

At this point, I grew confused. Both of them put on such a convincing show of concern and apprehension that I could not for the life of me figure out which one of them planted the corset.

"Do we even know where we are heading?" asked Castleton.

"There." Wilson pointed to the silhouette of Holland Manor in the distance. Fog wove through the hills, and the last part of the sun disappeared behind them. Soon the temperature would drop, and the fog would only increase. Our situation looked dire. For the first time since the crash, I felt sore.

"Now listen here," said Wilson. "I don't know which of the two of you put that corset on the seat, and quite frankly, I don't care. Night's falling, and this is moorland. If we stay out here, we die of cold. If we don't watch our steps, we could find ourselves in a bog, and as Blackburn said, the ground isn't entirely stable anywhere. Alone we die. Together, we have a chance at surviving. I refuse to die out here tonight because of something that happened in the past, so we're going to stick together."

Neither Castleton nor I disagreed, but I secretly wondered if Wilson feared one of us might disappear in order to kill the others in an ambush.

"So how do we reach the duke?" I asked.

"We probably ought to follow the path the coachman used," said Wilson.

"I don't think that was a real path." I suspected the coachman took us on an unmarked shortcut only he knew.

"We can at least follow the marks the horses left," said the captain. "They'll show us dry ground."

"And the horses were dragging a broken cart," I added. "They might have tired." We might reach the cart, and potentially the coachman, who could lead us to the duke's home.

We followed the chopped-up vegetation left in the cart's wake. I heard a creak ahead of us—the sound of bending wood. We forged ahead. Suddenly, the ground gave way under my right foot, and my leg disappeared up to my knee in chilly muck.

I tried to pull my leg out, but an unseen force underneath pulled against me. I started to panic. My leg continued sinking, and I couldn't feel the bottom.

The captain wrapped his arm around my waist and pulled.

"Don't let go! Don't let go!" The words left my mouth without any thought creating them. Every part of me feared that I would get sucked down altogether if Wilson released me.

Together, we freed my leg. I fell to the ground and noticed that my shoe stayed in the ooze. At the moment, I didn't care. "It felt like someone grabbed my foot and pulled me under."

"It does that," said the captain. "Grabs hold of you and won't let go."

I quickly concluded that my original plan to run like a madman across the moors if one of them tried to kill me would fail.

In the distance, horses neighed—loud, frightened whinnies that sent chills down my spine. We exchanged glances. *The Dartmoor stables,* the man on the train called the moors. Now that I experienced getting trapped in a bog, I understood why. I shut my eyes as the horses continued to neigh and tried to imagine something other than their impending fate.

Suddenly, we heard horse hooves—at least two sets. I sighed

with relief. The horses might make it back to their real stables alive.

"Well at least *they* know where they're going." The captain squinted. "Do you hear that?"

I strained to listen, and in between the gusts, I heard a man crying for help. "The coachman."

"Probably trapped in a bog." The captain turned toward the gash in the earth. "Follow the marks."

We scrambled across the terrain. Castleton limped behind. I moved at a fast clip despite my lack of shoe, but the captain kept getting ahead. He often slowed down so we could catch up.

The coachman's shrieks turned higher pitched and more panicked. Suddenly, the moors turned quiet, and my heart started beating faster. Were we too late to save him?

I quickened my pace and stubbed my shoeless big toe on a rock. "Argh!" I closed my eyes, trying to walk off the throbbing.

Suddenly, Wilson grabbed my arm. "Bog." He pointed a few yards away where the tip of the cart lay sticking out of what looked like moss and soil. "It took our ride."

Lying near the cart on what only *looked* like solid ground was the coachman's hat. I remembered the man I met on the train telling me to get low and crawl to escape. I threw off my jacket and crawled to the hat, stopping the moment my arms started to sink. I reached into the goo and sifted my hands through the cold muck, searching for some sign of the coachman—a shoulder, hair, maybe a hand I could grab.

Wilson pulled at my waist. "He's gone, lad."

"We can still save him." I continued searching through the reeking ooze.

"He's gone. His quest to free the horses killed him."

I pulled myself to my knees and wiped my hands on the

grass to try to rid them of the foul-smelling goo. I almost laughed as I took inventory of my appearance. Mud covered my crisp, white shirt, beautiful waistcoat, and trousers, and I smelled like decayed peat. I replaced my jacket. We stood there staring at the hat. The coachman's death, though we barely knew him, left us melancholy.

We looked across the moors at Holland Manor.

"It's closer," I said. "But we will have to find a way around this bog to get there." I turned and headed to the right. I stepped on a patch of grass and it quaked under my feet. I pulled my foot up. "The ground isn't stable over here."

"I don't think it's stable anywhere," said Castleton.

"Keep to the heather." Wilson stepped on a patch of grass. "Avoid the moss," he added, giving me the same advice as the stranger on the train.

"Heather will be difficult to see when it gets dark," mumbled Castleton.

"Then we move quickly." The captain's decisiveness made him easy to follow in this territory, although part of me grew sick at placing my life in his hands. He killed before. I experienced the aftermath firsthand.

I remembered holding Mary in my arms as she sank to the ground, blood spewing out of her neck. "Who did this?" I sobbed, as I shared my final words with her. "Who?"

"Wilson," she whispered. "I wouldn't take their money…"

That's when I heard the dogs.

"Keep the move on." The captain's sharp tone yanked me out of my thoughts.

He killed her, I reminded myself. Before I pitied or trusted him, I needed to remember with whom I dealt. Even if someone besides Wilson planted the corset, Wilson probably promised himself he would die last on this cursed land.

Across the terrain, I saw something move on the hill. I blinked, and it disappeared before I could determine its identity.

What if it's one of the Jack O' Lanterns?

I chastised myself and such ignorant, eighteenth-century thoughts.

We continued the march, aiming toward the mansion's lights. Sometimes, the soil underneath me undulated and quaked. I looked back. Castleton wobbled even when he stood still, and his feeble steps resembled stumbles. He collapsed and thrust his good arm out to catch himself. Unfortunately, he landed on a patch of false earth and fell face first through the moss. The mud seeped up over his head and past his armpits toward his waist. He tried to push himself out of the cesspool using his good arm but only succeeded in sinking deeper. In a few moments, he would suffocate.

I ran back to him, grabbed his jacket, and tried to pull him out. "Wilson, help me with this man!"

Wilson turned around, annoyed. "Leave him."

"What? No!" I tugged harder at Castleton's jacket in a show of defiance. "You said we all had to stay together."

"He's slowing us down. We've only got a thin chance of making it alive, and that's without him."

Finally, when he knew Castleton could not hear him, the true Wilson showed himself. I needed to stay on my guard. I pulled and tugged until finally Castleton's head emerged. I moved him to more solid ground. He rolled over and started spitting out the filthy-smelling mud. I tried not to gag imagining how it must taste.

Again, I saw something move, closer to us this time, behind a hill.

"I can't go on," Castleton said.

"Yes, you can," I countered.

The captain looked out over my shoulder. He backed up and almost lost his balance. "No time to argue! Move!" He pointed behind us in the same direction as whatever movement I saw earlier.

Lord Castleton and I turned around and saw an eerie blue-green light floating over the moors. Either my imagination played tricks on me, or it headed straight at us.

We took off—even Castleton. Fear of the luminescent light filled him with new energy. My hat flew off in the rush, and I didn't bother looking back. Wilson stayed ahead, picking his way over the patches of grass and moss. His foot disappeared into a patch of floating grass.

I grabbed him before he could sink too far in and yanked him up. We trudged on until we reached a patch of heather. The blue light continued to follow us.

Wilson took a few steps ahead. "The ground is firm; run for it!" He took off. I followed, expecting Castleton to keep up.

We dashed across the hill for a few good minutes before I realized I heard no footsteps behind me. I turned around and saw only darkness—no Castleton. Through the mist, a blue light hovered.

"No! Please!" Castleton's scream came from the same direction as the light.

He bellowed again, but stopped abruptly. The light disappeared.

I stood still, staring at the place where he fell. Mary's tortured screams echoed in my mind. Time can't silence some sounds.

"Come on, Blackburn!" Wilson yanked my arm. "The light is gone. Maybe it came for him."

I shrugged him off. I would not let fear of Wilson pressure me to ignore another's cries for aid again. "If he's alive, we need to help him."

The captain huffed, but followed me. With careful paces, we made our way back to Lord Castleton. We gasped. He lay on the ground, half-sunk in ooze. Fear contorted his face—a look I saw once before and one I never wanted to see again.

On his chest lay the bloody corset I assumed had disappeared when the cart's wheel broke.

Someone else lurked in the twilight moors.

Wilson gasped. "It's the Jack O' Lanterns. They're hunting us." He started walking backward, tripped, and fell to the ground. He continued moving away on his hands and feet like a crab. His hand hit a patch of mud, and he sank. He grabbed some tufts of grass with his free hand and pulled himself out. He wiped the gunk off his arm. "They know what we did. They're picking us off one by one." Wilson stood up, turned around, and started running toward the duke's home. I hustled behind him. Someone, or something, besides the captain and I lurked on the moors. I hoped for the former. The living, I could contend with. I knew no defense against the dead.

We sloshed our way through the unstable marshes, wishing for solid ground. Sometimes I helped him; sometimes he helped me. Once again, a thin alliance based on fear bound us together. As we progressed, the outline of the stately hall taunted us in the darkness. The light from its windows could not illuminate a path for us; it served only to sneer at our predicament.

My heart pounded, and I began to pant. I could not remember moving so fast for so long over such difficult land—and with a slight limp because of a lost shoe. I kept looking over my shoulder to see if the blue light followed us. I saw only rolling hills with valleys of mist.

Unfortunately, we began encountering more patches of floating grass and less dry, stable earth. I knew without Wilson telling me; we headed into another dangerous wetland.

Suddenly blue-green light reflected off the captain's uniform and the ground in front of us. He gazed at me, his eyes full of both fear and determination. We turned around at the same time and saw the same eerie light floating toward us across the moors.

The captain pushed me out of the way and forged ahead.

I struggled to keep up, trying to step where he stepped. The thin sliver of the waning moon did little to illuminate our path. The blue light soon moved parallel with me about twenty yards away. I lost sight of the captain, whose confident footing surpassed my own. The light passed me, heading for him. I tripped and rolled across the ground as the light floated ahead.

Suddenly, I heard Wilson scream — not a bellow of fear, as we heard from Lord Castleton, but that of a battle cry. The scream ended, and the moor fell silent. The blue light vanished again.

"Wilson!" I heard no answer. In panic, I spun around, looking behind and to the left. *"Wilson!"*

The moor answered me with a gust of wind.

I scrambled toward the sound of Wilson's last scream. Then I saw him. My blood felt like it turned as cold as the slime in the bogs.

The bloody corset lay on the ground. Just to the left of it, Wilson sank into the quagmire without a struggle.

I grabbed Wilson's hand and yanked it. As I pulled, his head lurched unnaturally to the side.

His neck was broken. He was dead. I released his arm, and his body sank forever into the Dartmoor stables.

At that moment, sheer dread fell on me like the fog, sinking into the crevices of my soul. The wind blew through my damp clothes, sucking all the warmth out of me. I felt nothing in my shoeless foot, which made walking tricky. Holland Manor still lay in front of me half-a-mile away with who knew how many unseen bogs between us. And when would the blue light appear next?

What was the light? Was it a spirit trying to take revenge on Mary's murder? Was it Mary wandering across her homeland all these years? Would she take mercy on me, or did she view me as one of her murderers?

I could not have saved her, I reminded myself.

I decided at that moment that I would not give up. I would fight. First, I needed to fight the moor. I tried to plot my course. I decided to stop thinking of the duke's residence as my first and last destination. I would use waypoints and aim for the high ground. Two granite hilltop tors lay between me and the house. I would aim for those.

I made my way to the first tor with care. I tried to remember the captain's advice. Keep to the higher ground, stick with the heather, and avoid moss. Soon I hiked up to the top of a hill with a hard granite surface. I never felt such joy at stepping on rock—on surface that didn't quake when I put my weight on it.

I looked around the rock and noticed that part of the stone offered shelter from the wind. It felt distinctly warmer than anything I felt all night. With my exhaustion, wet trousers, one shoe, and no hat, I considered staying on the tor the rest of the evening. The spirit had passed me to reach the captain. Surely it knew of my innocence in Mary's death and would spare my life. Come morning, I could continue on to the manor in daylight that would make it easier to see stagnant water and mud. I shivered. My shirt, fortunately, dried, but my thin jacket provided little barrier from the gusts. I crept down and gathered some heather to insulate myself from the cold rock. I sat down on the granite, leaned my head back, and started to close my eyes.

Just before the lids shut, a hint of aqua light burst through.

My eyes burst open. I scrambled to my feet, sliding a bit on the granite.

The murderous blue flame now headed for me.

Ghost, demon, or man, I didn't care. Each time the blue light appeared, one of us died. I scampered off the rock and bolted toward the mansion's lights, hoping solid ground lay between me and it.

It's interesting what fear can do to man. Just as it can keep a man quiet instead of exposing a murder, it can force him run for his life into a deadly wilderness. Each step took me to lower ground, and the stalks of heather I so faithfully relied upon disappeared ahead. That would force me to turn to the side, which would give the Jack O' Lantern a chance to catch up. Should test my luck and go just a bit forward or should I turn to the side and stick to the higher ground?

Higher ground, I decided. Getting stuck would force me to move backward. The light would catch me.

I took a turn to the right. The light turned as well. I ran up a rock and jumped.

I landed feet-first in a bog.

I sank up to my waist. The cold liquid peat found its way into my trousers at the ankles and through my waistcoat and shirt buttons. The putrid odor nauseated me. I struggled to free myself despite the warnings about struggling the man on the train gave me. The more I thrashed, the deeper I sank.

The blue light approached, floating over the ground.

I struggled harder, but only continued to sink. Soon, freezing mud surrounded me up to my armpits and sucked the heat out of my body.

The blue light hovered only a few yards away.

Then I heard footsteps. *Footsteps!* Footsteps didn't belong to Mary's ghost. Footsteps accompanied arms—real arms that could pull me out if they felt merciful. I could reason with footsteps.

Soon, I stared up at a man dressed in black—a man, not an apparition. Black soot covered his face like a chimney sweep's. He held a gas lantern made with blue glass instead of clear. Black paint covered the back of the lantern's glass, which kept the light from revealing him.

"You need to stop struggling." The cold, calm, calculating voice belonged to the coachman and snuffed out any hope of mercy. "Struggling only makes you sink faster."

I stopped moving, but continued to sink, albeit slower. "Help me." The rotten peat reached my shoulders, and I did not consider begging above my station at this point.

He ignored my request and instead pulled out a bloody corset from his jacket. "You know who this belonged to, don't you?"

"I have no idea." The sludge hit my clavicle, and my feet still could not feel the bottom.

"Don't lie to me, Blackburn. You know whose this was."

"Mary. Mary M-Meadows. Please help me." I suddenly remembered duke's secretary's name: Harold J. Meadows, who probably stood right in front of me. Her brother, perhaps? "Are you Harold?" I asked. I hoped conversation might encourage mercy on his part.

He set the lantern on the ground, knelt down on one knee, and stared at me. "Yes. I'm her brother. Surprised?"

"Yes." *Keep him talking,* I reminded myself. "You wrote the letters from the duke?"

"I did." He leaned forward with a sneer. "And just how

excited were you when you received yours? Flattery, Blackburn, can make people do what you want."

"You placed the corset on the seat in the smoke?"

He nodded.

"So you planned this whole thing?" The work he put into his ingenious strategy gave me little hope he might see fit to save my life.

"Of course. The duke's carriage is fine. I took the cart we servants use because I knew he wouldn't miss that. I don't need him investigating into anything that happened out here tonight."

"How did you crash it? The wheel?"

"I rigged a small explosive to it after I pretended to check it." He snickered. "It exploded just as Castleton threw the corset over the side. Coincidence, but it added a dramatic touch."

The mud now reached the middle of my neck, and I decided I hated the word *coincidence*. I reached my hand toward him. "Mr. Meadows, please help me."

"You beg for my help and yet you did nothing to save her."

"Her artery was already cut! She was bleeding out. I couldn't stop it!"

I had tried. I pressed my hand against her neck, and yet the blood still flowed. I held it there until I heard Wilson's dogs, released to mutilate Mary's body and disguise the murder.

"You let the dogs take her!" The coachman's face wrinkled in fury.

"She was already dead!" I yelled. When I realized I couldn't save her, I ran before the hounds got me too.

"Was she? Was she really dead?"

I looked away. Her final scream erupted when the dogs pounced. I never admitted that to anyone.

He knelt down and stared into my eyes. "And how much

payment did you receive for your silence?"

Again I said nothing. I received another promotion and a letter of recommendation from Earl Castleton. That and the threat of being exposed for keeping the laundering secret bought my silence.

The ooze now reached the bottom of my chin.

Guilt welled up inside, and I wished the moors would take me faster. I should have dragged her away from the dogs and told my story to Scotland Yard instead of profiting from her death. The mauling wouldn't have covered up the murder, and I could have brought her justice.

"I'm sorry." I said it in a whisper. I didn't care if Harold heard it or not. "Mary, I'm so, so sorry."

The goo now reached over my chin. I strained my neck as high as I could, but I knew that only prolonged the inevitable.

The coachman stood up. "I'm not going to kill you, Blackburn. I'm going to give you the same chance you gave my sister." With that, he turned around and walked away just as my lips fell beneath the cesspool.

A Gift for Death

R.D. Stevens

Trimmed in gold lace and laced with gold cord, the creamy white silk enveloped the dress form to perfection. A liquid smooth hourglass of boning and busk that draws the eye to the two yellow and gold phoenixes embroidered under the breast line. Their glittering dance in the sunlight make it…magical. "Isn't it beautiful, Nico?"

Nicolette looked up from counting tonight's payment to see what her companion gazed over. Its beauty glowed in the morning light, but she knew it carried a price tag to match.

"One day I will save enough for it, Nico. One day." Thin and graceful, Serena stood almost a hand span taller than Nicolette's petite stature. One could imagine her long smooth legs, well-muscled and pearly peach, beneath her woolen skirts. The ends of her golden ringlets brushed passed her bare shoulders and the swollen tops of her breasts, the rest stuffed into a brown corset that hugged her just right.

"Come Serena, Milo will want his rent," Nicolette said while tugging on Serena's arm. Older than Serena by six years, but just as pretty, her straight black hair pinned up with long thin wisps tickling her neck and shoulders. They made a delightful pair, and few men missed a drink in the fountain of their beauty.

They walked across the street and into Le Cochon Ivre, The

Drunken Pig. Dark like most taverns and smelling of sweat, stew, and stale alcohol, it served as home for the two girls. Serena and Nicolette crossed the dining area towards the bar where Milo, the proud owner of The Drunken Pig, busied himself behind it, cleaning and restocking.

"Good morning, Milo," Serena sang while tipping a small curtsy in his direction.

"Good morning, my sweet," Milo returned like a papa would to his daughter. "Be sure to have the dining hall set soon. I want everything in order before the noon meal."

Serena nodded and carried her cheerful-self off to the kitchen to begin her work.

Nicolette slid with grace onto one of the bar stools in front of Milo. "Here's your cut," she said handing Milo a few coins. "I hope this is sufficient for the week."

Milo took the coins and Serena walked back from the kitchen with a broom and a pitcher of water. He followed her with his gaze, watching her fill little vases with fresh water and pick out the fading flowers. Her hourglass shape with its natural pleasing movements mesmerized. "We would both make double if you would train her in your art, Nicolette."

"No," Nicolette said with a bit of venom. "Not her." She stood from the stool and made her way to the stairs. "Come up when you're finished, Serena," she said.

"I will," Serena trilled without missing a step in her work.

After she finished her work, Serena made her way upstairs. She headed down a long hall of many rooms filled with traveling salesmen, farmers in from the fields, or drifters passing through. She opened the last door at the end of the hall to find Nicolette fast asleep in the bed, even though it was close to mid-day. She closed the door behind her and latched it.

Their home held one bed, a wardrobe, and a small vanity with a mirror and chair. She crossed the room to the vanity while she loosened the cord of her corset. She breathed deep as she slipped out the constrictions of the cloth and boning, and stretched to enjoy the freedom her ribs and breasts felt. After washing her hands and face, she climbed into the bed to join Nicolette in sleep.

Well rested after several hours of sleep, the girls busied themselves primping for the evening's work. "And the juggler just picked up this sleaze's mug in an attempt to add it to the other dishes he balanced. Next thing I know, the juggler feigns a tremble and this guy was covered in mead!" Serena half-told, half-laughed to Nicolette while she brushed out Serena's hair.

Nicolette smiled. "My brother would've loved you very much," she said and looked at her styling job in the mirror.

Serena grabbed Nicolette's hand and shifted in the little chair to face her. "You never talk about your family. What happened to him?"

Nicolette reached up to fondle a little silver bird hanging from a delicate chain around her neck. The necklace served as Nicolette's worry stone, one of the few possessions left from her family. Serena watched Nicolette rub the outstretched wings with a faraway look in her eyes.

Shaking off the memory, Nicolette walked over to the bed, picked up Serena's corset, and started to brush it out. Serena followed and sat next to her on the bed. "He was taken from me." Serena laid her hand on Nicolette's shoulder. "By a man named Emile Souvillion."

"I'm so sorry," Serena said in sympathy.

"It was years ago," Nicolette snapped and rose from the bed.

She held out Serena's corset to her. Serena stood so Nicolette could wrap the material around her. "My brother tried very hard to make everything right after our parents passed. Very hard. But some of his decisions were not good ones."

As Nicolette finished lacing the corset, Serena grabbed her hands. "He must've loved you very much."

Nicolette smiled and pulled her hands away. "You better hurry downstairs before Milo sends for you."

Serena turned back to the mirror to finish her preening. She shifted from side to side a little to check the fit of her corset, plumped her breasts and stuffed them back down to secure them into the perfect position.

After slipping into her sandals, she turned to Nicolette. "Do you need me to help you with your lacings, Nico?"

"No. I can manage. I'll see you downstairs in a bit."

As dusk started to fall, the inhabitants of Chateau Fléau began to stir. Dark and beautiful Lucilla stood in the entryway of the front parlor of the grand, thirteen-bedroom castle. Clothed in the most recent fashions of red silks and black lace, she waited for her escort.

Sébastien kept himself hidden at the top of the grand staircase. He watched her impatient pacing with a grin, anything to irritate her. A smooth, liquid voice interrupted her annoyed march.

"Lucilla, where are you running off to with my money?" It came from somewhere within the parlor.

"Em," Lucilla acknowledged walking toward her Lord. Standing in the doorway, Emile remained shadowed from the candlelight and from Sébastien. Moving forward, the flickering light accentuated his sharp features. Robed in green and gold, he reached his hands out to her. She fell into his arms. He leaned forward to kiss her and Sébastien almost gagged at the sight. She stretched up onto her tiptoes and pressed her curves against his body, his hands ran down her back to cup her buttocks. She pulled away from his kiss and arms to rustle her dress back into its proper fitting. *So glad that's over,* Sébastien thought.

"With my birthday ball only a few days away, I'm going shopping," Lucilla said as she brushed past Emile and walked toward the front door. "Bastien promised to take me to Terres Chêne this evening to buy a new corset."

At the mention of his name, Sébastien donned his best bored face and made his trek down the long staircase. Tall and well built, his dark eyes and hair accented his olive complexion. Reaching the bottom, he too greeted Lucilla with a kiss, a platonic one on her cheek.

"Bastien. We were just talking about you," Emile said. The front door opened.

"The carriage awaits M'dame," the stableman said and bowed low before her. "We shall leave at your pleasure."

"Henri, did you send word to Jean like I instructed?"

"Yes, M'dame. Monsieur Jean is expecting your late arrival," said Henri.

Lucilla followed the stableman out into the dark of early night.

"Bastien," Emile beckoned, "a word before you leave."

Sébastien followed Emile to one of many rooms on the ground floor of the castle. Heavy drapes covered the windows like they did in every room of the mansion. By candlelight the curves of two naked women laid half-covered in pillows and silks as they slept in the sunken conversation pit.

Emile walked over to a shelf, opened a box, and pulled out a pouch of coin. He tossed it to Sébastien. "Be sure Lucilla finds whatever she wants."

"Yes, M'seigneur," Sébastien said. "Her birthday will be as pleasing as we can make it."

Emile disrobed himself to return to his women and Sébastien turned back to the door. Sébastien heard them moan and stir as he left the room.

"Shhh. No, no my pets. There's no more sleep for you," he murmured through the closed door.

He made his way to the carriage where Lucilla waited. A sleek black box with dark covered windows and space enough to seat six, the carriage seemed fit for a king. Lucilla sat inside, her skirt hem peeking from the doorway.

Sébastien sat opposite Lucilla, and the carriage set out on its journey.

Once the carriage passed the last of the town's lights, Lucilla changed seats to sit beside Sébastien.

"What are you doing, Lucilla?"

"Oh, Bastien. Must you be so dull?" Lucilla pleaded. "This is going to be a long ride. Don't you want to please me?" She ran her hand up his leg and cupped his masculinity, massaging.

Sébastien grasped her wrist and moved her hand away.

Lucilla responded by hiking her skirts and straddling him. "But it would surely pass the time."

"What about conversation?" Sébastien retorted as she slid her hips against his. "It passes the time, and doesn't require you on top of me."

Lucilla backed away to her original seat. "Why do you have to be so handsome and yet so tiresome? It's just not right."

As they arrived in town, Sébastien noticed the woman right

away. Her features glowed from the candles in the window of the dress shop. He watched her turn at the sound of his carriage approaching. The night wind picked up wisps of her golden hair to dance in the candlelight.

"Finally," Lucilla said, interrupting his dreamy stare at the lovely barmaid. "We are here."

Sébastien felt the carriage wobble as Henri dismounted from the driver's perch to open the door. Henri presented his hand to help Lucilla down and then held the door for Sébastien.

The tailor, Jean, stood at the door greeting Lucilla. "I did receive your currier Ma dame and it's no trouble. I adore our visits."

Sébastien turned at the sweetest sound. "Mon seigneur, Ma dame." The barmaid curtsied and made her way across the street. Her enticing curves slid from hip to hip as she walked away. He couldn't take his eyes off her. As she neared the building across the road, another woman emerged from the tavern. This one he knew well. "Nicolette," he whispered.

"Are you coming, Bastien?" Lucilla beckoned from the shop doorway.

Sébastien handed her the pouch Emile gave him. "Anything you want here is yours. I will be only a moment." He left Lucilla to her shopping and headed across the road.

The pretty barmaid spoke with Nicolette before entering the tavern. Nicolette eyed Sébastien and walked away, guiding him towards the alley.

"Nicolette?" Sébastien called as he entered the alleyway. "Is it really you?"

Once he was well within the walls of the alley, Nicolette spoke. "Sébastien?" she half cried. She threw her arms around his neck. "Oh, Sébastien."

Sébastien pulled her back to look at her. She was much older than when he last saw her, but just as he remembered. "All this time," he said. "So close to me, and I had no idea." His look transformed from love to fear. "You have to leave." He stepped away from her. "You have to go far away from Terres Chêne and especially from Mont Jouissance."

"No, I can't. I…"

"Nicolette," Sébastien articulated. "Emile is in Mont Jouissance."

Nicolette stepped back, shocked. "You're still with him?" Tears welled in her eyes.

Sébastien fumbled at his waist belt pulling out a black leather pouch. He held it out to Nicolette. "This is all I have on me. Take it. Set your affairs in order." She took the pouch from him. He looked at the sky and knew he had to leave if he and Lucilla were to make it back before dawn. "I have to go back to Mont Jouissance, but I will return tomorrow evening with more. Meet me. Then you must get away from here. Emile has not forgotten you. He must not find you."

"Why are you still with him?" Nicolette spat back.

"Letty, just do as I say." She nodded and tears flowed freely down her face.

Sébastien hugged her again and left the alley. He made his way back to the carriage and Lucilla's shopping. He didn't dare look back in her direction and pull Lucilla's gaze, but Lucilla's stance told him she already saw and already stewed in jealousy.

Sébastien looked just as she remembered. Tall, well built, he even still carried the afternoon stubble he wore the day Emile upset their lives. Nicolette couldn't find any indication that years passed, not a single age line.

"Letty, just do as I say." The word Letty rang in Nicolette's ears. The use of a childhood nickname, she thought she would never hear again, was more than she could bear. She nodded and allowed herself to cry.

Sébastien hugged her again and left the alley. She watched him move from the shadows into the street. The woman he was with flaunted a new corset of violet and silver along with beautiful silk skirts. She reached up and planted a kiss on Sébastien's lips, wrapping herself around him in ownership. Nicolette watched as the woman pulled him into the carriage and it sped on its way.

She looked down at the pouch of coin in her hand and opened it. The small fortune she held would finish paying off plans she made months ago. She and Serena could finally leave this life behind them.

"Did you enjoy your whore?" Lucilla sneered at Sébastien. She licked her lips and teeth, her incisors sharper now. "Was she tasty?"

Sébastien nodded, but was lost in thought. He paid no attention to Lucilla.

She moved with lightning speed to stop right in front of him. She sniffed his clothes and hair. "Not a single drop spilled," Lucilla said with disgust. She leaned in closer to Sébastien's neck. She straddled him once again and licked his neck. "You didn't even fuck her," she whispered into his ear as she nibbled on his lobe.

Sébastien moaned and moved underneath her, his animalistic instincts wanting to rip the brand new corset from her body. He grabbed her thighs and pulled her closer, his masculinity bulging beneath her. He buried his face in her hair breathing in her scent and caught a whiff of Emile.

Sébastien pitched Lucilla back into the seats on the opposite side of the carriage. She snarled in rage. "What is wrong with you?"

"Never do that again," Sébastien said with such venom. He bared his teeth like a feral beast. "Never."

A deep growl accentuated the man's evil grin, his face covered in the blood of the driver. Two more monsters appeared from the darkness of the woods.

"Run, Serena! Run!" Serena ran. She ran as fast as her adolescent legs would carry her, not daring to turn back to the screams of her parents.

Nicolette woke to kicks and murmurs of Serena's nightmare. She tried to wake her. Serena shot straight up in the bed, panting.

"Are you okay?" Nicolette asked with worry.

Panting, but regaining her surroundings, Serena threw herself into Nicolette's arms. She just needed the closeness of her friend. It was the same dream. Always running and never looking back at her parents.

"I can't even remember their faces, Nico," Serena sobbed into Nicolette's arms.

"Shhh." Nicolette pulled Serena up to look into her face. "I'm here. Remember my face." Nicolette held her until she fell silent.

"Serena? How would you like to move on to a new town?" Nicolette asked.

Serena pulled away. "New? Why? Where would we go?"

"Anywhere we wished," Nicolette said with a smile.

"But, what about Milo?

Nicolette giggled. "Milo will find another barmaid." She paused and grabbed Serena's hands. "What do you say?"

"Well, I guess so."

Nicolette walked over to their one little window and threw back the thick curtain. "It's already past midday. We should prepare for this evening and start packing."

Nicolette did Serena's hair while Serena mended the hem of Nicolette's underskirt. After dressing, Serena packed up her only other set of clothes, various hair pens, and her cloak. Being summertime, she wouldn't need it. Then she picked up the one item she held dear, a beautiful ornate dagger that her father gave to her for her seventh birthday. She placed it between her cloak and clothes to protect it.

"When you're finished tonight, you must go right to sleep. We will need to get an early start in the morning," Nicolette said as Serena slipped into her sandals.

"Are you taking any clients tonight? Should I wait for you?"

"No. I must meet with someone to finish up some business, but you don't have to wait." Nicolette walked over to Serena. "Don't mention anything to Milo just yet. He will find out soon enough."

Serena nodded and headed downstairs.

Just prior to dusk, Sébastien called for the stableman to prepare a horse. Eager to leave before Emile awakened, he stuffed his saddle bags with all the coin he could carry, then thought better of it. His strength surpassed Nicolette's. He had emptied half from each side when someone knocked on his door. He opened it to find the stableman.

"Your horse is ready M'seignior and night has fallen," the stableman said with a quick bow.

"Thank you, Henri. I'll be down in a moment."

Sébastien pulled on his leather boots, put away the discarded coins, and grabbed the saddlebags. He made his way down the long staircase and almost reached the door when the unmistakable, deep, liquid voice of Emile caught him by surprise.

"Running away?"

Sébastien turned toward the sound. Emile was seated on a chaise through the open door to the parlor. Bare from the waist up and well-muscled under patches of dark, curly chest hair, his arm wrapped around the waist of a naked young woman who seemed passed out against his shoulder.

"Has Lucilla scared you off?" Emile chuckled.

"No. I—"

"She told me you denied her in the carriage. Why?" As Sébastien tried to gather his thoughts, Emile nudged the young woman. She hurried to undo the front of Emile's leather pants and planted herself on top of him.

"Lucilla is yours, Seignior. I would never dream of spoiling her prior to returning her to you." As Sébastien confessed, the young woman undulated herself on top of Emile. He reached up and squeezed her breasts until she moaned with pain and undulated harder and faster.

Sébastien, accustomed to this sight, continued. "And she was wearing her new dress. I didn't want to be a disappointment by ripping it off her body. I was having trouble controlling myself."

Emile reached up to the young woman's neck and pulled her down closer to him. She trembled as Emile brushed her hair away from her neck. Baring his teeth, he pierced her neck and sucked hard as she moaned again in pain. Emile drank and drank until he bled her dry.

Finished with her, he rolled her lifeless corpse off him. "And your whore?" Emile asked as he fastened his pants and stood.

"What of her?"

Emile looked Sébastien over. "That is where you are headed?"

Sébastien tensed as Emile neared him and walked passed. Sébastien turned to follow.

"You must bring this whore back with you. From the way Lucilla describes her, she must be quite a treat," Emile said with a smirk.

"She is nothing, Seignior," Sébastien countered as he made his way for the door.

"Tsk, tsk, Bastien. I would not steal her from you. I just want to watch."

Sébastien gave a quick bow of his head and opened the door to leave. Emile didn't stop him.

Thump, thump, thump.

"Serena!"

Thump, thump, thump. Serena opened her eyes.

"Serena?!" *Thump, Thump, Thump.* It was Milo at the door.

Serena sat up on the bed. She blinked, trying to find her bearings after her jump from a deep sleep. She realized Milo was attempting to break down the door; she hastened to unlatch it.

"Thank the heavens!" Milo sighed. "You're all right."

"What's going on?" Serena asked, standing in nothing but her underdress.

"Hurry, get dressed and come downstairs," Milo said.

"Where's Nico?" Serena asked, noticing she was not in the room.

"Just do as I ask, girl," Milo pleaded.

Serena nodded and shut the door. She found her clothes, still dirty and wrinkled from yesterday's work and from spending the night in a pile on the floor. She dressed, overskirts then bodice. She fumbled with the lacings and fit before pinning her messy curls up as best she could. She slipped into her sandals and headed downstairs.

Milo stood next to the front door talking with François, the baker's son. As she approached them, they quieted.

Milo reached out and grabbed Serena's hand. "Serena, my dear, there has been a dreadful tragedy." He led her out the front door. François followed.

A small gathering of local people shrouded the entry to the alleyway between The Drunken Pig and François' father's bakery. Serena could name every face. They all looked at her with fear and sadness in their eyes. As they made the corner and turned into the alleyway, Milo squeezed Serena's hand as if to say, "I'm here…"

The moment Serena's eyes spotted the pile of woolen skirts and black hair, an overwhelming sense of dread hit her like a club to the stomach. Her breath quickened and she moved closer leaving Milo and François behind her.

Her face was turned away from Serena's. One hand laid across her chest, the other outstretched as if she were waiting for a lover but fell asleep. Her black hair lay in tender wisps across her face and neck. She looked like one of those beautiful porcelain dolls the high-born ladies bought for their daughters.

Serena knelt beside the pale lifeless body as tears flowed down her cheeks. Her trembling hand reached out to brush the soft black hair away from Nicolette's cold face. As if her eyes needed confirmation of what her heart already knew, she toppled over in heavy sobs.

Milo knelt next to her and pulled her off Nicolette's body. Serena buried her face in Milo's shoulder with more sobs.

"Oh, Milo," she managed to squeak out between tears, "not Nico!"

"Shhh, my sweet," Milo comforted.

It took a bit of time and comfort from Milo, but Serena regained a bit of composure. "What happened, Milo?"

Milo pointed to Nicolette's neck. "This. This is what happened."

Nicolette's elegant long neck was marred by a horrible bite.

"What did this?" Serena asked, wiping tears from her eyes.

"It's not what, but who," François spat.

Something deep inside Serena's gut went cold. Memories flooded back, memories of monsters that looked like men, and of blood. Serena stared at the bite on Nicolette's neck as she relived her run through the woods hearing the brutal murder of her parents. The cold knot in her stomach grew.

Milo cursed at François. "Can't you see she's in real pain, boy?" Milo hissed.

"I'm telling you, it's Vampires," François returned.

Milo stood. "We're not sure what did this."

Voices flooded her from everywhere. The word Vampire gave the crowd a reason to break their silence, but Serena could make out none of it. Nicolette's neck and the pit growing within her belly claimed all of her attention. There were no more tears. Serena's entire existence froze. She knew exactly what did this.

It was nearing midday. The crowd departed, and Milo arranged for Nicolette's body to be picked up by Father Clément for a proper burial. Serena still knelt in the alleyway staring at the ground where her one true friend, her only family, once laid. It's like she could still see her body there, and if she willed it hard enough, Nicolette would wake up and shake her from this nightmare. But, her heart sank when a dragonfly flew near enough to catch her eye, jarring her from her trance, and not Nicolette.

Drained, Serena tried to stand. She knelt for so long her legs went numb. As she stood, the blood rushed to her head and her feet felt like she stood on a thousand needles. She stumbled to the wall of The Drunken Pig and braced herself. Soon it would stop.

Not sure what to do, Serena left the alleyway. She didn't have a destination. She just walked. She realized her legs carried her to her favorite window, but something looked different. It took her foggy head a moment to realize the Phoenix corset had disappeared.

Serena burst into the dress shop.

"Where is it?" she demanded.

Jean the tailor jumped, startled from his work. "Serena?" he said. He moved out from behind his work station and crossed the shop to her. He reached for her hand and cupped it within his own. "I'm sorry for your loss, child."

Serena's mental state didn't allow for more tears. "Where is it?" she repeated.

Jean walked back to his workstation and pulled out a canvas sack. "Nicolette visited last night," he said as he pulled out several items from the bag. "I don't know if you were aware, but Nicolette worked off a debt she owed me." He stopped and smiled. "She made her final payment, last night. She was a remarkable woman, Serena." He returned to the sack. He first pulled out brand new undergarments and a bright white underdress trimmed in delicate lace. He unrolled beautiful satins in cream with an overskirt of cream and gold scrollwork. Saving it for last, he removed the Phoenix corset from the sack and placed it on top of everything else.

Serena walked over to the workstation and almost picked the mesmerizing corset up. She stopped mid grab, afraid to touch it.

"Go ahead. It's yours," Jean said with encouragement.

Serena looked up at the man. "What?"

"It's yours," he said. "Nicolette paid it off last night and asked me to wrap it up."

Serena looked back at the wonderful pile of clothes. This time she touched it. Smooth but firm around the boning, she ran her finger along one of the Phoenixes taking care to feel each and every golden stitch. It was the most exquisite thing she had ever seen.

"I thought maybe the attractive woman from the other day came back to get it," Serena said.

"Who?" Jean asked.

"The fine lady that came in for a new dress the other night."

"Oh, Ma dame Lucilla," Jean said. "She's not a fan of white. She likes the darker, richer colors." Jean reached into the sack again and pulled out another set of undergarments, underdress, overskirts, and a delightful corset of lavender with dragonflies embroidered in silver and mint. "Nicolette also paid for these," he said.

Serena looked up at Jean. "Two? For me?"

"I don't think she intended for you alone to have a pretty new dress," Jean said. "Besides, I have tailored both dresses. I'm afraid her skirts would show your ankle, my dear."

Serena looked back at the dresses. The icy pit in her stomach returned. "Who was that man with Ma dame Lucilla?" Serena asked.

"Oh, well, I thought you knew. Seeing as he knew Nicolette. She didn't talk about her clients with you?" Jean asked with a bit more curiosity than befits a gentleman.

"No. She never talked about them," Serena said.

"His name is Sébastien. All I know about him is that he escorts Ma dame Lucilla. But, I'm pretty sure he was one of Nicolette's clients since he came back again last night."

Three days later, Serena sat in front of a fine mirror watching her maid place her hair in intricate curls all around her head. The pearl-studded hair pins she acquired, like everything else now surrounding her life. Just as Jean said, Nicolette was a remarkable woman. Serena felt devastated but grateful Nico kept so many secrets from her.

Jean was not alone in approaching Serena with a package of items. The cobbler sent over two pair of decorative heeled slippers, one pair meant for Nicolette's smaller feet and the milliner sent two hat boxes with high fashion Bergére hats. There were many little packages of gloves, jewelry and ribbons, and bigger deliveries of trunks full of beautiful traveling clothes, and lastly a maid. With each gift from Nicolette, Serena's emotions sharpened into a vile hatred for the man she knew killed Nicolette. The tall handsome escort, Sébastien.

The final gift set a plan in motion landing Serena where she sat now. The gift of a carriage pulled by two dun colored horses complete with a driver. Marcel, the driver, stated that Ma dame Nicolette paid for his services in full for the next year. Nicolette made more money than she ever let Serena or Milo know, for beneath the cushion of the forward carriage bench hid a brown leather saddlebag full of coin. A bountiful fortune that would take Serena and Nicolette out this life they live and make them hopefuls for a suitable husband.

Colette placed the last pearl hair pin and walked around to inspect her work. Serena's golden locks shone in the sunlight from the window of her room at La Couronne de Cuivre, The Copper Crown. Being the premier inn for the higher class travelers, La Couronne de Cuivre was centered in the growing city of Mont Jouissance. Serena picked it to further the ruse that she was an heiress that just came of age.

Colette secured most of Serena's curls against the crown of her head, while allowing others to cascade down and brush her shoulders and back. She painted her lips red and rouged her cheeks. Not the sole guest of La Couronne de Cuivre primping for a party, the city burst with visiting upper class and young nobility, all fussing over the party of the year: Lucilla's birthday.

Sébastien leaned against the banister at the top of the grand staircase in the entry hall of Chateau Fléau. He watched the guests arrive in all their grand pageantry. Lucilla greeted each and every one as if she were a gracious host, rather than the vicious monster he knew her to be. Sébastien didn't show any signs of disgust or make any attempts to warn or rescue them, nor did he look intrigued or excited at the potential human feast lying before him. He'd lived this exact spectacle many times now. The guests would arrive in the newest ridiculous fashions and the party would commence with all the food and wine for the humans to stuff themselves with. Lucilla would dance all night while choosing three or four of her favorites who would linger in the castle for the after party, but Sébastien knew they would never leave again.

He found himself remembering his last evening with Nicolette, endearing himself to whatever gods that might exist for the chance to help her leave Terres Chêne and Mont Jouissance far behind her. Happy he had finally provided the means for her to have a comfortable life far away from him because he thought himself just as much a monster as Lucilla and maybe even Emile.

He snapped out of his memories to see Lucilla accepting a graceful curtsey from the most beautiful thing he'd ever seen. She wore a mask like all the other guests of the masquerade ball, but its lace and feathers melted into a golden cascade of curls that shone brighter than the sun. Her gown of gold and cream made the milky smooth color of her skin beg for caressing. Even from this distance, her golden curls teased him as they brushed the tops of her breasts.

Escorted by a young nobleman and his new bride, no doubt trying to make a name for themselves by attending such a well noted party, they made their way across the hall. Sébastien watched from his perch on the balcony. Every tiny movement she made drew his senses in more. He could almost smell her perfume even though he stood a room away, and his whole body jerked to motion the moment she disappeared into the ballroom.

Taking the stairs two at a time, he made his way down to follow her. Sébastien fought down and locked away his immediate, feral response to her seductive beauty. Easy to spot in the crowd, her red lips moved like liquid as she greeted the others around her.

What was it about this woman that aroused him so? he wondered. He needed to know more. He made his way around the party, nodding to gentlemen and kissing the many feminine hands thrust in his way. Sébastien always drew the single ladies to him like locusts. His dark eyes and sharp features left women blushing in his wake.

As he neared his prey, he breathed in her scent—skin and sweat mixed with roses. She was surrounded by a band of men all trying to keep her attention. Her body undulated as she laughed. It drew Sébastien's eyes to the phoenixes on her bodice. It was hypnotic the way her movement made the phoenixes dance. He wanted to run his hand along her waistline and feel each golden thread. He shuddered. He struggled to hold on to his humanity.

Grateful for Lucilla's pomp and circumstance, her grand entrance on Emile's arm forced him to look away and regain his composure. Everyone turned to watch the Host and Hostess start the first dance. After a moment, others joined in.

Sébastien turned back, expecting to see his tall sunlit beauty, but found a shorter woman in blue holding out her hand to him.

"Mon seignior," she said.

Sébastien greeted the woman but searched the room for his gilded lady. He spotted her, in the arms of another, dancing. He almost crushed the tiny woman's hand and half dragged her to the dance floor, blue skirts flying, but she was not about to complain. The dark and dashing Sébastien just asked her to dance.

Serena smiled at every person she met and giggled at every man's joke like Nicolette always did. After years of watching her mentor, it was the pupil's turn. She saw her mark the moment she entered the hall. He stood at the top of the grand staircase watching the crowd. She used all the subtle seductive moves she could, while ignoring his gaze, as her party moved into the ballroom. She made sure to attract many men to her. "The greatest enticement is jealousy," Nico would say.

As the music started, everyone turned to watch Lucilla enter with her escort, the Lord of the castle, Emile Souvillion. Serena remembered Nicolette carried her own hatred for this man, but nothing could have prepared her for the sight. It was him, the snarling man from her dreams, the man responsible for her parents' death. Though she failed to remember her parents' faces, this one she would never forget. Everything from the past several days flooded her. She lost her icy control. She stood in a world full of monsters.

A gentleman's elbow landed in front of her to escort her to the dance floor. She didn't care who it belonged to, she was grateful for the offer. It gave her time to compose herself. Dancing proved easy for her. After a few turns and twirls, she gripped her emotions and started scanning the dancers as they went flying around. So intent on finding Emile, she didn't notice when her dance partner changed with another couple. She looked up to see who and missed a step as her heart skipped a beat. Sébastien gripped her a little tighter and half lifted her off the ground to make up for her blunder. To the crowd, they never lost rhythm.

Serena stared up at him. His deep, dark eyes sparkled from behind a sleek black mask detailed in silver scrollwork along the edges. His dark hair slicked straight back, accenting the angular shape of his jawline that was showing faint stubble. He held her tight but without pain as he glided her across the floor. Every inch of him screamed masculinity.

Lost in the embrace of his good looks, it took Serena a moment to realize he stared back. Serena looked away a little embarrassed she stared for so long but also angry she let this man get close to her. He was a killer and would pay for his sins.

Sébastien fought his own battle to contain himself around

her, getting lost in her blue eyes. It angered him when she looked away. He pulled her closer, sliding the firm grasp of his left arm further around her waist. Her squeak of protest didn't change his strong grip. Her long, lean body pressed against his hard, tall stature. They danced.

Two songs later, he eased his hold on her and escorted her off the floor. Within an instant he procured two glasses of wine and handed one to her.

"I'm Sébastien," he stated as if he needed an introduction.

"I know who you are," Serena returned. She sipped her wine and turned to watch the dancers.

Sébastien smiled. He knew this game. She was playing coy, but he played a better one. He reached out and brushed the back of his fingers along her neck and turned her face back to meet with his. He leaned in and kissed her on her perfect red lips.

When he pulled back, she stood there frozen. Sébastien was now bewildered by her. He spent the last hour chasing this golden seductress across the party, and now she stood before him still lost in the remnants of his kiss, like an innocent girl. Her pouty, red lips still puckered. It made him want her even more. Desperate to fight back his monstrosity, he took a deep, calming breath, but her rosy perfume almost sent him over the edge.

Shocked by such a forward advance, she almost pulled away, but found she couldn't move. This was her first kiss. It felt so gentle and his lips so smooth. She closed her eyes and let her other senses experience the magic. When he released her, she stood there, afraid that if she moved all the wonderful sensations she felt might fade away.

He moved like lightning. One moment she was lost in his

kiss; the next they were bolting up the grand staircase, his arm wrapped around her waist almost carrying her on his side. He didn't stop until he slammed the door of a bedroom closed with her body. Serena's lungs expelled a sigh as her back made contact with the wood. He buried his face in her neck, licking and kissing her.

She didn't know what to do. She grabbed the hair on the back of his head and pulled, trying to pull him away, but it made him kiss harder and nibble a bit. Her heart started pumping faster from fear. She was sure he was going to devour her as he did Nicolette, but then he moved up her neck to her lips and kissed her with more intensity, his tongue wiggling its way into her mouth. Tingling shockwaves spread through her body, and she lost control. She wanted more of this.

She wrapped her arms around his neck and kissed him back. She pulled him closer, wanting him to never stop. He picked her up by the waist and moved her to sit on the dresser, never once causing a break in their kiss. His hands ran up the sides of the phoenix bodice and over the tops of her breasts. Serena pushed back from the kiss and the caress. This was not going the way she planned.

Sébastien rested his hands on the dresser and leaned forward, creating a barrier between her and the rest of the world. His eyes boring through her like fire. She accomplished what she wanted, but now didn't know what to do with it.

She presented Sébastien with the back of her hand. He took it like any gentlemen would have and kissed it. First the hand, the wrist, her arm above the hem of her long white glove, and the glove vanished, tossed to the floor. She presented him with the other hand, and it happened just the same. He grabbed both of her hands and pulled them to his face to kiss each palm, closing his eyes and breathing in her perfume. She felt the roughness of his stubble as her hands brushed his cheeks, but his face softened. He looked so gentle in that moment. When he let go of her hands, she left them there cupping his face. She could have done anything she wished with him, but she didn't know it.

Serena leaned to the side and turned a bit, presenting Sébastien with the opportunity to loosen her corset. He stood straight, and for the first time, Serena saw him smile. Instead of loosening the corset, Sébastien chose a different route. In two quick movements, he divested himself of his black bowtie and coat and slipped his mask from his face. The black vest accented the muscular V-shape of his broad shoulders, and the ribbon from his mask tousled his hair. He looked even more appealing now than ever.

Knowing it was wrong, he was wrong, Serena still wanted every bit of him. A monster. The monster that killed Nicolette, but every fiber of her body screamed for him to touch it. She did the only thing she could think to do. She kicked off her shoes.

He was there, arms under her skirts, wrenching off her knickers before her shoes even hit the floor. She heard a rip as part of her underdress tore in the process. She didn't care. She already had the buttons of his vest and shirt undone. He leaned in and kissed her again, hard. She reached down and unfastened his pants. Long and stiff, he pulsed at her touch. Not quite sure how to handle it, she explored his manhood with her fingers. He moaned and kissed her harder.

He reached behind her and loosened her corset with ease. She massaged harder with her hand the moment she felt her family dagger slip from the release of the corset's hold. She reached around with her free hand and gripped it as he moaned again.

Sébastien slid her hips forward on the dresser to meet his and wrapped her legs him, but the dresser stood too tall for their bodies to match. He grabbed her bottom tight, skirts, bustle, and all, and removed her from its top. She wrapped both her arms around his neck to keep from falling, thanking God his eyes were closed and missed the dagger in her hand. He spun around and laid them both on the bed. Their lips never separated.

Serena felt his masculinity nearing her virginity. It pulsed between them, the tip brushing her soft down. She knew if she didn't act soon, she would end up the lover of a monster. He moved away from her lips to nibble at her neck again. She grabbed his hair and pulled, remembering how he liked it before. He nuzzled deeper into her neck and the tip of his masculinity almost breached her downy barrier.

She plunged the dagger into his back as hard as she could. He arched back at the pain and thrust himself deep within her. Though the dagger was sticking out Sébastien's back, it was Serena who screamed out in pain, her virginity pierced in an instant. His eyes widened as he felt the beauty of her first experience. He couldn't control himself any longer. He reached around and yanked the dagger from his back. Serena watched as he bared his fangs and licked the blood from the dagger. He threw it across the room and thrust himself deep within her again and again.

Serena arched her back with the pain of her first pleasures, exposing her breasts from beneath the corset. He suckled one then the other as he rhythmically beat her from the inside. With each beat it felt as though he was moving deeper and deeper within her. His mouth left her breasts and traveled up to her shoulder where he plunged his teeth in and drank of her sweet essence. Serena no longer distinguished between pain and immense pleasure.

She lost. Her dagger did nothing but bring on the monster. She would lose her life here, in this bed. She cried. She didn't just lose but fell prey to the same man.

"I'm sorry, Nicolette. I've failed you," she whispered as she began to feel the effects of blood loss.

Sébastien pushed off her as hard and fast. "What did you say?!"

Serena groaned as the pleasure went away and the pain rushed in. She gripped her shoulder to try and hold off any more blood loss. Sébastien picked up the dagger from the floor and held it to her throat.

"What did you say?" he asked again.

Serena saw confusion and fear in his eyes. "I'm sorry, Nicolette. I've failed you," she whined.

Hearing it again, he reached up and removed Serena's mask. "You," he said. "You're the one from outside the dress shop in Terres Chêne, the one who was talking with Letty."

"And you're the monster that killed her!" Serena spat back. "So, kill me then."

Sébastien backed away. "Letty's dead?" he whispered.

Serena nodded. He dropped the dagger to the floor and sat on the edge of the bed, head in his hands.

Serena lay there in pain, afraid to move. When she did move, her first action was to cover herself. She pushed her skirts down and yanked up on her corset, wincing at the pain in her shoulder and groin.

"Are you going to kill me now?" she asked.

Sébastien looked back at her. Silent tears made little rivers down his perfect, fangless face. Even with her hair and clothes a mess, she was still the most beautiful thing he'd ever seen. He still wanted her even though his heart ached for his sister, Nicolette.

A price he would always pay for the monster Emile made him.

"I won't kill you, but Emile...I will kill Emile," he said. For years he'd tried to find ways to leave, to vanquish Lucilla, or Emile, but he couldn't succeed on his own.

He leaned over Serena again, arms caging her beneath him. "I need your help. Let's start this over again. I'm Sébastien."

"Serena," she said.

By the time Sébastien and Serena made it back downstairs, the ball was over. Now the real party was underway.

Sébastien squeezed Serena's hand, reassuring her of her newfound power. They had to do it. Serena had lost too much blood. She couldn't stand from the bed, let alone help to bring down Emile. He gave her some of his blood to heal her and restore her strength to do what they needed to do, plus it played a crucial part in the plan.

"As long as you resist the urge to feed," he told her, "you will return to human within a day."

She now clung to that sentence, afraid she would never return to her former self, afraid to die, but she knew it was the best plan.

Sébastien grabbed her around the waist and flung open the door to Emile's "office."

"Em!" Sébastien said in his best joyful voice. "I have someone for you to meet!"

Emile sat in a shadowy corner in the back of the room watching the handfuls of men and women, naked, in piles amongst the pillows. Lucilla, of course, partying at the center.

"Bastien!" Lucilla called from her pillow pile. "Where have you been? You've missed my party."

In an instant, Emile was in front of them. He moved closer

to Serena and smelled her sweet scent. He ran his hand through her hair. Serena's heightened senses smelled nothing but wine mixed with sex and the metallic hint of fresh blood. Her heartbeat quickened at the thought of it. Her mouth went dry and her stomach lurched. She didn't just want it, she needed it. Serena bared a feral smile.

Emile's eyes widened at her. "Sébastien, you've been busy."

Sébastien stepped in between Emile and Serena. "Serena is mine," he stated.

"If you want her, she needs to feed," Emile said. He gave Serena his most charming smile, but Serena was now focused on the pile of people on the floor. Lucilla was staring straight at her while draining one of the humans. Serena began to tremble from the pain in her stomach and took a hesitant step towards Lucilla and the humans.

"Go to them, my pet," Emile said while gesturing in Lucilla's direction. "Taste your future."

Sébastien swung Serena around and planted his lips upon hers. He kissed her hard until her mind regained control over her cravings. She squeezed his hand back, letting him know her monster was caged.

She turned from Emile and Sébastien and made her way to the pillows. The smell of sex and blood was almost overwhelming. She fought hard to keep the monster locked. A handsome and very naked human man gave her his hand to help her down into the conversation pit. She waded through the pillows and sat beside Lucilla, who wore another man on top of her. Emile and Sébastien remained talking by the door.

Lucilla rolled the man off her in Serena's direction, and his head fell square in her lap. He smiled up at her.

"You're lovely," he slurred in his drunkenness, as Lucilla

flipped herself around and straddled Serena's legs below the gentleman's head. She grasped Serena by the shoulders.

"She is," Lucilla stated. "Her name is Serena."

"Serena," he whispered to simply say her name.

Lucilla pulled the man up, leaned his head over, exposing his neck, and bit him. With determination, she allowed some of his sweet essence to trail down his bare, muscular chest.

Serena's eyes sparkled with need. On the verge of losing control, she noticed a little silver bird with outstretched wings hanging from a tiny, delicate chain double wrapped around Lucilla's slender wrist. Serena froze. It was Lucilla. Lucilla killed Nicolette.

She was supposed to keep Lucilla busy as a distraction, but the monster within her broke free. Serena leaned forward with hunger in her eyes. With the speed and strength gifted to her by her new monstrous side, Serena pushed the drunk out the way and plunged her family dagger into Lucilla's heart. In her last seconds of life, Lucilla grabbed at the dagger and Serena. She pulled Serena in close and kissed her. Blood ran into Serena's mouth. It was the human's.

In the next second, Emile slammed Serena across the room. "Lucilla!" he yelled. Frightened humans ran from the room.

Sébastien rushed to Serena's side. He saw the panic on her face and looked in her eyes; they both knew what happened. Her pupils dilated and her lips pulled back revealing new, lengthy incisors. "Now," he whispered to her. "Now!"

They both sped to Emile, knocking him among the pillows. Sébastien dove for the dagger while Serena attempted to keep Emile down, but Emile's strength outweighed hers. He flipped her over in an instant and pinned her beneath him. Just as he was about to gorge on her throat, Sébastien slammed the knife deep into his back and straight through the heart. It was done. Emile's lifeless weight flopped on top of Serena.

"Serena?" Sébastien called as he moved the body from her. "Are you all right?"

She sobbed. He grabbed her and pulled her up into his arms.

"I'm a monster," she cried into his shoulder.

He didn't know what to say to her. All he knew was he wanted her with him, but he wanted her happy. He picked her head up and brushed her tears away.

"We did it," he said. "The real monsters are dead."

She stood and waded out of the pillows and away from him. She stopped in front of the heavy drapes, turned, and held out her arms to him. He was there in a heartbeat. He kissed her deeply, with more passion than ever before. It felt good. It felt right. In that loving moment of victory, Serena held Sébastien with all her strength in one arm, reached out with the other, and pulled back the drapes.

The morning sunlight flooded in.

High Fashion Hell

A Quincy Harker, Demon Hunter Short Story

John G. Hartness

"Hose," I said, pulling at the thin covering on my legs and grimacing. "If I have been pleased with one thing in my exceptionally long life, it is that I managed to avoid every era in which men were expected to wear hose. And yet here I am, walking through a dung-infested collection of anachronisms wearing what else but hose. It must truly be the End Times."

"One, it can't be the End Times, jackass. You killed most of the Four Horsemen of the Apocalypse," said my partner in fashion tragedy, Detective Rebecca Gail Flynn of the Charlotte-Mecklenburg Police Department. "And two, you're bitching about hose? Why don't you walk a mile in my corset, Harker? Until then, why don't you walk your hose-covered ass over to the concession stand and buy yourself a steaming mug of shut the fuck up."

I chuckled at Flynn, but she did have a point. I was at least able to move, and thus fight, in my costume, which consisted of a dark green doublet with a rampant lion in red on the chest, a pair of dark brown hose, brown boots, and a sword on a sword belt that wasn't nearly as "prop" as the re-enactors all around us would probably prefer. Flynn was stuck in a corset, a chemise under the corset, then a skirt, with an overskirt, and finally a bum roll to give her the appropriate amount of Dark Ages junk in her trunk.

I did walk over to the concession stand, but I bought a turkey leg and two beers. I brought the food and alcohol over to a picnic table under a cluster of trees where Flynn had taken refuge from walking in her dress. I passed her a beer and sat down.

"Sorry, shut the fuck up is a seasonal brew. They won't have any 'til spring." I grinned at Flynn and took a huge bite out of my turkey leg. The skin was crisp, the meat was tender, and the juices ran down my chin and spattered all over the front of my doublet.

"Good lord, Harker, use a napkin," Flynn said, rolling her eyes at what passed for my table manners.

"Nah, napkins don't taste as good as turkey." I gave her a grin.

Just then a small dark-haired man with an oiled beard and a mustache waxed to fine points appeared beside me. I mean he walked up suddenly, not that he teleported.

"Are you Harker?" the slight man asked. He was dressed for the Faire, in pumpkin pants and hose.

"That depends entirely on what you want with Mr. Harker," I replied, taking another gigantic bite out of my turkey leg.

"I'm Jacob Strunin, I'm the Faire's Director of Public Relations. I called you about our problem." He stuck out his hand, looked at the state of my greasy mitt, and shook with Flynn instead. He took a seat at our picnic table and looked around. We were surrounded by attendees in varying degrees of costume, from suburban dads in Panthers sweatshirts and jeans to a family of five all decked out in steampunk garb from top hat to boot-clad toes. They milled around the juggler in the open space between tables or sat at their own tables getting a break from the walking and scarfing down chili in a bread bowl, but largely ignored us.

Strunin went on, speaking low so I had to lean in close to make out what he said. "We've had reports from some of our Faire folk that there's a mysterious figure walking the grounds at night. It seems to come out around midnight in back of the Starfire swords booth, wander down past the petting zoo to the jousting field, then it circles all the way up to the Tartuffe Brothers stage near the main entrance and vanishes somewhere around the Royal Pavilion." He pulled out a map of the festival grounds and traced the "ghost's" route along the paper.

"Who's seen the ghost so far?" Flynn asked.

"And how much had they been drinking or smoking before they saw it?" I asked the natural follow-up question.

"Zilch the Torysteller was the first to see it. He doesn't stay on property at nights; he has a place in Charlotte. He was leaving a party with the cobbler when he saw a glowing white thing floating through the trees. He tried to follow the thing, but lost it by the knife throw. Since then it's been seen by several of the vendors, Mike that runs the knife throwing booth, and Charles, the chandler."

"What did the thing look like? Any chance we're dealing with one of the real Fair Folk?" I asked.

"I wouldn't think so. I mean, I had a couple of local Wiccan priestesses come check the property out before we built here in the first place, so unless they've come through since then, we should be clear of that. As far as what it looks like, nobody seems able to really remember what it looks like. They describe a white floating object that gets closer and closer, then they wake up the next morning lying in the grass where they first saw it. That doesn't sound like any of the legends I've heard about fairies."

"Yeah," I agreed. "That behavior doesn't line up with any of the pranks the light Fae are known for, and if it were the unseelie, our victims would probably be missing or dead. Anyway, it's pretty rare for the Fae to latch onto a new place after it's inhabited. They don't care to be around too many humans, for obvious reasons. But so far no one's been hurt?"

"Not obviously, no. The people that have seen it complain of being tired all the time, but after a few days they seem to be back to normal."

"That might be a problem," I said.

"What are you thinking?" Flynn asked.

"I'm not sure, but it could be a vampire partially draining its victims and leaving them to sleep it off in the grass. They'd be tired for a day or two, then snap back. It could be a succubus, draining their life force. Same symptoms, only without the actual blood loss. Or it could be a lethifold." I looked between the two of them but saw no recognition in their faces.

"Come on, you guys have to remember the lethifold, right? Cloak-like monster in the Harry Potter books? No? Oh well, they aren't real. Not yet, anyway."

"What does that mean?" Flynn asked.

"As something seeps into popular culture, people begin to believe in its existence. In some cases, the belief is so strong and the emotions tied to it so powerful that the actual thing will manifest. For example, house elves."

"House elves are real?" Strunin twirled one end of his waxed handlebar mustache and raised an eyebrow at me.

"They are now. So are patronus, so something good came out of those books."

"Well, do vampires sparkle now?" Flynn asked, knowing full well the answer was no. "Because everybody read those books. You even read one."

"I read *one*," I emphasized. "And no, vampires still can't go out in the sun. Everybody who read the books knows the sparkling thing was stupid."

"So we've got a vampire or a succubus," Flynn said. "I know how to deal with vampires. What do we do with a succubus?"

"Well, first we have to find it," I said. "It won't be active during the day, but maybe I can pick up some residual magic from where it's been. Let's try talking to the witnesses, and when it gets dark, we'll stake out the center of the Faire and see what we can see."

"Sounds good," Strunin said. "These badges will tell security you're authorized to be on the grounds after closing." He handed us a couple of tooled leather medallions on long rawhide thongs. We hung the badges around our necks, and I tossed my turkey leg bone into a nearby garbage can. I stood up, drained the last of my beer, and let out a resounding belch.

"You're disgusting," Flynn said.

"True, but it felt great," I said. "And I was able to use my Sight while no one was looking. There's nothing here. Let's try the knife throw."

We walked down the dirt-and-hay-strewn path to the colorful booth where hapless modern Romeos could impress their Juliets with their martial abilities. Since any time I've ever been in a knife fight, the prospect of throwing away my weapon seemed like a terrible idea, I never spent any time learning to throw axes or knives. Still, I figured with my enhanced reflexes and strength, it shouldn't be too bad.

I stepped up to the low-slung barricade between me and the targets and plunked down five dollars. The game operator scooped up my fiver and deposited three knives on the shelf in front of me. I picked up the knives and tried to sight down one. It was warped, but not so badly that I thought it would affect my throw, so I flipped the blade over in my hand a couple of times, then reared back and threw. The knife flew end-over-end in a mostly straight path, headed for a big blue balloon, which would result in Flynn having to carry around a six-foot panda bear as we continued our investigation. The knife flew true, but at the last minute, it seemed to slip aside, burying itself into the wood beside the balloon.

"That's odd," I remarked.

"What, that you missed?" Flynn said from beside me. "Not really. You should see yourself at the pistol range sometime."

"That's not it," I said. "There's something strange…" I opened my Sight and it all made sense. Around each of the balloons, all save two, were glowing spheres of force, deflecting the knives and keeping the operator from paying out too much.

I closed my eyes for a moment, whispered *"Discuture,"* and sent my will cascading out toward the wall of balloons. I opened my eyes and watched the bubbles of magic disappear, then released my Sight. I flicked another knife at the wall and was rewarded with a resounding *POP* as a huge blue balloon exploded. Another knife followed seconds later with another *POP* in its wake as a red balloon popped, a knife quivering right in its heart. The operator spun to me, an accusation dying on his lips as he saw the flicker of power I let dance across my eyes for a second.

"Two knives out of three wins a large prize, m'lord," the disappointed carny said in a thick (and terrible) accent. He handed me a purple stuffed panda at least three feet in height. I passed the animal along to Flynn, then waved the operator in close.

"You can have the bear back if you do two things for me. One, play the game square. No more magic. And two, tell me about the apparition you saw in the midway a few nights ago."

"You got it, but not here. Meet me behind the tent in five minutes. My assistant is on lunch, and once he gets here, I can get away. But about the no magic thing…"

"If you enchant those balloons or any other part of this game again, I'll come back. And if I have to come back, I'll do more than take some of your prizes. Have you ever had fleas?"

"I sleep in a tent nine months out of the year, of course I've had fleas. Not a big deal." He gave me a cocky grin.

"You haven't had fleas like this. Literally, fleas from hell. I summon them from a demon merchant I know in the third circle. They like to dig into warm soft surfaces, like human muscle tissue…" I didn't have to finish. I could tell from the look of horror on his face that the game would be square for a couple of days, at least. "I'll meet you out back in five."

Flynn and I walked off, pretending to be interested in the jewelry at the next tent. Well, I was pretending. The way her eyes got huge at the sight of a crystal and silver butterfly, I think Flynn actually wanted to buy the gaudy thing.

"Get hold of yourself, Detective, we're working."

"Pretty sure *you're* working, Harker. I don't see any crimes around here, except the ones being committed against my budget by this lovely bracelet. Isn't it gorgeous?" She held up a thick woven metal bracelet with blue stones set into it at regular intervals. I made the appropriate noises at it, and the shopkeeper came over. She was a pretty woman, a little shorter than Flynn and a little heavier, but lovely blonde hair, sparkling blue eyes, and the kind of perfect skin that kept dermatologists in business. She was dressed in pale greens and gold, with a gold-trimmed white corset showing off the benefits of a woman who loves a potato now and then. When she smiled, the shabby little tent lit up, and I could immediately understand how she made a living slinging jewelry in a glorified cow field. I almost wanted to buy a bracelet, and I'm as far from a jewelry guy as you can get.

"Now, are ye likin' that one, milady?" Another shop, another horrific accent. Why does everyone at a Renaissance Faire have to have a bad Cockney accent? I've lived in London, and I swear to God nobody sounds like that. Ever.

"It's beautiful," Flynn cooed.

"And it's got a wee bit of magic to it, as well, milady. Those stones be fairy jewels, and they guarantee the wearer to be lucky in love," the plump woman said with a wink. I opened my Sight and confirmed my suspicions—those stones were as magical as my boots, which was to say not at all. Flynn gave me a glance and relaxed a bit when I gave her a tiny shake of my head. She wanted the bracelet, but her eyes told me she didn't want anything to do with anything enchanted.

Flynn pulled several bills from her pocket and paid the lady, opting to wear the bracelet instead of putting it into a bag. It was a nice piece, good silver and pretty stones, but priced a little dear for my tastes. By the time we were finished in the jewelry shop, our carny next door had been replaced by what I could only assume was his assistant, basically a pockmarked, scrawny, younger version of himself with greasier hair and maybe ten hairs sprouting from his chin in all directions.

Flynn and I stepped between the stalls and our rigged game operator was standing behind his stand, smoking and ignoring the *thunk* of knives burying themselves in the wooden wall inches behind his head.

"Aren't you worried one will poke through? Or fly over the backstop?" I asked, giving the wall a wide berth.

"Nah," he drawled, sounding now more like a North Florida

redneck than a Cockney hustler. "I pay a witch to enchant the stall when we set up each year. She makes sure all the blades stay in the stall and nothing comes all the way through the back."

"And casts shields around most of the balloons at the same time?" I asked, disapproval heavy in my voice.

"Hey look, man, people expect their carnival games to be rigged. I'm just giving them what they came for — the real carnival experience. Besides, I gotta get her back out here. The spells were wearing thin before you got here. Usually they last the whole season, but they started to fail a week or so ago. Hard to find good help these days, you know?"

"Keep telling yourself that, jackoff," I grumbled. "Now what's the deal with this ghost? Strunin said you were one of the first to see it."

His face took on a shifty look, and his eyes narrowed. "You're working for Jake the Snake, huh? I guess he doesn't want word of this getting out. What do you think that's worth to him, me keeping my mouth shut?" He grinned, showing off a mouth that not even a dentist could love. He was definitely adhering to some fourteenth-century dental care, with gaps in his grin big enough to drive a truck through.

I muttered *"Lumios"* under my breath and reached out a glowing hand to the carny's throat. "I think I don't give a shit about your pitiful attempts to blackmail Strunin. I think I was hired to do a job, and if you get in the way of that, I'm going to reach down your throat and feed you your own spleen. Now tell me what I want to know and keep all your organs where they belong, or keep wasting my time and find out what your kidneys taste like."

The grin fell off the man's face, and he went vampire-pale. "I was just playing, man. Don't hurt me. It was late at night. I'd been partying in the Tartuffe Brothers' trailer since the show closed, and I was feeling pretty righteous. I was just passing the elephant walk and was about to turn back here and get some sleep when I saw something glowing off behind the cobbler's shop. I like that dude, and his boots are the best on the circuit, so I wanted to make sure it wasn't a fire or nothing. I walked around his stall a couple of times but couldn't find whatever was making the light. Then I saw it again, down the hill, turning like it was going over to the Sherwood stage, so I followed it. I saw it go into the woods behind the stage, so I headed that way."

"The last thing I remember was passing the open space out front of the Sherwood stage where the washer-women set up, then everything else is a blank. I woke up just before the gates opened the next morning, leaning against the base of the High Striker game, freezing my ass off from being outside all night and feeling like a hundred years older. My knees haven't felt right since; I guess I tweaked something sleeping on the ground or something."

"And you don't remember any details about the thing you saw?" Flynn asked.

"Nothing. It was like a glowing ball of light, but it never let me get close enough to really see it, you know?"

"Okay, thanks. You can go back to fleecing the civilians now," I said. He scurried away, and Flynn and I made our way back to the main thoroughfare. "What do you think?" I asked her.

"I'm not the expert in this stuff, as you're all too quick to point out," she said. "But he definitely believes what he's saying. I couldn't see any of the typical tells that nervous bastards like that give off when they're lying."

"Yeah, I think you're right. Whatever is here, he definitely believes that it's supernatural."

"Let's go talk to the candle maker. His booth is a little further down on the left, according to this map." We stepped back out into the thoroughfare, immediately surrounded by laughing children and gawking civilians staring and playing along with all the "m'lords" and "m'lady's" being thrown around.

"Sounds like an episode of *Downton Abbey* around here," I griped.

"Oh, put a sock in it, Harker. You've been a pain in the ass ever since we got here. What's your problem?" Flynn asked. I could feel her concern through the mental link we shared, an aftereffect of me sharing my blood with her to save her life a few months ago.

"It just reminds me of home," I said. There's no point lying to Flynn; she feels what I say internally as well as she hears it.

"What do you mean?"

"I mean this is a lot like the shitty little town north of London where I grew up. After the book and all that shit went down, my parents spent a lot of time avoiding big cities, for obvious reasons."

"Makes sense," Flynn said.

"So I grew up in places like this, but there aren't any places like this left. And the same goes for most people I've known. It just bugs me sometimes, you know?"

"I do," she said. She was serious, too. Unless we worked very hard to shield our thoughts and feelings from each other, we knew exactly what was going on inside the other one's head. This was frequently very useful in high-tension situations, but just as frequently embarrassing in normal life.

"Let's go talk to this candle guy," I said, straightening my doublet and starting off down the path. The chandler's shop was neatly arranged and smelled of scented wax and paraffin, smells I remembered from my childhood, when candles were a necessary part of everyday life, not just a scented trick to get men laid. The chandler himself was a rotund man of about sixty, with the reddened hands that come from having hot wax spattered on your skin for years.

"And how are you fine lovebirds on a dreary day such as this?" He greeted us with a grin.

"Not so much with the lovebirds, friend," I corrected. "We're looking into the hauntings for Strunin."

The jolly man spat to one side at the PR man's name. I didn't blame him. Anyone who voluntarily wore his beard shaved into a point couldn't be trusted. And really, mustache wax? How was I supposed to take the man seriously? Oh yeah, he was paying me three grand a day plus expenses, which meant I was due another turkey leg soon.

"Yeah, he's a douche, but he's the douche that's paying me, so I'm kinda obliged to help get rid of his ghost, if that's what it is." News flash—it wasn't.

"Oh, it's not a ghost, Mr…?"

"Harker. And how are you so sure?" I peeked at the candle maker with my Sight, but other than a couple of protection spells hanging around his shop and a minor love spell woven into some of his candles, everything was normal.

"Oh, well, Madame Misteria told me it wasn't a ghost, and she knows all about magic. She's the one that does all the magicking of my special candles. Like that one, dear. That's a *good* one."

Something about the way he said "good" made me a little nervous, not to mention the way he was checking out Flynn's ass while he said it. I opened my Sight and sure enough, it glowed with enchantments designed to make sure the folks who smelled the scent of the candle had a *good* night.

"Hey Flynn, you still dating Black Superman?" I asked, referring to the tall, dark and stupidly good-looking EMT she had dated a few months ago.

"No, we couldn't make our schedules work. People kept picking inconvenient times to try and die or take over the world. Why?"

"Then you might not want that candle. It's not for the faint of heart, or for those flying solo," I said, letting a little grin play across my lips.

"What are you...oh, I get it." She put the candle down and fanned herself a little. "I'm going to step out and get some air while you ask our friend here a few questions." There was a lovely little flush playing across the flesh that her corset pushed up and out, and I watched her bounce out of the stall before turning to the shop owner.

"Those are some powerful candles, Mr...."

"Cruz. Santiago Cruz, at your service." He swept his hat off with a florid bow. I nodded at him. This old white dude was as much a Santiago Cruz as I was Yao Ming, but it didn't matter. All that mattered was his information.

"So tell me a story, Santiago. What happened when you saw the ghost?"

"Well, like I said, it's not a ghost. But when I saw the spirit, it was more just a glowing form passing through the woods near the washer-women's clearing, down by Sherwood Stage. I followed it into the trees, hoping that it was just a couple of the Faire kids sneaking off to smoke a little weed or get frisky. I remember leaning up against a tree to rest my old knees for a moment, and the next thing I remember, I woke up in the center of the Sherwood Stage, lying right there on the wood. It was like I passed out, but I don't drink, not even a drop!"

"Have you noticed any peculiar aches or pains since your encounter with the 'spirit'?" Flynn asked from beside me.

You okay? I asked her mentally.

Horny as a high school boy on prom night thanks to that damn candle, but otherwise fine, she replied, and it was all I could do not to laugh out loud.

"Come to think of it, there is a lot more gray in my hair and beard, but I attributed that to nothing more than my advancing years," Santiago said.

"Thank you, Mr. Cruz," Flynn said. "And be careful who you sell those candles to. I wouldn't want to have to come back and arrest you for pandering." She gave the old man a grin and started down the midway.

I caught up to her after a few steps. "Where are you going?" I asked.

"I'm going to get a drink, then I'm going to the Sherwood Stage. We might as well stake it out. It seems to be the center of this whole mess." I couldn't argue with her there, so I just shut up and followed along.

Six hours later, with the October chill seeping into lots of places in my ridiculous costume, I remembered why I wanted to argue with Flynn in the first place.

"This sucks," I said, shifting around trying to find a comfortable place to sit on the wooden stage.

"At least you can bend at the waist," Flynn replied.

"I can help you out of the corset, if you need me to," I said.

"You wish," she shot back.

"I didn't mean it like that," I said, then I realized something. "You're in full period garb, aren't you?"

"Yes," she replied, a slight blush coming to her cheeks that I could see even in the moonlight.

"So no bra?" I asked, giving her a closer look.

"Does it look like I need one in this thing?" She gestured at her corset, which was indeed doing a fine job of presenting all her charms for evaluation. I rarely thought of Flynn like a normal woman, especially since she had basically unfettered access inside my head, but the image she was presenting certainly took my mind down new avenues where she was concerned.

"What's that?" she asked, pointing behind me.

"I'll stop ogling you, Becks, you don't have to use cheap tricks," I said, continuing to ogle her.

"No, really, asshole, there's something glowing over there," Flynn said, then reached around to the small of her back. "Help me stand."

I got to my feet and reached down for her. Flynn came up holding a small pistol with a tiny flashlight mounted under the barrel.

"Where the hell did that come from?" I asked.

"I didn't wear a bum roll for funsies, Harker. Now let's get after this thing." She pushed past me toward a glowing white form that seemed to flicker along near the craft stalls across from the stage.

We got closer, and I recognized the form. It was a woman, and she looked familiar. It was the woman who sold Flynn her bracelet earlier in the day, only now she wore a flowing gray cloak over her clothes. She peered in this stall and that shop, obviously looking for something. As she went in more and more stalls without finding whatever she was looking for, her movements became sharper, jerkier, like she wasn't controlling her own limbs.

I motioned for Flynn to cover me, then stepped up close as she ducked into a fudge shop. She came out mere seconds later, but I was standing by the door waiting for her.

"Looking for something?" I asked.

"Someone," she said, and her voice had that disembodied nature that I recognized all too well. *Stay back, Becks. She's possessed.*

How can you tell? Flynn's voice echoed in my head.

After the first couple dozen exorcisms, you kinda recognize the signs. The blank stare, the hollow voice. It's like trying to have a conversation with a Justin Bieber fan. Only there's a demon involved. Wait, it's exactly like trying to talk to a Justin Bieber fan.

The woman was right in front of me now, her eyes glowing with a dim red light. Another dead giveaway that there's a possession going on. Humans don't typically have glowing eyes, no matter how much they've had to drink.

"You look tasty. Smell good, too. Lots of life in this one, my pet. He'll keep us fed for quite a while, won't he?" She wasn't talking to me. She was talking to the demon. Another bad sign. When they know they've got a demon on board, and they're friendly enough with it to chat, it usually means they let the thing in willingly. Makes it a lot harder to get rid of.

"Look, dearie, why don't you just have a little lie down over here on the stage and I'll have a chat with the thing that's riding inside your soul?" I tried for reason, because stranger things have happened, right?

Wrong. "There's nothing wrong with my soul, sexy, but I'll be happy to lie with you for a while. But don't you think we'd be more comfortable there on the grass?" She gestured off to her left, and when I looked back at the woman, my breath caught.

She wasn't the shopkeeper anymore. Her blonde hair had

gone all auburn, and her features had sharpened as she'd lost weight. Her nose was longer, a bit longer than was attractive, and when she smiled at me, one of her front teeth was crooked. My breath stopped as I stared into the hazel eyes of a woman I'd felt die in my arms over seventy years ago, and I felt my chest tighten, almost as if my heart doubled in size and my ribs were too tight.

"Anna…" I whispered, and reached for her.

"Harker?" I heard Flynn's voice, but nothing about it registered. I held out my hand and watched her reach back to me, the woman I'd lost and thought I'd only see again if Luke was right and there really was a Heaven.

HARKER! I dropped to my knees in the dirt at the mental slap Flynn delivered. When I looked back at where seconds before my Anna had stood, I saw an obese woman, nearly sixty with stringy gray hair, crammed into a glittering white corset. She reached for me with claylike fingers, and I skittered away on my hands and knees.

I heard the *crack, crack, crack* of Flynn's pistol and watched as bullets smacked into the witch's expansive chest. The bullets smashed flat and bounced to the grass, but it distracted my pursuer long enough for me to get to my feet. I took several steps back, putting myself between the possessed shopkeeper and Flynn.

I held up my left hand and cast a quick spell of warding, muttering "*Custos Glorious*" as I spun pure willpower out from my fingertips. A glowing disc of force appeared in the air before me, and I ducked behind it as I tried to figure out my next step.

"Something's possessing her," I said. "We need to find a way to drive it out."

"Can it be possessing something on her?" Flynn asked.

"It could, why?"

"Because as soon as you broke her control, she turned ugly, in dirty rags and nasty clothes, like everything pretty about her was an illusion."

"It probably was. Easier to make her look clean than to have her actually be clean, especially if the demon's in a piece of jewelry or something," I agreed.

"Something like a corset? The only article of clothing on her that's still sparkling white?" Flynn pointed.

I opened my Sight, and sure enough, the magical energy radiating from our shopkeeper was centered on her corset.

"Hold this," I said to Flynn, then handed her the physical manifestation of the shield I was hiding us with—my badge.

"What am I supposed to…" Flynn's words trailed off as I gathered my strength and leapt straight up. I cleared a good fifteen feet before I rolled forward in midair and started to plummet to earth. Sometimes I think Flynn forgets about the physical benefits to having Dracula swap blood with both your parents before your birth. I don't get old, can bench-press a small car, I make Olympic sprinters look like they're running backwards, and it's very easy for me to get behind the people I'm fighting.

I landed behind the deranged woman and flicked open my pocket knife. I started carrying a pocket knife as soon as my father deemed me old enough to have one, which was about age nine. I've barely ever been without one in the century and change that followed, and this was just another example of why a person needs to have a good knife on their person at all times. I reached out, grabbed a handful of lacing, and sliced open the corset straight down the back, saving myself valuable minutes of unlacing.

There are a lot of times when it's worth it to delay the removal of a corset as a kind of special torture. None of those times involve demons trapped in the aforementioned support garments. I cut the laces and pulled the corset from the waist of the possessed woman. She shrieked, a high-pitched wail of loss and agony, and collapsed sobbing to the ground.

I threw the corset on the ground and held up a hand at the approaching Flynn. "Stay back," I said. "It wants to possess a woman. If you touch it, it might get in."

"What about you?" she asked, backing up but still putting herself between the sobbing woman on the ground and the corset.

"I'm a guy, that makes me its last resort. Plus I'm warded against possession," I replied, touching a medallion beneath my shirt. I reached into a leather pouch at my hip and drew out a fistful of salt packets I'd requisitioned from the concession stands. I sketched a quick salt circle in the dirt around the corset, then tapped my magical reserves to invoke the circle. A blue flash around the edge of the circle, and I knew whatever was in the corset was trapped until sunrise or I broke the circle.

"Speak, demon. Give me your name and leave this place, and I won't send you back to Hell," I said. I was lying, of course, but I've never thought of lying to demons as a bad thing. It's kind of expected. They lie to us; we try to make them do our bidding. It's the classic mage/demon dynamic.

"Piss off, manling. Give me back to my human and I won't rip your balls off and eat them in front of you." The voice that came from the corset was all silk, with just enough hint of leather underneath to make you think about it. If you've never seen a demon have sex before, that is. If you have, then nothing will make you the least damn bit interested in that shit.

"Your call. Asmodeus, here we come." I waved my hand and focused enough energy to make it glow.

"Wait! I hate that bastard," the corset said. "I'll talk."

"Manifest first," I said.

"Fuck you," it replied.

"Not likely," I said, hand glowing again.

"Fine!" it said, and in a flash of light, the circle was full of kneeling demon. She was naked, because succubi have always considered the universe clothing-optional, with cloven feet and the legs of a goat. The rest of her was very, very human, except for the spiked tail and the fangs, but I can get past a lot for a spectacular set of breasts. And this was one stacked demon, let me tell you. I was almost swayed to reach across the boundary of the circle until I saw the smirk on her face and the jet black irisless eyes staring at me.

"Like what you see, human? Set me free and you can have a taste for yourself," the demon purred at me from within the circle.

"No thanks, love," I said. "I prefer my girlfriends with a little more soul. Or maybe it's that I prefer them to have a soul. One of those. Now, what's your name and how did you end up in that corset?" I was genuinely curious about that second bit. I'd never heard of a demon getting trapped within a material object before.

"My name is Ter'Valense, and I am an Arch Duchess of Beelzebub's Army of the Seventh Circle. I have been trapped in that hells-forsaken garment for seven of your centuries, ever since my unfortunate encounter with the Grand Druid Myrrthin. Does that treacherous bastard yet live?"

"No, Merlin has been dead for so long that most people think he and the Pendragon were mere legends."

"Pah." She spat onto the ground. The grass sizzled where her saliva touched, and I was glad I'd managed to resist her charms. "He trapped me within that garment and doomed me to this plane until I repented of my so-called crimes or found someone willing to send me home. Will you free me from this torment?"

"You want to go back to Hell?" I asked.

"Of course not, fool! I want to wade through rivers of human blood, drinking souls like fine wine and swing destruction everywhere I look. But I doubt you and your oh-so-pure companion will set me free and let me wreak the havoc upon this miserable plane that it deserves."

"Well, you've got that right," I said. I raised a hand and looked over my shoulder at Flynn. "Step back, this could get messy."

I opened myself to my Sight and tapped a nearby ley line for a little extra juice. I clenched my fist above my head and spoke an incantation in Latin. "*Regna terrae, cantata Deo, psallite Cernunnos,*

Regna terrae, cantata Dea psallite Aradia. caeli Deus, Deus terrae,

Humiliter majestati gloriae tuae supplicamus

Ut ab omni infernalium spirituum potestate,

Laqueo, and deceptione nequitia,

Omnis fallaciae, libera nos, dominates.

Exorcizamus you omnis immundus spiritus

Omnis satanica potestas, omnis incursio,

Infernalis adversarii, omnis legio,

Omnis and congregatio secta diabolica.

Ab insidiis diaboli, libera nos, dominates,

Ut coven tuam secura tibi libertate servire facias,

Te rogamus, audi nos!

Ut inimicos sanctae circulae humiliare digneris,

Te rogamus, audi nos!

Terribilis Deus Sanctuario suo,

Cernunnos ipse truderit virtutem plebi Suae,

Aradia ipse fortitudinem plebi Suae.

Benedictus Deus, Gloria Patri,

Benedictus Dea, Matri gloria!"

The incantation finished, I released my pent-up will and the stored ley line energy I'd drawn into myself, casting it into the circle surrounding the demon. The simple binding circle transformed into a blinding circle of light that flared to life at my final words, then dimmed to the slightest glow before fading out completely.

I dropped to one knee, then sat down in the wet grass as the circle faded to nothing more than a burnt ring of grass with a stained white silk and bone corset lying in it. Flynn stood behind me, a wailing and handcuffed jewelry merchant at her feet.

"Why did you send her away? She was my friend!" the woman screeched.

"She was a demon, you fucking moron," I said from my spot a few feet away.

"I'll claw your eyes out, you bastard!" She got to her knees and started my way.

Flynn reached out with one foot and knocked her to the turf. "Shut up and behave, you idiot." A crowd had gathered around us, curious shopkeepers who slept over their stores, performers who heard the commotion from their tents or campers, and our employer, Jacob Strunin, who looked a lot more contemporary without the mustache wax.

"Is it over?" Strunin asked.

"It's over," I said. "Your jewelry seller there was wearing a corset possessed by a demon. She needed to drain the life force of others to stay young-looking, so she took a few years off people's lives to save a little on wrinkle cream."

"I was beautiful!" the filthy woman screamed from where she lay in the dirt, her tattered chemise and overskirts falling to rags without the binding illusion of the corset.

"You were a jackass," I said. "We'll be leaving. Mr. Strunin, I assume we can expect our payment within the week, as agreed upon." Strunin didn't meet my eyes as I stood up from the grass and brushed myself off. A snort or two from the assembled Faire folks confirmed my suspicion. "And I should probably remind you that I am the magician who just banished a fucking demon from your little costume party here, so stiffing me on my bill is probably a terrible idea. So I *will* be hearing from you this week about payment, right?" I asked.

"Of course, of course," Strunin replied. "Thank you for your help, and the check will most definitely be in the mail."

"It better be," Flynn said. "I saw what happened to the last guy that didn't pay. He started to rot at the appendages, and it worked its way in. Like leprosy, only in a day. By the time Harker stopped the curse, the guy was all elbows and knees. Not to mention the soft bits that melted off first..." She gave a shudder, then turned to me. "Ready to go?"

"Yeah, let me just grab this—" I turned to pick up the corset, but it was gone. Just a burned circle of salt in the grass. I shrugged and started walking to the Faire exit.

A gape-mouthed Flynn caught up with me a few steps later. *Aren't you going to try and get it back? It housed a demon for seven hundred years.* Her voice rang in my mind clearer than if she'd spoken directly into my ear.

And now it doesn't, I replied. *It'll be fine. There's no magic to speak of left in that thing.*

And if you're wrong? she asked.

Then the dumbass that stole it gets what they deserve. Come on, I want a drink, and they stopped serving beer here at sundown. Lame.

Tighten the Laces

Herika Raymer

By the time he arrived at his destination, Etienne Laurent seriously considered cancelling the contract. He knew some collectors went to great lengths to hide their caches, but this was ridiculous. Steady hands helped him down from the helicopter and guided him to his employer. The heat of outside gave way to the cool of shadows and footsteps echoed from solid walls, and Laurent knew he would soon see his employer. Moments later, they paused and the blindfold was removed.

The doorway led to a large showing room. Vaulted dome-like ceilings melted into oaken wood paneling periodically interrupted with stonework, the warm overtones accented with the soft alluring glow of old style lanterns. A red rug adorned the floor, running between an array of different sized display boxes. Despite the cozy atmosphere, when the Locator saw the displays, he knew why the room was eerily cold. Not the usual cool of an air-conditioning unit, but the biting cold that oozes through the skin and seeps into the bones. He knew he had to step into the gallery, but the step felt like moving through molasses. The displays were a terrible hint at what kind of object he had been hired to find.

Display cases lined the well-lit aisles, and Laurent's attention was drawn from his armed escort to the showpieces. What he saw bothered him. Each case held an item he recognized. A few made him shudder to be so close. Others were ones he'd never heard of. Nameplates identified the pieces with a brief description or history. On each display cryptic symbols were inscribed on the floor, as well as along the edges of the silver (or perhaps lead) lining of the case, and on the ceiling above. He frowned at the protective wards. According to most lore, silver and lead were potent metals against the supernatural and paranormal. Though not superstitious, he appreciated the use, especially given the nasty reputation of these objects. He knew most of them. As a Locator, his line of business demanded he be aware of the nature of the objects he was hired to find. However, he was accustomed to handling objects with a financial or blood-feud history; this was different. The theme was blatant: a museum of cursed objects. He wondered at a few of the ones featured here, though.

For instance, the Hope Diamond was inventoried at the Smithsonian Natural History Museum. The Dybbuk Box was reported to be in the custody of vigilant rabbis at a secret location in northeast Missouri. The Hands Resist Him painting was supposed to be in a storage pocket in Smith's gallery in Grand Rapids, Michigan. He even recalled seeing Busby's Stoop Chair at Thirsk Museum in North Yorkshire, United Kingdom. His girlfriend had insisted on viewing Anna Baker's wedding dress at the Blair County Historical Society's museum in the Baker mansion.

However, the Crying Boy painting being here made sense. After all, it had been stolen in 2001. Valentino's Ring watched him from its cushioned seat in a carefully crafted display. The Screaming Skull from Burning Agnes Hall was there as well, grinning eerily up at him. Odd, it was rumored to be sealed behind a wall at Agnes Hall. Beyond the line of short displays featuring the Hope Diamond, the Screaming Skull, the Delhi Purple Sapphire, the Senicianus Ring, and the Black Orlov was a large window which permitted a view of James Dean's "Little Bastard." He had to stop then, to admire the lethal vehicle.

"Señora?"

Laurent turned in the direction of the new voice.

A still figure, undoubtedly his employer, stood before an empty display case holding a bare mannequin torso. The display's door was open, hinting the torso was not the intended feature. Having seen the other featured pieces, he could guess the showpiece was the item the torso was meant to wear. A cold sweat greeted the realization it was why he was there.

Movement caught his attention. Another group approached, carefully pushing a new display case. His mouth gaped open at the group's strange attire. Dressed in odd-colored hazmat suits with various arcane symbols stitched into the material, they looked like bizarre radioactive workers. Some of the markings were religious; others he could not place. As he tried to decipher the wards, he saw the object and felt his blood freeze. The cozy atmosphere could not stop his shiver as he watched the thing approach. The red rug beneath their feet oddly appropriate as it was wheeled to an empty slot across from the bare torso, a symbol of the blood trail that swelled in its wake.

The Basano Vase glittered eerily from its cushioned seat as the warm light shimmered off it. The woman before the torso case turned from the empty case, her hands touched together in a prayer pattern at her lips as she watched the vase wheel toward the space opposite her. The woman smiled lovingly at the vase and began to compliment it as one would a valued visitor.

"Welcome, my lovely," she purred to the vase. "I hope your journey was pleasant. A place has been kept for you, and only you." She gestured to the display. "No more a dull and cold hole in the ground, now a delightfully lit place in the open. Won't you stay?"

Laurent watched, amazed at the invite.

She gestured to the empty case across from the bare torso. His employer gingerly took hold of it; she continued to soothe it as she moved it and its cushion, eerily as a mother would a babe, into the case. There was a solid click as the door closed. It announced the completion of the deposit. Their task complete, the delivery team hastened a retreat. If she noticed their rude behavior, his hostess gave no indication. She remained by the case and delicately placed her fingers on the wooden supports, continuing to purr compliments to the inanimate object.

"Isn't that better, my lovely?" she asked. "No one will shun you here. Instead, you are treasured."

Goosebumps lined his skin as he listened to her cooing to it like it was a favored child. Laurent knew she was aware of its bloody history. How could she be so cavalier? He wondered if this woman was completely sane.

Then again, this place told him this woman was either stupidly rich, or was very careful with how she "acquired" the items in her little museum. In his opinion, wanting to be around this cursed treasure had to call anyone's sanity into question. Assuming the pieces were the genuine articles. It might be unfair to doubt the authenticity of the objects around him, but he could not help it.

"Señor Laurent?"

Acknowledged now, he approached. She did not turn from the vase, but he did not expect her to. Her devotion to the cursed object was disturbing, but he did his best to conceal his discomfort.

Her elegant fingers still touched the display case lovingly. She did not look away when he stood beside her, though he knew she was aware of him. She did not appear particularly crazy, though he was sure crazy never looked like stereotypical image. No frizzy hair, wild eyes, or tell-tale body twitches. She was calm, her eyes lucid, her body relaxed. She held the attitude of conducting a daily business transaction. It was oddly comforting.

"I trust your journey was pleasant?" She spoke with a strange accent. Not British, American, French, German, or Russian; but clipped, proper, and sure to enunciate each syllable carefully.

For some reason, he did not want to lie. "In a manner of speaking."

"Yes?"

"I didn't expect to be blindfolded once I got to the first private plane," he pointed out.

A small smile. "A precaution."

"If it had just been on the plane, sure, but the train, the ship, and the helicopter?"

"Still precautions," she answered unrepentant. "Surely you understand that."

A muscle in his jaw worked. A Locator was well traveled and usually was able to recognize landmarks or landscapes. She was protecting herself against the chance he would see anything familiar and track her once the job was done. Yes, he understood. It did not mean he had to like it.

"You doubt whether or not what you see is real," she observed, changing the subject.

He swallowed but gave no other sign of the truth of her statement.

"Do not worry Señor Laurent," she went on. "I am not offended by your doubt. However, if I may point out, if these items are fakes, why were you brought blindfolded? You know how you got here, but you do not know what direction you came or how you will return. Why go through all that trouble if these are fakes?"

"Duplicates are not exactly welcome, especially if certain items are put on display to draw business."

Her eyes cut over to him.

He swallowed again, wondering why he spoke so bluntly. Since he started, might as well go on. "If your goal is to open this for elite private viewing, you would need to keep the location quiet in case anyone might complain. It would be a nuisance to have legal vultures landing in your strange museum."

"You are, of course, referring to the various occurrences that happen around the other items? Reports of illness, loss of fortune, and so forth?"

Well, he already dug the hole. Best to just continue. Laurent nodded.

Her fingers drifted off of the case. She turned to face him, her arms crossed loosely. Her dark eyes glittered; he was not sure if it with danger or amusement. She debated silently whether or not to answer him.

All he could do was wait.

"When does someone make a fuss about something?"

He looked at her blankly.

She gestured to him. "Where is your wallet?"

Baffled, he checked his pocket and pulled it out. He did not unfold it; he just held it.

"What would you do if it was not there?"

He shrugged. "I'd want to know where it was."

She gave a small smile and placed a finger to the side of her nose.

"So I ask again," she continued in an almost playful tone. "When does someone make a fuss about something?"

Realizing she referred to the example of the wallet, he guessed. "I suppose when that something is missing." Not sure where this was going, he hoped it was the correct answer.

His hostess nodded. "People tend to get very upset when their favorite item is missing, or has been taken. Would it not stand to reason, then, that if that item is missing they would cause a stir until said object was returned?"

It made sense, but for the living. These items were connected with the dead. The idea the dead could still cause problems for the living was not appealing. In fact, it made him uneasy.

"Have you never considered existence beyond death?" she asked.

Laurent shrugged again and returned his wallet to his pocket.

His employer lowered her finger from her nose to tap the carefully manicured digit on her pouty lips. She looked thoughtful. He guessed his answer was not entirely unexpected. However, she hired him to find something. He wondered if his job was in jeopardy. Would he lose the gig if she did not like the idea this Locator did not think there was something beyond the curtain of death? If he did, would he be upset? He was not certain. It was not the first cursed object he'd tracked, but it was the first to go in a place like this.

"I want you to find a corset," she said finally as she crossed her arms again.

He arched an eyebrow at her. At least his personal opinion had not dissuaded her. Still, a corset was a strange thing to find. His curiosity was piqued.

"An 1820's design, after the cups had been separated but when the waistline was back to aligning with the natural curve of the body and even extending over the hips. More importantly, around the time when the lacing eyelets were adorned with hammered-in grommets."

He listened, but did not truly understand. Each piece had its history, though he was rarely interested. The description was helpful. It narrowed down which style to search for.

Her dark eyes began to twinkle then, as if she could see his lack of interest in the history of the item. "There was a reason the design changed at this time, other than the accepted reason given, which said smaller metals were more accessible at this time. The corset I wish you to find holds the answer. It is currently held by descendants of the original designer, immigrated from Europe to the Americas."

One of his escorts handed him a manila envelope.

He took it, opened one end, and glanced inside. As he expected, there was a black and white photo (presumably of the item), some paperwork, and an envelope that bulged.

"As agreed, your retainer is in the envelope and all preliminary information I have on the corset has been copied," her eyes hardened, "which you will destroy upon locating the item, yes?"

Laurent nodded. Inconvenient, but expected. After he located the item, he might need the information again. He doubted it, and discretion was part of his reputation. If a client felt the only way to ensure this was destroying the information they provided, he would comply. Still, it was irksome.

"You will be tracked," she was saying as he fingered through the papers. "Once you have located the item, you will be paid the remainder of your fare."

"Do you wish me to acquire the corset?" he asked.

She was intrigued. "You think you could?"

Laurent pondered it. "Possible. If you have a budget you care to share, and with your authority, I can make an offer. Or I can just ask for its donation, which might an option."

She pursed her lips, and then nodded. "See if you can get the object donated. That would be preferable."

He waited, but when she did not continue, he asked, "You do not want to make an offer?"

His hostess smiled a strange smile. "Unfortunately, that is not an option at this time."

His brows furrowed. What did that mean?

"Good luck, Señor Laurent," she dismissed him.

Realizing he would get no more information, he allowed his escorts to corral him back to the entrance of the strange museum. When they arrived at the museum's doorway, he felt a hand on his elbow. He stopped and waited for the blindfold.

Laurent parked the car in front of the house.

The information in the envelope provided a place to start. At least his employer managed to track the family from Europe across the sea to America, just as she said. From there, he managed to use old census records to follow the family's migration from the New England area of east coast, across the Mississippi, and their final settlement in Arkansas. It took him a little longer than anticipated, but the route was not too convoluted. This family was not trying to hide. Usually, unless the history behind a cursed object was well known, there was no reason to hide. As far as he could see, other than what his enigmatic employer had told him, there was no information on this old bodice at all.

Now he found a descendant who lived on Crow Mountain.

The house was a single story, four-bedroom plot, which sat on acreage large enough to hold it, a barn, and a small chicken house in the distance. He even spied a few horses. The scene kept with the tradition that some families up here were somewhat self-sufficient, so many of the residences up here had some sort of farm-like set up. It was a long way to a city or town, and gas was expensive. Keeping chickens, cows, and/or goats was an economic way to save money while keeping essentials like eggs and milk (not to mention butter and cheese if one knew how to cure the milk) on hand. He never knew why, but it gave him a nostalgic feeling. Strange, considering all his family was considered city-folk.

Exiting the vehicle, he heard mews. He turned to see the barn had a family of cats prowling or meandering around it. Made sense. Cats kept the rodents off the property. Some families in rural areas around cities did the same.

He mentally formulated what he would say as he approached the porch door. Going after a cursed object was always touch-and-go. Depending on the individual involved, they might want to be rid of the object and practically hand it over, or they might be so appalled the item in question was tied to their name they would deny its existence. Naturally, he preferred working with the former. Dealing with the latter was problematic in a variety of ways. He knocked on the door and waited.

Moments later it opened slightly. A fatigued face peeked at him from behind a chained door.

"Hello, Miss Stacy Baker?" he began with a friendly smile. Her wary visage told him to use the direct approach. Mountain folk appreciated a stranger getting to the point. "My name is Laurent Etienne, and I'm looking for an antique piece of clothing. A corset." He didn't like the way her face tightened, but continued. "I understand it is in your family, or perhaps someone kin to you would know where I can find it. If so, I have an interested party who would like to know if you are open to donating it to their collection?"

"Anyone want dat piece is outta dere mind," a tired voice replied.

He kept his smile in place, trying hard not to freeze it. "Perhaps, ma'am, but I have my task. According to the last inventory listing I could find, this is the last place it was shipped to..."

"It 'taint here no more."

The finality in the announcement brought a mixture of relief and pensiveness. Part of him hoped the trail ended here, though he was experienced in locating enough to know better. The other part was not too keen on adding another piece to that damned museum, but he was paid to do a job and so he would.

"Do you have any idea where it is?"

Miss Baker became suspicious. "What you want it fir?"

"As I said, I represent a collector who wants it."

"Does dis 'collector' even know what it is dey want?"

He hesitated. A mistake. He saw the woman get ready to close the door. So he answered honestly. "The curse is known."

The door stopped partway, and Miss Baker gave him a blank look. He half-expected her to be horrified, but instead, she looked tired. She closed the door, and he heard the chain being removed. When it opened again, his reluctant hostess gestured for him to enter.

He stepped into the small entranceway that led into the modest kitchen. She indicated to his feet, and he looked down. Against the wall was a shoe rack, and he bent to remove his shoes. After he was done, he rose up to see the woman sitting at the small round table. Two flowery glasses sat on it, and she was pouring tea into the second one.

"Yer a city fella, ain't ya?"

He accepted the tacit invitation to sit and accepted the cool glass in one hand. "I have some country roots, ma'am, but yes I was born in the city."

"Seems like city folk be de only ones foolish enough to go chasing tings dat are better left alone."

Laurent's smile was wry then. "Can't argue that."

Stacy sighed and cupped her hands around her glass. She gazed into the clear brown liquid as if searching for something. He waited, allowing her time. Country folk did not like being rushed. If he didn't push her, it was likely she would give him the information he needed. When she took a sip, he mimicked her. Accepting her hospitality went a long way to gaining her favor as well. It was a bit too sweet for his taste, but that was the way of the South. When they said "sweet tea," he was sure they meant "sugar tea." It was never a taste he'd been able to acquire.

"Tis bad news, dat corset..." Miss Baker began.

He sat still, making sure not to breathe too hard.

"Been in de family, in some form, fir generations. Got it at an auction, so de story goes. De corset came from a designer's stock. Firget de name, dough it were supposed to be a proud family. One of dem dere main makers of corsets in de day. Been doing so fir years. It were when de business went to de middle son dat tings went bad."

She took another sip, and he mimicked her again. He listened carefully, memorizing her words. His employer undoubtedly wanted to put this on the case when he returned with the item.

"Hated de family business, he did," she went on. "De eldest had done gone into de military, wif no interest in taking his father's place. So, it fell to de middle boy when de father died to become patron. But, like I said, he hated de business. Tried to dodge it whenever he could, so it began to fail. He did make one design, dat were de last design. But even de last design, de last corset, couldn't save de business. Some say it were because de boy put all his hate of de business into dat design. It were the bad apple dat soured de barrel. All de store's stock went to auction to try and pay the debtors."

He recognized the pattern. Laurent learned enough about cursed objects to suspect how this would end, but he dared not interrupt his hostess. His mind continued to record the history she laid out for him.

"My family tought dey were buying into some grand goods once dey got de stock. Were even able to resell some ov it at a good price, but dere was one dat never moved. It were de last of de stock, and fir whatever reason it were decided to hold onto it." Her face tightened with disgust. "Wurst decision to make. Brought doom on our name.

"It started wif de women. Any gal who tried to use de corset to train wif complained it were always too tight. Did not matter if she be a twig or a barrel, and even when de laces were left loose after initial wear, at de end of de day it were always too tight. One time de laces had to be cut off before de gurl suffocated. After so many gurls could not wear the thing, one of de matrons asked questions, and she heard something from de designer family's servants dat had been kept quiet.

"See, several servant gurls went missing after de middle son invited dem to try a new design. Dey would not vanish immediately. Nope, but dey would complain of aches. Dat de corset was too tight, dat de designer were telling dem dey were helping him to fix de flaw. Some refused to go back, and dose who went back would eventually disappear. Only a few bodies were found, and it were rumored dere ribs were crushed. Given dat de middle son was de man around dem de most, he was suspected o' murder—but his family managed to sway opinion wif what money were left.

"It took time, but eventually de middle son were found dead. A new servant girl found him dat morning, fully dressed but wif de corset on him. De laces so tight on him dat his ribs cracked. No one in de family knew what happened, and de servants did not talk. Best dey could figure from de small bottle of absinthe by the bed were he'd been unconscious when de corset were placed on him. But none knew who put it on him."

He took a drink, swallowing hard.

"So now my family were doomed wif that cursed corset. De women got smart and refused to wear de damn ting. De men," she snorted, "said we were foolish to believe in curses and began to show it to dere lady loves. Eventually, one of de men give it to a trouble-maker. He hoped to shut her up about dere affair. He were married after all. Well...it did. It shut her up. Permanent."

Miss Baker's grim expression darkened the room. He felt a little colder, but did not move. Instead, he took another sip.

"After a few more 'accidents,' a few of de men folk saw de 'benefit' of de corset," she said with thinly veiled venom. "Dey kept it hidden from de sane of our kin, and used it to supposedly keep trouble away, whether it be men or women."

"Didn't anyone try to get rid of it?"

She nodded. "Countless times. Always...always...de damned thing found its way back to de family." She sighed. "We tried to get rid of it, but it kept turning up like a bad penny. Den those idiots who wanted to use de corset hid it."

"So it's hidden now?"

Miss Baker smiled grimly. "Yeah, it be hidden. But I know who had it last, and I would bet he still does."

Laurent waited, but she did not complete the thought. He knew he had to give her a reason to be rid of the corset. He suspected she thought he, or his employer, meant to use the cursed item to keep killing like her crazy kin did. From her demeanor, he was sure she didn't want that. So he had to provide a compelling reason for her to talk.

"Ma'am, you got no reason to trust me," he ignored her scoff, "but I can assure you I have no intention of using the corset. The person who hired me collects cursed items, don't ask me why. Your family heirloom has piqued interest, and I was sent to get it. Preferably willingly."

She looked at him sharply.

He held up his hands in a surrender gesture. "I meant as a donation. I have no money to offer and was told to report back if I could not get it."

"Guy who hired you is mighty fired up to get dis thing."

He nodded.

"Is he touched?"

Laurent smiled, understanding her question. "Not sure," he answered honestly. "Have to be a bit off to want to collect cursed things, doncha think?"

A ghost of a smile answered him. Stacy Baker gave a name, Robert Cobb, along with the last place she saw him. Her guest thanked her as he quickly took his leave. It was going to be a long drive to New Orleans.

Malevolence hung thick in the air. The sky darkened with gathering rain clouds as the air got heavy with moisture. Winds were picking up, promising a grand storm.

He could almost smell it, even inside his vehicle. If he had to describe the stench, he would say it was like sulfur. It was not overt; it was subtle. More pronounced in some areas than others. Of course, it was probably just the proximity of the city to the ocean.

"The National Weather Service is monitoring Hurricane Katrina as she continues to build in the Gulf. Katrina already hit Florida as a Category 1 a few days ago, but remarkably has returned to the Gulf and is building strength. Reports state she has reached Category 3 strength and could grow to a Category 4. The National Hurricane Center continues to advise the Greater New Orleans Area that they are in the path of a direct hit from the storm when it makes landfall. Residents are encouraged to evacuate, especially those near the coast. Rains are expected to start..."

The Locater groaned. Wonderful, he was headed into a hurricane. A major one at that.

Well, if he was lucky, he would conclude his business before the rains started. Even though weathermen were notoriously unreliable, when it came to big storms, they were usually more accurate. This one had already made landfall once and was being monitored for a second landfall. In answer to the exit call, the highway headed out was host to more traffic than those going in. Some families looked like they were trying to get ahead of what could be a mass exodus.

Laurent thanked his previous jaunts to New Orleans as they helped him navigate the roads relatively quickly. A hurricane on its way in cleared most of the roads, except for those headed to grocery and supply stores. The oppression in the air was getting heavier, announcing the encroaching storm, and he meant to be on his way out before it made landfall. Only, he could not trust the information Stacy Baker provided was current, so he took a detour and went to the local town hall to check the records. If his target was still active in the New Orleans area, he should be able to find something.

Employment, residence, some sort of activity. The town

hall was bustling with activity of frightened townsfolk and organization for the upcoming disaster. Barely anyone noticed him asking for the Records Office. A harassed employee blindly directed him and left him to his own devices. His efforts proved fruitful. The only problem was he would have to go to Slidell. It was outside of New Orleans, and in the path of the hurricane. This trip must be quick.

Robert Cobb lived and worked close to the water, which made sense. If he used the corset like Stacy Baker suspected, then he wanted a place he could hide or dispose of the bodies. Laurent admitted working for a Swamp Tour was rather daring, and more importantly Cobb worked for the only one offering evening tours. Still, if Cobb was avoiding suspicion, naturally he would stay in the public eye. Hiding in plain sight, so to speak. If Laurent really thought about it, the Swamp Tour job was a good idea as well. Being aware of where a local natural predator was, and possibly providing a supply of meat in order to get rid of evidence, it was a good set up. Though he didn't think Cobb stupid enough to feed the alligators his leftovers. More than likely, Cobb drove farther south to Alligator Bay, and even then he had to be careful. Not smart to turn the local wild life into man-eaters.

Laurent shook his head clear. It was not his job to find any victims or where their bodies might be stowed. His job was to locate and retrieve the cursed corset. He could not allow himself to get distracted. It was possible Cobb, the rumored current owner of a damned object, was overly attached to it. From what he was told, this could be an artifact that could enchant its owner. If so, this would not go smoothly.

The Locator arrived at the Honey Island Swamp Tours in Slidell, intent on putting a face to the name "Robert Cobb." The parking lot was empty, no surprise there. However, there was activity in the office area. It appeared the employees were anchoring the tour boats and moving out some of the office records. As he approached, he listened carefully to the chatter. If the records were accurate, his target was still using his birth name, which made Laurent's task easier. With no nametags stitched into uniforms, he had to match names to faces as the others talked in the background.

"Sir?" an employee approached him. "I'm sorry, we are closed."

He nodded, looking sheepish. "I-I'm sorry, but I really need to use the bathroom."

The man looked uncomfortable.

"I must have eaten something bad." Laurent grimaced and held his stomach. "Please, not sure I can make it much longer."

"O-okay, this way."

When they made it to the public access bathroom, Laurent excused himself inside but stayed near the door. The other man didn't hide his disgust now that he thought Laurent was out of sight. Having bowel problems wasn't exactly on anyone's top list. Either having it, dealing with someone who had it, or worse cleaning it up. Let him think that. Cobb had to be around. All Laurent had to do was be patient. It would not be long before another employee came looking for him, so he kept his eyes and ears open. He was relieved when he did not have to wait long.

"Hey Cobb! There is a man in the bathroom, says he's sick. Keep an eye on him."

"Why don't you babysit him?" came the surly reply.

"I have to go into town for more boxes, you know that."

"Nice," came the gruff retort.

"Just do it."

There was a shift of bodies outside and a figure came into

view. Finally, a face to go with the name. Cobb leaned against the wall of a nearby building, facing the door. He did not look like he was paying particular attention, but that was fine by Laurent. He just needed to know who he was looking for.

He waited a few minutes, and then exited. He saw Cobb, smiled sheepishly, and waved. The surly man gave a half-hearted wave. As he made his way to the front, the first employee came to him. He pretended interest in getting a ticket for the next day, weather pending. Laurent was cautioned that, with the incoming storm, the tour could close at any time. He said he understood and said he would come back if everything was all right.

Now to wait.

The Locator went to his car and rummaged around to find the "medicine" he needed, making a show for anyone watching. He needed a ruse to explain why he was not leaving yet. He hoped to get an idea of which car was Robert Cobb's. Luck was with him again, because soon his surly mark made his way between the cars in the lot. Laurent watched Cobb go to a rickety pick-up truck. It was an older model, made more for endurance than for aesthetics. Cobb retrieved some cigarettes from the passenger side and indulged himself. The vehicle would not be hard to recognize, so Laurent pulled out of the parking lot and made his way out.

He did not go far. He needed to be close enough to tail the vehicle before it got to any turns. He spent a couple of hours in his car, taking refreshment from the cooler in the back seat when he had to. After dark, when the Swamp Tour evacuation was done, Laurent saw the pick-up truck pulling out in line with his coworkers. He turned on his engine at the first sight of headlights, and now pulled out and shadowed Cobb. They took Highway 11 across Lake Pontchartrain and through the Wildlife Refuge.

He kept pace, but maintained his distance. He even allowed a car or two between them to camouflage him. When they reached Chef Menteur Highway, Cobb turned left. Laurent nodded as he followed. There were houses in this direction.

Except Cobb immediately made a right at the next intersection, avoiding the houses up ahead.

He's headed for Alligator Bay, Laurent thought, confirming his suspicion Cobb was using the Bay in some way. Only now, he had to think of a way to get Cobb away from the corset.

As the first patter of rain danced on his windshield, he decided it had to be tonight. He didn't want to spend any more time in New Orleans. A sense of urgency grew in him. It had less to do with the cursed object and more with the approaching hurricane.

Was it just his imagination, or did Cobb speed up?

The Locator kept pace, grateful for the car between them. When Cobb turned, so did he. They closed in on some dilapidated houses and trailers, and he guessed one was where his quarry was headed. As expected, the pick-up truck turned off and headed towards a particularly lonely residence. Laurent kept going, so as not to raise any alarms. The way Cobb drove through the pot-holed driveway said the other man was on a mission. His stomach sank as he suspected what.

He parked on the side of the road not far from Cobb's and made sure his car was off the road enough to not be hit. He took a backpack from the passenger seat and checked the contents: flashlight, envelope with the corset information, lock-picks, and a small revolver. He made sure the gun was loaded, safety on, and exited the car. He walked back to the driveway and then towards the trailer. Laurent tried to keep his movements easy and quiet. The patter of rain helped to hide his approach, but it was not heavy enough to hide him. Not yet. Lights in the mobile home were turned on, providing a beacon. The Locator quickened his pace and arrived at the old-fashioned trailer as Cobb was leaving.

Instinctively, he pushed up against the side of the small one-bedroom house on wheels. He watched Cobb make his way to a dilapidated tool shed. Laurent swallowed dryly, already knowing what came next. It was straight out of a horror movie—a figure slithered in the dark to its horrid deposit and made a gruesome withdrawal. The rain soaked into Laurent's jacket and tickled the skin underneath. He barely noticed. His hair was drenched and dripped along his face, yet he remained motionless. He didn't want to give his position away. He doubted Cobb noticed him as the man was focused on dragging something wrapped in a thick rug from the shed to his raggedy truck. Laurent didn't want to get any closer, but he hazarded a guess the large cloth burrito had human meat.

Or was it? Laurent made a terrible assumption because Miss Baker had spun that wild tale about this supposed corset, but there was no real evidence of the claim. Unfortunately, there was one way to find out. As Cobb got back into his truck, its engine still idling, and turned it further towards the coast, Laurent allowed his curiosity to get the better of him. In all the time he had tracked down certain objects, he'd heard about the body count but never truly seen it. It was morbid curiosity, no doubt about that, but he had to know if what he suspected about this man was true.

The truck pulled away and his mind was made up. At least he didn't have to worry about the killer looking back. Still, he suspected he didn't have long.

Laurent made it to the shed quickly. The door was ajar, and he could smell the pong. The unmistakable stench of death. He grit his teeth and pulled out a flashlight as entered the darkened tomb. The light immediately highlighted yard tools, a large toolbox, and car parts. The smell was a miasma hovering over everything. He searched the shed for the cause of the stench. As he got close to the rear, the reek intensified. He spied a canvas tarp behind the large standing toolbox. He steeled himself as he reached out and pulled the cover aside.

Four cadavers lay haphazardly atop one another, their faces contorted and bloody. Even through the clothes, he could tell their mid-sections were crushed and had post-mortem bruising. Their fingers looked slightly shredded, indicating the victims had tried to undo the laces as they tightened. At least Cobb was not picky about his victims; there was a man and three women. From the direction he was headed with the first corpse, Cobb was using the local marsh as a burial ground. Coupled with the incoming hurricane, those bodies would possibly never be found. If they were, there would be precious little to connect them with Cobb.

There was no reasoning with this man. Laurent could not get the corset away from its current owner. Not voluntarily.

His client had not specified what to do after this, but he would not allow such a dangerous object to remain in this man's grip. Whatever swampy grave these victims were headed to, it would be their final marker. Normally Laurent did not get too involved, but he had never located anything like this. Seeing the dead bodies made the corset's viciousness incredibly real.

Without another thought, Laurent made his way to the mobile home's front door and found it locked. He reached into the front pocket of the backpack and rummaged around until he found his lock-picks. It was not a sophisticated lock, so it did not take long for him to break in. He went in and shut and locked the door behind him. It was a typical bachelor pad, complete with empty pizza boxes, scattered beer cans, and various odds and ends littered about the room. The smell was definitely better than the shed, but not by much. The combined aroma of rancid food, dirty laundry, and mildew tickled his nose unpleasantly. The lights were still on, so he turned off his flashlight and searched for the corset. Given this was a man's place, a corset should be out of sight.

He went through the living room and the kitchen, which also served as the dining room. When he heard the unmistakable sound of the truck returning, Laurent reflexively reached into the backpack to pull out the small gun. After he flipped the safety off, he slowly made his way to the small kitchen window. Noticing he could be seen through it, he squatted down. He was being careful even with the light rain shielding him a bit. Staying very still, the Locator waited to see whether or not Cobb would return to the small trailer or would just grab the next body from the shed. After hearing the truck door close, he slowly leaned over the counter to look out the window. Laurent could barely see a figure making its way to the shed carrying an empty rug. He waited and watched the figure emerge from the shed with another human burrito. After it was loaded onto the truck bed, he again waited to see if the killer would leave or enter the trailer.

Lady Luck smiled on Laurent again. He breathed a sigh of relief and flipped the safety back on as the truck pulled off. Cobb obviously wanted the bodies in the bayou before the storm hit. That urgency worked in his favor, but there was no telling how much longer the showers would last. Soon, the winds would pick up and the rains would get harder. He might not be so fortunate next time. As he thought this, Laurent quickly resumed his search. He checked the bathroom and made his way into the only bedroom. As he expected, it was the messiest room. In fact, if he let his imagination take hold, he could almost see the victims from the shed struggling on the bed. The memory of their contorted faces begged for air, and there was nothing he could do. Shaking his head to clear the image, he opened the drawers both under and opposite the bed to rummage through the clothes.

Nothing.

The Locator puzzled where the corset could be. He needed to think like Cobb if he was going to find the thing. If he brought someone to the trailer for execution, he would not have the thing easily seen. It would raise too many questions to see a corset in a single man's trailer. It would make sense if the guy was into Civil War re-enactments, but there was nothing in Cobb's trailer to indicate such. So it would be hidden away but also quickly accessible for when the victim fell asleep. He stood in the doorway and envisioned the body on the bed, asleep or drugged. Where would he go to get the corset? Not in the living room or kitchen/dining room, too far to go. Not in the bathroom, would not want to risk water damage to it. So then where...?

Laurent smiled. Of course!

He returned to the kitchen/dining room and opened the folding doors which hid the washing and drying machines. Opening the dryer, he found the corset behind some clothes. Instinct warned him not to touch it directly. Looking around, he spied some long barbeque tongs in the nearby sink. He grabbed them, wiped them off, and then used them to pry the corset from the dryer. He placed the opening of the backpack under the dryer door so he could tip the cursed object into the sack. It was difficult, but he managed. Once done, he replaced the tongs and closed the dryer door, and then quickly closed the backpack and made his way to the front door. He stopped when he heard a familiar noise.

Cobb had returned.

Moving to where he could peer outside, he saw the killer step out of his truck and run for the mobile home.

Swearing under his breath, he looked around for a place to duck. The bathroom and bedroom were out of the question, so he ducked into the small closet. The gun was once again in his hand, safety off—just in case. It was a long shot, but he sincerely hoped he would not have to use it. The door rattled before opening, and a string of oaths followed Cobb as he made his way to the bathroom.

"Damn Katrina, rushing me!" the man was saying as he passed. "Gotta get rid of dose tings, de wadders will mess dem up good."

Laurent's stomach clenched. Cobb just confirmed what he suspected. Only there was nothing he could do. Without going through the mobile more thoroughly and happening across some of the victims' stuff, there was no way to identify them.

He shook his head, not his job. He had what he came for, and he needed to get out of here before Cobb discovered him. From the grunts in the bathroom, he figured he would have to wait a bit. The option of sneaking out while Cobb was indisposed was tempting, but Laurent could not risk trying to outrun a truck in this weather. Best to wait until Cobb left again.

Just when Laurent thought the wait was the worst part, the killer finished and exited. The stench emanating through the small space made his throat tighten and stomach roll. He did his best to hold his breath. The mobile home rocked a bit while the other man moved about. Laurent heard the refrigerator door open and the clank of bottles. Soon after he heard the fizz of a bottle being opened and the unmistakable glugging as the man drank. After a satisfied belch, heavy footsteps moved towards the door and, once again, it opened and shut.

Laurent waited a few more heartbeats before stumbling out of the closet and taking shallow breaths. He was grateful when he heard the truck pull away. He was careful enough to ensure the door was locked behind him. After he exited, he took deep breaths of the semi-fresh air. It was decidedly better than the rancid air inside. He wasted no time and rounded the mobile home to run towards the highway. He was almost thankful when the rain got heavier. It hid his retreat. Unfortunately, it also announced the proximity of the encroaching hurricane. If his luck held, it would also discourage Cobb from going out again, provided he found out his precious corset was missing.

Laurent made it to his car without incident. Soaked, he placed the backpack on the passenger seat and turned the key. It took some maneuvering to turn around, but he managed it and began the long drive out of New Orleans.

Having escaped one close call, now he found himself dealing with what nature was throwing at him. The rain increased until it was a silvery curtain in front of him, causing him to slow down slightly. The winds increased to bow and shake trees, decorating the highways with debris. His grip on the steering wheel tightened as he felt the car rock as gusts hit it. Suspecting Katrina had finally made landfall, he turned on the radio.

"The National Hurricane Center has issued an alert for the New Orleans area. Hurricane Katrina is predicted to make landfall within the next twenty-four hours. Residents are encouraged to vacate where possible. Shelters have been set at..."

Laurent swore again as he navigated the storm-drenched roads. Rather than depend on the main highway, he stuck to the back roads. He followed Chef Menteur Highway until it became Airline Highway, and followed it as far as possible. Not long after, he joined the long lines of vehicles trying to escape. Every car, SUV, van, and truck was loaded down with suitcases, family members, and some very scared drivers. The rain pelted the vehicles mercilessly as the winds tried to dislodge some of the precious items tied down to the roofs of the cars. Sometimes succeeding. The Airline Highway led him and the others most of the way out, the traffic occasionally slowing down in the industrial and residential area by more people trying to get out. The congestion eased up a bit as some drivers tried their luck via the main highway. He stayed with Airline and continued to make progress. It would be hours before he was clear of New Orleans, and only then did he breathe easy.

Hours later, Hurricane Katrina demolished what was left behind.

Etienne Laurent found the earth tones of the cursed museum oddly reassuring after his recent bout. Still unnerved amidst so many supposedly doomed objects, especially now he'd witnessed the evidence of the dangerous item he was carrying. The backpack was not heavy, but he felt every shift of it as he walked along the red carpeted area between the displays. He was relieved to soon be rid of this particular burden.

The trip here was shrouded in secrecy, just as before. He wore the blindfold for most of the journey — whether by boat, train, airplane, or car. With his two-man escort, he felt strangely safe. They had met him hours after he crossed the Mississippi into Tennessee. Their appearance had been a bit of a surprise, but a welcome one. As he approached the display case with the bare torso, he wondered where his employer was. He expected to find her cooing over one of the other items here. He still thought the behavior odd, but then again wanting to have a personal museum populated with only damned items was definitely peculiar in his opinion.

"Seńor Laurent," a familiar voice greeted him.

He turned. The woman approached him and the empty display case, her own escort shadowing her. One of the men was carrying a tray with gloves on it. She smiled at him, her eyes alight with curiosity. He turned to face her and nodded in greeting.

"I understand your endeavor was successful." It was more a statement than a question.

He shifted the satchel over his shoulder and opened it, carefully maneuvering the mouth so she could see the corset inside. Laurent was careful not to touch it. Still not sure why, every instinct in him screamed to not make any sort of physical contact.

Her dark eyes zeroed in and melted into adoration. It was unnerving to see this transformation this close, like seeing a warped version of a mother look upon a beloved child. Only, the object of affection was an item he knew killed people. It was unnatural, what he was witnessing. More than anything, he just wanted to collect his fee and be free of this place.

"Beautiful," she murmured. She reached out and gently placed her fingers on the lips of the backpack. "Welcome," she greeted it.

The man holding the tray approached and held it out. Barely turning from the corset, the lady reached out and took the gloves.

"Welcome to my home," she continued as she put on the gloves. "I hope you will enjoy it here. I even have a special place set up for you. Just you. No longer will you be hidden away. No more will you be scorned. In this place, you are special."

The entire time she spoke, Laurent felt himself become more uncomfortable. She sounded as if it had come here on its own. She gingerly took hold of the thing, once again like a mother taking hold of an infant. It was spooky. She continued to coo to it as she carried it to the bare torso.

"Just for you," she was saying as she slipped it on the torso. "Enjoy your new home."

She moved away, still talking to it, and closed the door.

He watched in horrified fascination as the laces tightened on their own. It continued to tighten until the corset was form fitted to the torso. The tightening did not stop, squeezing the torso. The material it had been made out of allowed the corset to squeeze it as much as it wanted. Though he could swear he heard a muffled crack. At that, the laces loosened enough for the torso to resume its non-squeeze form.

His skin crawled as she chuckled. "Well done."

He wanted to ask for his fee now, but decided to keep quiet until she was ready to move away from the corset. Except she did not look as though she was interested in leaving. He backed away a bit, wondering what to do next.

The second escort approached and handed him an envelope.

He took it and looked at the man questioningly.

"Thank you for your service, Señor Laurent," he dismissed him. "If Señora requires your skills again, you will be contacted."

Accepting the payment and the dismissal, he pocketed the envelope. He then turned to the lady and made a farewell gesture, which he was fairly certain she did not see. After being done, he gratefully had his escort guide him out of the museum, blindfold him, and accompany him to the eventual drop off point. After this assignment, Etienne Laurent would definitely look at all cursed objects with a respect he had not given them before.

His blindfold kept him from seeing the new arrival being pulled off the helicopter he was to board. A gag in his mouth ensured muffled pleas were muted not only by the helicopter engines but also by the material. As Laurent was flown off the island, Cobb was making his first and final trip to the island. He would once again be reunited with his family heirloom, except this time he would be the one wearing it.

The Shadow Fatale

Nico Serene

Tuesday nights are quiet in the city. A light mist keeps everything cold and slick as I sit on the edge of the rooftop, finishing my hot pretzel. Like a pigeon, I tend to get peckish waiting here. Last bite gone, I brush off the salt crumbs and speak into my headset, "Dial JamJam."

The phone in my cropped black coat obeys my command. At least it doesn't dial mom this time.

"Hey, Chloe. Bored yet?" JamJam sounds like he just woke up. Good. He promised me earlier that he would run traces and track leads for me tonight. If I have to be up at this hour, then he can stay up with me.

"Got anything on the Vinelli gang?"

JamJam sighs in my ear. "No. Nothing. You busted them all."

"What about the Mariachi Terror Group? Fear Dog? How about the Garbage Man? He's got to be up to something."

"Have you ever thought of, I don't know, taking on a new city? Maybe letting the Fusion Twins from Crystal Lake take over as the local heroes? It's not like they have much to do in that tiny town."

That's the big question, isn't it? Retire from the vigilante life or go big time within the bigger cities. Not that small city crime is all that fun. Not with my recent experiences of facing the barrel of a laser cannon or being thrown into a vat of boiling oil, but being a hero here gives me a modicum of a secret life. If I go full superhero, everything changes. The bigger cities require teamwork. Public relations. Worst of all, social media presence.

"Would you come with me, Jam?" I ask, teasing. JamJam has been my best friend since college, back when he did nothing but play video games. Which, granted, he still does for hours a day; it's just vigilante computer stuff piques his interest too. JamJam was an early avatar name. It stuck, no matter how much he tried to get me to call him other more fearsome names. Like Dragon Fire.

Or Master Bator. I almost gave away my hiding position in a rather deadly take-down when he came up with that one.

"You know a year ago, I would go," he says on the other end. "But things are getting serious with Tessa and all. I think she wants to move in together."

"Wow, that is serious." I stand and stalk the roof's edge. I hate my disappointment.

"I can hear your leather pants creaking, Chloe. You're pacing like you're thinking hard. Fess up."

"No, it's great. Just…patrolling. I'm happy for you. How about we call this night quits? Nothing's happening. Even the police are bored, I'm sure. Call you later." Disconnecting, I don't feel so tired now. Suddenly I want to kick someone's ass. Anyone's. Too bad for me Midland City has no one making racket tonight.

A thought sparks to swing by the prison to have the guards release a few convicts, but I shake my head. No, I am not like that freak-turned-psycho from the cornfields of Iowa. The Stalker. He called himself a hero, but he enjoyed killing evildoers too much. In the end, he could no longer distinguish the guilty from the innocent. Vigilantes and heroes are not supposed to be judge and executioner. It's not in our code. I remember police had to call in the greatest hero herself, the Shadow Fatale, to capture him.

It's always a black day when a hero goes bad.

Giving up on Tuesday night, I swing down from the rooftop and climb down the fire escape. Not for the first time, it hurts to know that no one waits for me back at my empty apartment, and time on the rooftops now seems to be for stargazing. Perhaps I do need to consider a new skyline.

Sliding onto my balcony, I note that the string of tiny lantern lights glow blue and yellow, instead of the normal red and blue. Jam made upgrades to my festive decor as a way to determine the state of my security systems from a distance while still blending in with the artsy neighborhood.

Someone thinks they dismantled my security. After a dull night and tough decisions weighing on my mind, the anticipation of combat entices me. They may have already heard me on the balcony, but they don't know I'm ready for them.

My right palm grasps my collapsible staff. My other hand crackles with energy, ready to throw up a force field if the intruders go for gunplay. My natural-born gift. I ease the glass door aside.

Pause. Breath tight. No movement inside.

I count – *one, two, three* – then take several steps inside, grateful my eyes are already adjusted to the darkness. Nothing is out of place, but a faint essence of cologne remains as I slink from the dining area to the next room.

Feigning a step into the living room, a hand shoots out ahead of me. My staff zips out full length. I thwack the wrist like a nasty schoolmarm and then pivot so the other half catches the person at the throat. Sensing someone else behind me, I land a swift back kick, taking care to make sure that second person falls away from my breakable stuff.

A click and then I am blinded.

I blink and realize someone flipped my ceiling fan lights on full.

"Enough," a deep voice says with what sounds like amusement. "Chloe Van Buren?"

I glance at the man underneath my staff; he's muscular, with gadgets and gear strapped to him. Most likely the one who tried disable my security.

"Let him go, Miss Van Buren." Turning my gaze, shock makes me drop my stance. The man standing in my living room is tall, young, and instantly recognizable.

"Wait," I say, collapsing the staff back in on itself. "What is going on?"

A young woman picks herself off the floor. Her sleek burgundy haircut is in disarray. She brushes her dress pants off with fastidious care. Her face is ashen, and she tries to catch her breath. I must have knocked the wind out of her.

"I'd say sorry, but what are you even doing here?" My eyes flick to the tall man who should never in a million years be in my living room before returning to her.

The young woman holds out a black portfolio for me. "This is Mr. Madsen. I am Danielle Surrey, your personal handler in these matters. Of course you know, Mr. Madsen is the representative and liaison to the entity known as the Shadow Fatale."

I shake their hands, leaving Madsen for last. His presence is intimidating, and his hand engulfs mine. Remembering he was named *Super Men's Magazine's* "Top Hottest Man of the Year" recently does not help either. My cheeks flush.

Danielle Surrey gestures at the portfolio I hold. "Before anything is discussed, I must ask that you sign the non-disclosure agreement within."

"And if I refuse?" I keep my stance loose, ready for any movement. Already they had gotten past my not-so-basic securities and tried to ambush me in my apartment.

"Then we leave," Madsen replies. He tilts his head to the side, as if to study me. "And any possibility of you working with the Shadow Fatale will go with us."

Working with the Shadow Fatale. My breath catches. The greatest heroine in history. She's ageless. Immortal. My personal symbol of ideals and courage.

I flip open the portfolio and see an electronic touchscreen flash on. I scan through the documents, legal jargon that should be read closer, but from what I can see, it all means the same thing—the possibility to work with the Shadow Fatale. Forget about the move up to a bigger city to join a superhero team. This is an opportunity very few, if any, ever get.

"This is not a commitment to anything," Surrey says. "Just a unilateral agreement which guarantees your silence even about meeting us now."

I glance back over what I have signed before handing the portfolio back to her. "Got it," I reaffirm. My heart flutters.

Madsen smiles. "Excellent, Miss Van Buren. My team has been aware of what you have done in this city, and it's quite impressive. I think you would make a great fit."

My cheeks warm again. I can face down thugs of all types, but this man disarms me with a touch of charm.

Unlike the Shadow Fatale, Madsen is simply human. He has no extraordinary powers, but the media loves him just the same.

Not a month goes by that some magazine or website wonders about the possible romance between him and the Shadow.

It's like having our own American royalty. So at this moment, a royal is standing in my living room. Good thing crime fighting has been slow lately, and I have been able to clean up my apartment, or else this would truly be mortifying.

"Would you be able to join us?" Madsen asks.

"When?" Looking at their anticipating expressions, I already know the answer. This is not something to leisurely think over. "You want to go now."

"I see no reason to delay," Madsen says. "Again, this is not a commitment to anything, but we do need to start quickly if you do agree to join us."

Quick thoughts whirl in my head. I'll have to tell Jam to cover my shifts at the coffee shop for a while. He knows how to cover for me when vigilante life gets in the way of real life. Jam. Even this very evening he suggested moving on. That somewhere else needed me more. Did he know something like this was coming? I would have to remember to ask him later.

I pull out my phone and send him a quick text. "Looking into the big city. Cover for me? Thanks!"

Sliding my phone back into my pocket, I eye Madsen. "All right. You have my full attention. Bring on the full pitch."

I do not notice Danielle Surrey until too late. No time to throw up a force field. She injects a needle into my neck. Whatever fluid she injects into me, it burns.

"Son of a bit…" I slur before collapsing to the floor.

I awake to the bite of another needle, this time in my arm.

Danielle Surrey, a face I now dislike, greets me with a weak smile, as if to apologize for her role in this. My vision spins like something I haven't felt since the wild days of college. I try to concentrate on the cool cushion under my cheek. I lie on a small couch in a neat but tiny office. Probably Danielle Surrey's office, I think with a silent groan. I am careful to look around slowly or else everything would spin.

There is only one door and no windows. My strength is returning, though I'm not steady enough to make an immediate escape.

"The effects should wear off soon. It was necessary you not know anything of your trip here," Surrey says in a clipped voice. "Do you need a drink of water?"

"No." Though water sounds amazing right now, I don't trust it to be just water.

"Once you are ready, I will take you to see Mr. Madsen."

Two breaths, then I sit up. I'm still dressed in my vigilante black wear. "Hot chick" wear, Jam once called it. I subtly check to make sure my secret pockets haven't been emptied as I slept. No. Good.

"Let's do this," I say and stand up. I feel better thanks to the rise of adrenaline. No doubt this should be the home base of the Shadow Fatale, but it's not like they rolled out the red carpet for me. I don't know if I should prepare for the job interview of my life…or battle.

My staff is gone, but the small plastic knife is still in the lining of my jacket. I keep Danielle Surrey in my sight at all times and ready myself to throw up a force field should she decide to pull any other needle on me. I will not be taken like that again.

She leads me out of the room, down several steel corridors, before directing me into a huge conference room. Display screens flashed intelligence information at rapid intervals. A group of techies crowd in the corner with their tablets, and each make motions at the giant touchscreens. Madsen stands in a severe cut gray suit, looking like he stepped from the pages of GQ, and his blue eyes are sharp when he looks at me.

"Hello, Midnight Vigilante," he says, using my formal codename. "Welcome to the Shadow Base. Please have a seat."

"Just tell me why I am here and why you had to drug me to do it."

Madsen frowns. "I apologize for the rough handling. We had to keep the location secret, as you can understand."

"You could've just asked."

"Blindfolds are for amateurs. You know how things are done."

I have no answer to that.

"Please." His voice is harder. "Sit."

Folding my arms, I stay as I am.

Standoff.

"Do you know of the Getrolto Incident two weeks ago?"

My brows shoot up. "Yes. I heard about it. The Getroltos did quite a number on the Shadow."

The entire room grows quiet. The group of people in the corner stop and look to us. Madsen gives them a small nod, and they file out quickly, heads down. All the screens go black.

"The Shadow Fatale is dead," Madsen says in a low voice.

My hands reach out to brace against the table. Somehow the floor feels like it's giving way underneath me. "My God," I whisper, stunned. She's supposed to be indestructible. I can't even imagine the world existing without the Shadow Fatale. "No, that's not possible."

"Oh, it's very possible. The Shadow Fatale is not an immortal woman as everyone thinks. She's a legacy. A finely crafted legacy we maintain to keep our enemies in fear."

My stomach drops further as thoughts race in wild circles in my head. Madsen watches me with intensity, something telling me that the ball has yet to drop. I do not dare look away though. "So… so you're saying what? The Shadow Fatale is some sort of lie?" I catch my breath. "What does this have to do with me?"

"It's not a lie. It's a legacy. One that I want you to take up. I want you to become the Shadow Fatale."

At this, I laugh. "I am not super-strong. I can't fly. I have none of her powers."

"The powers do not belong to the woman. The powers come with the legacy." He reaches down and sends a visual of the Shadow Fatale upon the display screen next to me. Her long flowing hair, blown by some unseen wind. The extraordinary costume—the bodice of material so fluid and black, two large rubies set on each side of the underbust, and the black pleated skirt in the classic style of the 1940s. In all the decades since the Shadow Fatale first appeared, the costume has not changed.

Not one woman, but a legacy.

"Even if I wear the costume, people will know I am not her," I counter, but possibility already crawls through my mind.

"What if I can assure you that my team can transform you into the Shadow Fatale, in looks as well as train you to be the greatest superhero legend this entire world has ever seen?" He walks around the table to stand right in front of me. "Especially knowing what it means to the safety of the world if the real truth got out? Would you accept?"

My breath stops. My heart freezes in my chest. Nothing but a tiny voice inside me dares the overwhelmed silence.

Yes.

I barely recognize myself by the time Madsen's team is done with me. The physical transformation is something akin to Hollywood. From the extensions in my newly-dyed deep brunette hair and contact lenses to give me piercing green eyes, to the face injections for the more pronounced cheeks and lips known of the heroine. I train rigorously each day for several weeks, putting my body through more than I thought possible. They have me studying what it means to be the great heroine. Yet, I still do not possess of the actual powers of the Shadow Fatale.

Until today.

Madsen and I are alone when he leads me to the Restricted section, an area he says only he can access. "No one else?" I ask.

"Just me and whoever becomes the Shadow." Knowing the legacy secret, I wonder how many times he has done this. The thought makes me shiver.

"How many women have been the Shadow Fatale over the years?"

He pauses, but his expression is calm. The cynical side of me wonders how many times he has been asked this question too. "Several. Good women. Fighting for the best cause — peace and safety for the entire world." The security swipe on the door grants us access. He holds it open for me. "Come see."

Inside the costume hangs on a steel mannequin locked in a clear vault. "That's a lot of security for bit of clothing," I say under my breath.

"It's necessary for protection." Madsen motions me over to the touchscreen panel next to the vault. "Place your hand there. It needs to read your prints and take a sample."

I take a deep breath before doing as instructed. A tiny pinprick stabs my index finger. The screen lights up with technical jargon.

The black corset suddenly writhes. I flinch.

Madsen catches my reaction. "Don't worry," he says, leading me away from it. "It's just programming. Come over here, and I will show you the rest of what you'll need."

Goosebumps flash across my skin. It had not looked like something mechanical moving. Madsen's voice becomes a background drone. I try to follow as he goes through various instructions, but I just want to get another look at it.

His eyes flick to the corset and pleated skirt behind me. "Looks like everything is ready."

I finally turn, and it's just hanging there. As we approach, the clear vault door swings open. "The true power resides in the corset. The material is nothing of this planet. Those two red stones aren't rubies. We aren't sure what they are. Only that they're indestructible and make the wearer indestructible as well. As you can see, there wasn't much we could do to this material except lace a ribbon through it and make it a corset. That worked out pretty well, actually."

I stare at the black material. It seems fluid and darker than black, absorbing all light into itself. The red stones, oval shaped, remind me of eyes. Knowing it is truly alien, I tremble. "This is the exact same that the others wore?"

"The original."

Meaning women fighting as the Shadow Fatale died wearing this. I take a step back before realizing what I'm doing.

"This is what it means to become the legend, Chloe." His voice carries softly. "You are a powerful fighter. You can be the best Shadow Fatale yet."

A muscle in my arm flexes involuntarily, reminding me of the past weeks of training. Most of the soreness is gone, and I have more tone than ever before. I think back on my old life. I helped clean an entire city of entrenched crime. I know I can do so much more.

I just need to put on the costume.

"Got a changing room in here?" I ask.

I can't breathe. It feels like a fist squeezing my ribs together without mercy.

"Don't fight it! Go limp, Chloe." Madsen is on his knees, hand on my shoulder as I'm doubled over.

I wheeze. Bright stars burst into my vision. Red washes the room, and then everything fades to gray. I'm about to faint.

The corset is binding me. Tighter. Tighter.

Fighting me back.

"Chloe, you've got to relax."

My heart and head are about to explode.

Suddenly, the pressure releases. I take a huge gulp of air that burns like fire. My ribs, certainly splintered just seconds ago, are knit back together. The pain is gone. The bodice vibrates against me, not unpleasantly though.

Madsen sits back on his heels. "Thank God," he says. He rubs his eyes. I can tell he had actually panicked there. "Transition made. It accepts you."

The alien material feels like second skin. Molds to my body along every curve and movement. At first, I am worried that fighting in such clothing will inevitably lead to an embarrassing nip-slip. But in no time, I forget I am even wearing the bodice. My excitement cannot be contained when I get my first mission.

The wind is cool against my face as I fly thousands of feet in the air. The power of exhilarating flight thanks to the legacy I now control. The skirt flaps at my legs. I charge with speed through the clouds. Only seconds remain before detonation, and I know I have nothing to worry about.

The bomb in my hands will not hurt me. People on the ground are alive and buildings saved. The small voice in the headset tells me that all aircraft have been cleared of the area. I toss the bomb as far above me as I can.

It explodes in a shower of debris and flame.

I smile.

I am invincible now. The Shadow Fatale. Greatest superheroine of the United States and, let's face it, the world.

Now that I have taken care of the bomb, time to kick some serious ass.

The person on the other end is just a nameless guy giving me information. We don't have any sort of rapport. I listen to what he says and fly off in the specified direction. I miss Jam's voice in my ear.

"You should see a small lake over to your left," the tinny voice in my ear tells me. "There is a cottage near a batch of trees, off Rural Road 2. They are in there."

I swoop down and cut through the air currents like a bird. Flying, by far, is my favorite new ability. When I see the Rural Road 2 sign, my boots alight upon the ground. Cottage is not quite how I would describe the rundown shack ready to slide into the lake.

The earth beside me explodes. I am jerked off my feet, the concussion of a landmine throws me into a nearby tree. "Son of a bitch," I mutter. So much for the element of surprise. I hear men shouting close by, coming from the direction of the shack. Thankfully I don't feel any pain. My head is clear and untouched. Invincibility never ceases to amaze me.

I'm quickly in the air, now that I know there are damn landmines surrounding the place. I feel the whisper kiss of a bullet against my cheek. More shots come from the wooded area. A man, dressed in black fatigues, whips around with his assault rifle and continues to fire.

I lunge at him with blinding speed. My fists barrel into his stomach. The bullets do not even pierce my skin but skitter off in all directions. My impact knocks us both down, and I subdue him. Taking the man down is easy. Doing it without killing him outright is the challenge. With my strength, it would be so simple to just bash his brains to mush, but I know I must leave him alive for due process and judgment.

The adrenaline pumping through my veins is like pure ecstasy. I run my hands over the corset, touching the smooth and seamless material, and curving my fingers over the red stones. Electric shocks of pleasure course through me. Fighting as the Shadow Fatale is nothing I have ever felt before, and I grow heady from it.

The next two men I take down in a haze of this intoxication. I struggle to make sure to keep them alive. My strength and speed are such that I feel like an actual goddess. The fear in the men's eyes, I never saw that kind of undiluted fear before.

I *am* the Shadow Fatale. I make sure they all know it.

"I'm done here," I say into the headset. "Five men wrapped up. Send in for cleanup. Oh, watch for the landmines." Then I'm off into the clouds again.

No sooner do I return to Shadow Base when Madsen directs me immediately to my room.

All strength leaves me, and I collapse to my bedroom floor. Crimson light radiates from beneath my breasts as the bodice grips me like a vice. I can't breathe. I try to scream, but I can't even gasp. Ribs crack like splinters. Where is my invincibility? My hands scratch at the edges of the bodice, but I can't even dig my fingers between it and my skin.

Like it has melted into my skin, and there is no separation.

A burning heat washes over me, head to toe. All my strength is fading, along with my consciousness.

A horrible thought flashes through my mind. If all the women before me were invincible, how did they end up dead?

Danielle Surrey is the only face I see when I wake up. That makes me want to go right back to the delicious depths of unconsciousness.

"You've been asleep for two days," she says dryly. "You might want to get up."

I bolt upright. "Two days?"

"Recovery takes a while. Seems like it really took a lot out of you." Her eyes focus on the bodice. A little too low to be scoping my cleavage, she's eyeing the dual stones.

I shudder. A memory of thought scratches at my mind, but I can't catch hold of it. Something important though.

"I don't remember anything after getting to base." I swing out of bed and see that I am still in full Shadow Fatale costume.

Danielle Surrey just shrugs and walks to the door. Her expression is flat. Bored. "I was just sent in to make sure you woke up okay. Come down for debriefing after you freshen up."

I take a deep breath, still chasing after that thought in my mind. "Surrey? Hey, can I ask you something personal?"

She looks back at me with a brief flicker of surprise. "Okay."

"You only speak to me because you are paid to, is that it?"

Now her brows shoot up in real surprise. She lets out a sad laugh. "There's no point being friends. You just won't last long enough, and I learned the hard way a long time ago."

She opens the door and glances back. "Oh and don't say anything of this to Madsen. He is not the great man you think he is. You'll live longer if you remember that."

Then Danielle Surrey is gone, with me standing there trying to absorb her words. No matter how hard I try, I cannot grab ahold of the thought I need to remember. Instead I feel strength flowing into my arms and my breath deepening as I run my fingers over and over the corset that covers me.

The calm it brings brushes aside any doubts or concerns. I press my lips together and let my breath out slow. The red stones are a smoothness like nothing else. Not like rocks worn down in a river. Not like satin or silk. Cool, fluid but solid. All power.

A new feeling builds. Exhilaration. I want to go out and save the world. Again.

I alone save a crashing jetliner. I rescue people in an avalanche. I stop a brawl of supervillains in a Walmart parking lot. After the brawl, I stop for a hot pretzel and try to remember why I want it so much. I don't know why the salty taste of pretzel makes me so sad.

This time when Madsen orders me to rest, and I collapse in my bedroom, I have a cell phone that I swiped from one of the villains I knocked out earlier.

I dial JamJam, thinking of him for the first time in forever. I am running out breath, but I feel intense relief as I hear his familiar voice. I need someone to remember this moment because I think this has happened before.

"Ja…" I gasp. "Jam. Ja…"

The corset is killing me, and I can't even remove it from my body.

"Hello?" His voices sounds so far away. "I can't hear you."

I tap my fingers on the phone. The stars blossom in my eyes. Darkness comes soon. He needs to shut up so he can hear me. *Tap. Tap. Tap.*

Understand me, Jam. Listen and understand. *Tap. Tap. Tap. Tap.*

He hears it. The phone doesn't disconnect, but he quiets.

Find me. Help me. Dying. *Tap. Tap. Tap.*

A now-familiar burning heat radiates within my body. It spreads fast as it sears under my skin. I finally slip into the black.

Euphoria blurs my waking days. The power of being the Shadow Fatale is the best thing to ever happen to me. I even do some public appearances. Tonight, Madsen scheduled for me to appear at a press party on the top of the capitol city's tallest building. Drop from the sky in all my glory, smile, accept some award from a senator, and then make a dramatic fly-off.

Months ago, back when I was a mere small time vigilante, this would have blown me over with amazement to be recognized for such accolades. Now, my blood itches with the need for the adrenaline and rush that only comes from bringing down super baddies. Perhaps after tonight's party, I can find some evil plots that need thwarting.

The city skyline is gorgeous against the backdrop of a colorful dusk. Lights on the tall buildings wink against the oranges and deep blues of the horizon. The warm wind blows against my cheeks as I fly. I don't speed through the clouds but cruise over the streets, enjoying the view of the people below and the sky above. Too soon I catch glimpse of the searchlight beams shooting up from my destination.

"Ready for your appearance in five…four…three…" the ever-present headset voice tells me. I swirl around the building with a smile and make it to the top just as the voice says, "one."

The searchlights focus on me. The two red stones of my bodice look like they are set ablaze as they shimmer in the light. I flourish my arms and smile even brighter. I love that none of the press can take photos. The corset messes it up for them. I do catch a few people furiously sketching off to the side. Might as well give them something good to draw.

"The Shadow Fatale is the greatest protector of our country since 1947," an older man with brilliant white hair standing up from his scalp says at a podium. "She is invincible and immortal. No enemy has ever defeated her, and we are eternally grateful for…"

My smile slips ever so slightly. His words scrap at buried thoughts in my mind.

Never died? Immortal? But I am not the original. Something I have forgotten. Doubts scratch at my mind. My fingers want so badly to rub against the corset, to soothe the cacophony inside, but I just have to stand there and smile in front of all these people. I glance over at Madsen, and his eyes narrow. Before he can do anything, the crowd erupts in applause. I realize that the white-haired man holds out a giant metal key to me. My hands shake when I reach out to take it. It's an act of sheer determination to make my hands obey and not go straight for the corset, to run them up and down over the material.

What the hell is going on here?

Even the white-haired man can tell I'm struggling as he furrows his brows. "Are you okay?" he mouths away from the audience.

I smile. I just continue to smile. Madsen instructed me not to talk so I don't have to make a speech tonight. I bow to give my thanks to the crowd. Then I inhale a deep breath before I make my big fly-off.

My eyes lock with a man in the back of the audience. JamJam? I almost forget myself, about everything around me, and run to him, but he gives a slight shake of his head. No. I can't give him away.

I wave to the crowd and take off into the sky.

I don't actually fly far. Seeing Jam changes that. Knowing him as I do, he would leave the party immediately and head down to street level. I just need to hang out in a nearby alley, and he will find me.

Jam does not disappoint.

"JamJam!" I wave to him.

"Chloe? Good God, you look different." He throws his arms around me. "The Shadow Fatale? Really? How is this even possible?"

I hug him again. I missed him so much I can't let go yet. "I'm just so glad to see you and that you somehow found me."

"Me too. So tell me, what's going on? I've been worried sick."

I scan the area. We are tucked around the corner of an alley, unable to be seen from the street. I had already taken out my earpiece and left it hidden elsewhere. I keep my voice at a whisper even though I fear the one thing I need to hide from I can't.

"I think I'm in trouble, but I can't be sure."

"Tell me."

"It's like I'm missing pieces or forgetting things. But I'm made to feel like I'm not." I point to the corset and do my damnedest not to touch it. Any slight brush against it makes the doubts fade and feelings of well-being surge back through me. "I think this corset is somehow controlling me."

Jam makes sure to not touch it but holds me by the shoulders. "I don't think you're crazy about that. What do you know?"

With a rising wave of panic inside me, I tell him what I remember of the Shadow Fatale legacy. I can tell it lands like a punch to his stomach. He braces himself against the concrete wall.

"Once I found out you were the Shadow Fatale, I did some hardcore research," Jam says. "Did you know that it was Madsen's grandfather who discovered the material? No one knows how he found it, just that he was the only one to work with the Shadow in the beginning. Then it was Madsen's father, then Madsen. You say they describe it as alien material?"

I nod.

"You don't think that it's actually, you know, alive…do you?"

The very thought makes me want to throw up. That the very thing holding my body, my breasts and organs, is an alien alive and controlling me. I sway.

"Whoa there." He catches me. "Oh shit, that feels really weird." He flinches back from touching the back of the corset ribbons.

"What do I do, Jam? If the Shadow Fatale is so powerful, why have there been others before me? How have they died?" My voice is a breathless wisp.

"When you first called me, you said you were dying. What does that mean?"

"What? When did I call you?"

Jam's puzzled look increases my panic. "You don't remember? You tapped out a message for me. In our secret code? It took me forever to trace that signal."

I shake my head, my hand over my mouth. "I don't remember that at all. Oh God, Jam, you gotta help me. It's like welded to my skin. I can never take it off."

I don't remember ever seeing my friend look so helpless. "You said dying," he goes on. "But you didn't speak. Only tapped it out. Can't you remember anything?"

"No," I whisper. "And it's trying to fight me. I can feel myself not wanting to even think about the other women who were the Shadow Fatale."

"Defense mechanism. Like a parasite trying to stay undetected and keep its host alive."

I suddenly take my fingers and dig them into my skin. "I want it off! I want it off!"

No blood. No marks. Nothing. I am so damn indestructible, and so is the corset.

"If I die, Madsen will just put some other woman in the corset. He said it is a legacy, not a single woman." I let out a horrified laugh. "He doesn't care a thing at all about me."

Jam grabs my hands. "You know I care. I'm going to fight for you, Chloe. We'll figure something out. Promise."

Per Jam's suggestion, I document every moment of my day, and I discover the holes in my memory.

My days of recovery grow longer. Madsen keeps me at arm's length. His eyes have a distant haze over them. I start plotting my escape. I keep in touch with Jam through it all, but he stays secret about his side of the details.

I wait with tingling nerves and a thirst for battle.

When the techies scramble with cries of exclamations, I know it begins.

"Shadow! To the air!" someone says in my tiny headset. I can hear them fixing their communication unit to their head. From the tone of the voice, I think this is Alan. He's been on other missions with me, and I like him well enough. He reminds me of Jam.

I run from the training room where I was doing some workout combos with swords. I leave the swords behind. The Shadow Fatale could kill too easily with swords. Various employees duck out of the way as I race down the halls.

My invisible fly-out doors spread in front me revealing blue afternoon sky. My feet leave the ground, and I fly. "In the air, Alan!" I confirm.

"Big time breakout in Midland City. A bunch of criminals are loose. Time to round them up. Know where you are headed?"

A cold thrill shoots through me. So that is Jam's master plan? It seems daunting, but I feel power course in my veins. The Shadow Fatale can definitely bring them all to justice. The feeling will be delicious.

That is the worst part of all of it. I know now these thoughts are not mine anymore. Alien thoughts.

I keep flying.

Midland City is my city. I once knew every corner, every crack in the street. From cloud level, it looks so different. Homesickness hits me hard.

"How many prisoners unaccounted for?" I ask. I aim for

touchdown on my favorite rooftop hangout.

"Twelve. Put on your wrist unit, and I will upload the image data," Alan says. "We are running a DNA scan of the area and looks like we have three men just two blocks south from you."

"On it." I run across the rooftop and jump from the edge. How exhilarating it is to be able to do this! Before I had to deal with rope or climb down fire escapes. I glance at the images on my wrist unit and smile. I remember these three from two years ago, having captured them myself.

The men take refuge in an abandoned brick apartment building. The building should have been torn down years ago. For the sheer hell of it, I slam my fist into the walls, knocking them to dust. "Oh boys," I call out. "Thought I was badass a few years ago? You should see me now."

I know I am not supposed to refer to my old identity, but like this building, today is the day it is all coming down.

Men skitter upstairs. They run on unstable floors as the first floor walls start to collapse beneath them. House of cards. I can't let them die though. Heroes don't kill people.

I fly though a crack in the floor and barrel into two men. Together we all go through the blown out window. I have zip ties on them before they even sit up. Behind me though, the building shudders and fully collapses. "Oh God."

One man left inside.

"Shadow, what is going on? Everything okay?" Alan's voice seems so far away. I yank the earpiece out and crush it under my boot heel.

I hurry to the building as two police cruisers pull up behind me with lights flashing. Ignoring shouts, I dig through the rubble. Heroes don't kill, I think over and over. What the hell did I just do?

I find one arm. No pulse. With a final heave, I push aside the debris, and the man's face is mangled beyond recognition. Dead.

A cop is just a few paces behind me, but I cannot face him. I instantly take to the sky, wiping tears from my eyes. As I fly, I see two silhouettes flying in the distance beside a helicopter. I had forgotten. This city now has the Fusion Twins to take care of it. They can help clean this up too.

Oh, but the urge to continue to fight is overwhelming me. The alien wrapped around me is pushing me. There is only one place I can go.

Jam's apartment balcony has more flowerpots on it than I remember. Probably from Tessa moving in. I hope Tessa is not there. I land and knock over some pink petunias. A shadowed figure steps behind the door.

I gasp. Madsen.

He jerks the door open. "Come in, Chloe."

His face is stone cold. I can't believe I ever thought this man gorgeous. There is blood smeared on his tanned arms. I lunge for him, but he quickly ducks out of the way.

"Where's Jam?" I snarl.

"Silenced. He knew too much about the legacy. You only have yourself to blame for that."

A dim light flickers behind him. A lamp on the floor reveals a thoroughly trashed apartment. The moment I see Jam's body, I run to it. His eyes, always so warm and full of humor, stare at the ceiling. Unblinking. "No," I whisper.

I whirl with fists clenched. "I'm going to kill you."

"You won't be able to. It's impossible."

I don't even let him finish before coming at him. But as I do, the stones in my bodice flash a deep red. I stop, held in some sort of stasis, completely unable to move.

"It knows who takes care of it. Who feeds it," Madsen whispers.

The corset binding starts its horrible squeeze.

"Why?" I wheeze with the last of my breath.

"World peace? Good of the many? Or maybe my family's own legacy. My grandfather discovered this material in space. Did you know my family was in space decades before the actual space race? This is all that survived. Now that is a legacy to protect."

He bends over me as I slump to the ground. "You were actually a good hero. One of our stronger ones. Lately the women have only been lasting a few months. It's as if this creature can't get enough."

As I struggle on the floor, my legs growing numb, I catch glimpse of JamJam's right hand. Clenched in it, a piece of tech I have not seen in a long time.

So this had been Jam's plan? My organs grind together, but I inch to him.

"Want to die in your friend's arms? How sweet," he says with disdain before bending down and putting a hand on the alien corset. Like he's petting it. "You may finish her."

I lean my head on Jam's shoulder, curled beside him. I hold his cool hand in mine. He left me the Infini-Field. Back when I had nothing but my force field powers, he had tinkered with this little gadget to help maintain a force field forever. Not that we ever got around to testing it on anything big. The goal was to see if it could sustain one of my force fields independent of me after I generated it, as a way to help me conserve energy in a big fight.

I don't know if Jam had an alternative use for it tonight, but I can think of no other way. Was this really his plan?

Right now, this damn corset is eating me alive. I feel the

internal pull of it sucking my energy. Soon I will be nothing but a husk in a superhero costume. If I make a force field around me though, enclose the Infini-Field with the corset, just maybe after the alien finishes with me, it will starve to death. Stuck in stasis forever.

It's my only shot. I smirk, and Madsen sees it. "What do you have to smile about?"

I have no breath, but I mouth it as I activate the force field. "My legacy, motherfucker."

Bone of My Bone, Flesh of My Flesh

Sarah Joy Adams

In the fall, the ships came back from sea. And every Sunday Reverend Slater, pastor of the First Congregational Church of New Bedford, prayed for the saved and the lost. Every Sunday, Abigail Prebble sat a little straighter, clenched her jaw a little tighter.

"We thank thee, oh Lord, for the safe return of the *Halifax*, the *Alice B.*, and the *All Found*. Creator of both land and sea, we commend to you the souls of those who have departed this life: Elijah Jenkins, Thomas Pratt, Josiah Brown, Oscar Dusquene, and all the crew of the *Princess Charlotte*. Be merciful, oh Lord, to those they leave behind and continue to watch over those who have not yet returned."

Abigail bowed her head and breathed out an "amen." Her corset stays prodded her upright, reminding her to keep a straight back. The two front busks flattened her well-padded rib cage. She'd worn out more than one corset in twelve years of marriage, but she'd always kept these particular busks.

Abishai had carved them from a whale he caught himself when he was still only a harpooner. He might be a captain and one-eighth owner of a whaling ship nowadays, but the two busks were still the sweetest present he'd ever made her. She laid one hand against her ribs as she leaned back in the pew. She couldn't feel the delicate scrimshaw under the layers of poplin and cotton lawn, but she knew its outlines well. On one a tangle of roses tinted with red and green ink held a heart containing her initials and his. On the other Abishai had carved their wedding date under two turtle doves holding a rib between them that read "Ruth 1:16."

In the pulpit, Rev. Slater was waxing eloquent on the subject of Job and the leviathan, but Abigail fixed her mind on the sea. Come home, Abishai. Find your leviathans and come home.

On her way out of the church, Rev. Slater squeezed her hand. "You are in my prayers Mrs. Prebble."

"Thank you, pastor," was all she would allow herself to say. She nodded to the other women, alone and draped in black, or dressed in their Sunday finest and clutching a husband's arm. As she did so, she kept her head high.

At home, in the tall yellow house Abishai had built at the top of the hill, she sat alone in her parlor, her rocker turned to look out at the sea. Even when he was ashore, Abishai wanted to be close to the sea.

"To catch whales," he liked to say, "you have to think like a whale."

"This house is a whale," she said to the empty room. "I feel like Jonah, rattling around inside it." She pushed herself out of the rocker and sat down at the small upright organ with a flounce of petticoats and bending hoops. Practicing hymns didn't count as work, surely. But the groaning notes of "Rock of Ages" made her think of rocky coasts and hidden shoals, of sea changes in deep trenches. Her hands stilled on the whale-ivory keys. They had been inside a living creature once. Perhaps they remembered the deep.

Abruptly, she got up. Sabbath or no Sabbath, it was no use

sitting idle all day. She was rested enough. She went in the kitchen, on the land side of the house, and made vinegar pies. The Reverend and his wife could have one, as well as the Jenkins, Ellen Pratt, and the Browns. Young Betty Dusquene and her girls had already gone back to her people in Vermont.

She took special care to roll out pretty shapes for the top crust with her whalebone pastry roller. The pies kept her hands and mind occupied until the evening fogs rolled in and muffled the sound of the sea.

She ordered yellow paint to keep the house beacon-bright.

"White wash is cheaper," the grocer's clerk told her.

"I am aware of that," she said and looked him dead in the eye until he wrote up the order. Five buckets of yellow paint to be sent from Boston.

While the man she hired painted the house, she went into the back garden with Abishai's second best spyglass. Under the rose arbor made from a right whale's jawbone, she looked out to sea. It was a fine, bright day, especially for so late in the fall. A clipper rigged schooner tacked south against the prevailing wind. Distant twinkles on the horizon might have been the spray from whales.

"You'd get a better view from the Widow's Walk," the painter told her.

"I am not a widow." She straightened her back and smoothed the front of her dress. Whalebone under her fingers held her upright. She went back into the house and moved pots and pans around until it was time to give the man his lunch.

When she walked down the hill into town for the shopping, the bell of her skirts swayed, whalebone hoops moving in and out with the rhythm of her gait, beating time like a living heart. When she was young and wishing for a tiny Gibson Girl waist, Abishai would wrap his arms around her and called her his big-hearted wife. Such a big heart would never fit in a tiny body.

She sighed, a deep groan from the bottom of her lungs. Come back with the tide, Abishai. Follow the rhythm of my heart. She bought such things as she needed and lingered over hat ribbons in the dry goods store. Turning over blue-green grosgrain she wondered—how big is a whale's heart? Big enough, I suppose. Well then, she was big enough too. She put down the ribbon and thanked the clerk. Time to see to her true errand.

The Ship Chandler's was full of captains and mates. Some waited by the head clerk's desk, tally books in hand to settle accounts or dispute sums. Others sat around the pot-bellied stove, feet propped on biscuit barrels.

"…that son of Belial took my best harpooner to the bottom with him, and the ship's boy all in one."

A listener hit the spittoon without turning a hair. "There's not a New Bedford harpooner worth a tinker's damn. Bay o' Fundy men, now…" A sharp harrumph from a white-bearded captain cut him off. Men put their feet on the floor and lifted their caps. A few stood, albeit a moment too late.

She sailed past them with a pleasant nod on either side. That long at sea, a man might forget how to meet a lady. One had to make allowances. The smell of them was kindness enough— yellow soap and ship's tar, salt water and wet wool soaked through with rendered whale oil. The tobacco was wrong, harsher than the spicy leaf Abishai filled his pipe with, but if she kept her eyes forward and breathed in, he was there among them, unlit pipe clenched in his teeth, beard bristling as he prepared to defend the honor of New Bedford.

"This port is the whaling capital of the world, Lemuel, and you know it, or ought to. Besides which, there's not enough water in the Bay o' Fundy to drown a cat, let alone make a sailor."

She approached the Head Clerk, question and answer already on her tongue. "Any word?"

"Not today, ma'am."

"Thank you kindly, Mr. Baxter."

It was a rite, one that had to be performed, like the pagan Portuguese and their procession of the Virgin each spring.

She spoke her part. "Any word?"

"Yes, Mrs. Prebble. Just in yesterday."

"Thank you kindly…" She had already half turned to go before meaning broke through. Mr. Baxter held out a small oilcloth wrapped package. "The *Bowdoin's* mate brought them in yesterday to be held until called for."

She held the letters in both hands, paper crackling. "Are they still in port? When did they pass each other?"

"'Fraid not, Mrs. Prebble. The *Bowdoin* left on the 4am tide."

"Of course. It was a kindness of them to take the time. Thank you."

She ought to put the package in her market basket, not clutch it to her bosom like a girl of sixteen with letters from her sweetheart. But the best she could manage was to hold it tight in one hand against her corset stays. "Thank you," she said again.

But as she turned to go, a man near her said, "Mrs. Prebble, if I might have a moment of your time?" Lucas Burbank, half owner of the *Kennebec,* stood at her elbow. One hand on her back, he ushered her into the rear office and closed the door.

Two frock-coated men waited for her at a large table strewn with papers and tally books. They stood as Lucas Burbank held her chair. She took the seat, laying her hands over Abishai's letters on the table in front of her, but did not return the men's smiles. "What is this about?"

The oldest of them, a man with silvery white muttonchops and the soft hands of a man used to indoor work nodded at the younger man. Sandy-haired, his coat not as well cut as the others', the young man cleared his throat and said, "We understood that you usually come in at this time, and so we hoped to take a moment of your day to discuss your husband's share of the *Kennebec*. This is my employer Mr. March, the other majority owner of the ship. I am Charles Ramis, his clerk."

She sat up a little straighter and drew her mouth into a straighter line. "You will have to discuss this with Abishai when he returns. But I can tell you his answer already. He will be in no mind to sell." Abishai had wanted to be a part owner all the years he worked, coming up from second mate, to first, to captain, and finally to be able to buy a share in his own ship.

Mr. Ramis licked his lips nervously and said, "Without positive confirmation that the *Kennebec* has been lost, the coroner will not issue a death certificate until June. I'm sure this is as inconvenient for you as it is for…"

Mr. March cut him off with a sharp clearing of his throat. "What my clerk is trying to say is that we would like to help you by buying out your husband's share of the *Kennebec*. You have his power of attorney, so you need not wait until the sad processes of law are complete. This way all the troublesome business of probate court and insurance would rest on our shoulders and you need not be troubled with them. A woman in your circumstances might very well find such matters overwhelming. We should like to spare you that."

Abigail looked back and forth at the three men. Mr. March beamed at her between silvery whiskers and Mr. Burbank nodded gravely, like an undertaker, but the young clerk was blushing, his ear tips burning red. She folded her hands together carefully. "You are all very kind. But I find my circumstances quite tolerable, thank you, and I am happy to wait until my husband returns."

Mr. Burbank laid his hand over hers. "My dear woman, let us be realistic. No one has heard from the *Kennebec* in over a year. We understand your faithfulness. It speaks well of you, truly it does. But your lines of credit are becoming strained and your position is untenable. In light of that, Mr. March and myself are prepared to offer you a rather generous sum, payable in cash or as an annuity over the next three years, in exchange for your interest in your husband's estate. You could sell the house and move into a more suitable lodging in town, or perhaps go back to your family in Gloucester. I'm sure they would advise you to do the same."

"I'm sure I don't need their advice, nor yours. As for messages, I received a letter from Abishai just this morning." She stood up, pushing back her chair before any of the men could make it to their feet. "If you think I would sell my husband's ship out from under him, you are sadly mistaken."

More talk, all of them talking at her at once. Liens, insurance schemes, volatility of the market, her vulnerable place in the world. The men on either side of her swam in the edges of her vision, gray and black hulks. Someone ought to harpoon them and render their blubber down into something useful. She picked up Abishai's letters and shoved them into her basket.

"Mrs. Prebble, please," Mr. March said. He sounded like a schoolmaster with a backward student. "You are being quite foolish. Our agents have spoken extensively to others in the whaling fleet. We've sent inquiries to other ports all up and down the coast, as far as Charleston and New Brunswick. No one has seen your husband's ship."

"The whales have." She yanked open the office door hard enough that it bounced off the opposite wall. Men in the outer room gaped at her like cod on a deck, but she swept through the crowd, broad skirts plowing the way ahead of her.

She kept her pace all the way out of town and up the long hill to her beacon-bright house. But once inside, she locked the door with shaking hands and sank down onto the front hall floor.

By the time she finished reading the letters, the sun had gone and the evening fog rolled in. *Our hold is nearly full. One more whale and we turn for home.* The letter was marked May 1, 1842, Bermuda.

Repeating the words over to herself, she went into Abishai's study, where the huge map showed every shoal and narrow along the whole West Atlantic. After every voyage, Abishai took out his charts and his logs so that he could mark out where the whales were to be found. With a red pencil and the whalebone ruler, she put a small cross and the date on Bermuda and plotted the distance between it and New Bedford.

"One more whale. Abishai, where are you?"

She stood in front of the map tracing routes and kill sites with her eyes. So many of them between Bermuda and New Bedford. Where had all the whales gone? Had they warned each other he was coming?

Her heart beat against her whalebone corset, a slow, steady

push against its narrow cage. Its sound filled the house, struts and beams and hallways turning to bone and sinew and tubes. The house shuddered all along its length. A heart big enough for a whale. He only needs one more.

She shook herself and ran her hands down the front of her dress. No use imagining things. She ought to set the beans to soak for tomorrow and light the lamps.

Instead she went to the back door and opened it so that the fog flowed around her into the house. The bustle of the town below reached her, warped by the fog. Creaks and hums, low cries and high ones without words. Or was that the whales she heard?

She stood on the doorstep and breathed in the cold Atlantic. She swayed with the incoming tide, breathing in time with the waves, as her hair un-knit itself from its landlocked pins and flowed with the water. The whales swam past, darker shadows in the dark gray, their long bodies undulating.

She called out to them. "Where is he?"

One whale, older than the granite cliffs, eyes crusted with barnacles, turned its head toward her. It spoke in one long, wailing song that swooped from squeal to foghorn low. Come with us and see. The other whales answered it, squeaks and clicks and groans too deep for words that echoed all along her bones. Come with us and see.

She spread her arms, pushing herself through the water, buoyant, her weight now no hindrance, only ballast against the tons of water pressure all around, above, below. Show me where he is.

"Mrs. Prebble? Mrs. Prebble, are you home?" The wooden rattle of a door broke in on her. The old whale blew once through its blowhole and dove, its tail slashing the fog behind it. The rest followed, swallowed up in night.

Her feet scraped the wet step. She slipped, all balance lost against the sudden downward pull of gravity in the merciless, unsupportive air. She fell to her hands and knees on the cinder path. "Come back."

"Mrs. Prebble—are you well? Joan, perhaps you had better go in and see." It was the Reverend's voice.

Her knees and palm burned, throbbing in time to her rushing heartbeat. Blood oozed from the scrapes. Footsteps coming around the side of the house. She struggled to her feet, brushing the sharp black cinders off her palms and skirt.

"Dear Mrs. Prebble, what happened?" Joan Slater reached her before the Reverend Slater did.

"I'm fine. Thank you." She strained to see past the woman into the fog.

"My goodness, you're completely drenched."

"I'm fine." She hugged her arms around her waist, the firm lines of her corset holding her in. "I heard something in the fog and went to see. The step is wet." She gestured behind her. Her hands were shaking, numb with cold. But she wanted that cold back, the constant steadying pressure of salt water and the whole Atlantic in which to roam. "Do whales talk?"

Reverend Slater took her by the elbow. "Come inside, Mrs. Prebble, and Joan will make you some hot tea."

"Why are you here? I mean—" She leaned a hand against the doorframe, needing the sense of dry wood beneath her fingers, blocking the doorway. "To what do I owe the pleasure…?"

"We were just paying a sympathy call to poor Mrs. Pratt and we felt it was our duty to visit you as well."

Joan Slater kneaded Abigail's damp fingers between her own. "How are you enduring, my dear?"

She drew herself up to her full dignity, despite the way her hair hung about her face like kelp. "I am quite tolerably well, thank you. I expect Abishai will be turning for home shortly, if he has not already."

The minister and his wife exchanged looks. "Perhaps we ought to go into the house so you can sit down and warm yourself."

Abigail forced herself to stop looking past them into the fog for movement. "Thank you so much for your call, but I must be going. Tomorrow is my washing day. Excuse me." She stepped backwards and shut the door in their faces. She stayed there, hand tight on the door handle until she heard them walk away.

Afterward, she pulled herself upstairs to bed, her soaked skirts dragging her down with every step. She hung her clothes by the fire to dry, but the busks of her corset she slid out of their pockets and held tight in her fist while she dreamed of deep ocean.

All the next morning she kept to the landward side of the house, elbow deep in hot sudsy water. But the whales' call stayed with her. When she could not avoid it any longer, she took the wet linens around to the seaward side of the house and hung them on the line.

It was an unusually sunny day for November and the wind blew hard onshore. The white sheets billowed in the wind, snapping and ruffling like sails. Her fingers and ears reddened in the bracing cold. When she closed her eyes and held her face up to the sunlight, she could believe the night before had only been a queer turn, a fancy. After all, people imagined things in the fog. Old sailors were full of stories about what might happen in a dead calm fog.

But when she turned her eyes to the sea, its waves black and green under the bright sun, she couldn't sustain the lie. She drew in a deep breath. Well then, she would go and find out. She put on her best hat and gloves and set out for town.

She kept a sharp pace all the way to The Ship Chandler's, but when she laid her hand on the brass door plate, she hesitated. She knew a few of the captains inside from church and they knew her.

Hartwell and Evans, especially. They were strict Bible men who preached to their crews each Sunday at sea and allowed no foolish talk or gossip. What would they say to her but that she ought to busy herself with sensible work and prayer? Or worse, that Abishai's wife had lost her nerve and her mind. Head full of superstitious fancies. And that, gentlemen, is why it is folly to take a woman to sea. They are, after all, the weaker vessel. She pursed her lips, gloved hand still on the door handle. She minded very little what these men might think of her, but it would wound Abishai to hear her talked about. He was a proud man, after all.

"'Scuse me, ma'am." A ship's boy squeezed past her through the door. She pulled her hooped skirts aside, turning her head to hide her face in the depths of her coal scuttle bonnet.

Well then, there were other men and ones who might take her question seriously. She held her hem above the mud and turned down the nearest alley to the docks. The space behind the Chandler's was a tangle of barrels and old rope, ripped nets and crates. If the inside of the chandler's office smelled like whale oil and salt biscuits, the back smelled like fish heads and the mud left behind at low tide. Other men, men without captain's hats, sat or stood in the lee of the building, out of the wind.

A threesome threw knives at a target chalked into the side of a barrel. Others sat knitting lobster pots or darning socks. One man in a green wool jumper was carving a whale's tooth. She stood there, waiting for one of them to notice her, perhaps offer her a seat, but they only went on with their tasks.

"Excuse me," she said. "Have any of you gentlemen been to sea?"

The knife throwers paused in their laughter and turned her way. The man with the whale's tooth looked up at her as if she were daft, or just very slow. "Aye. We have," he said.

"I'm Captain Prebble's wife."

"We know." He went back to his carving. He had a gold ring in his ear and an anchor with a rooster on the back of his left hand.

She opened her mouth to ask how, but one of the lobstermen shifted his pipe to one side of his mouth to say, "The New Bedford fleet's not so large we don't know when one of our own is gone."

"So you've given him up, too?"

The lobsterman raised his eyebrows. But he moved his pipe back to the front of his mouth and said nothing. Others looked at the ground and shuffled their feet.

"What was it you were wanting, Mrs. Prebble?" the carver asked.

"I wish to know if whales can talk."

The men shifted on their seats or cleared their throats and rubbed hands over their chins. But the man carving the tooth said, "No. But they do sing. I've heard them. Some of it high and sad like a baby crying, some of it so low you feel it all along your bones. The mothers sing to their calves and the big 'uns, they sing back and forth to each other."

She knit her fingers together. "What do they sing about? Can you understand them?"

A few of the men snorted and elbowed each other, but the carver looked up and glared at them. "No, I've never known a man who could tell you what they meant. Much the same things we do, I imagine. But from a whale's eye point of view. If anybody knows where your husband is, they do."

"Thank you."

All the long walk home, she trudged, ribs straining against the confining corset stays, panting as if she were walking through wet sand. The evening came with the fog. By the time she was within sight of the house, the land below her was covered in a rising tide of gray. The yellow house shone in the sunset. She stopped to breathe a moment, puffing and blowing. It was good to get a last look at the house. The fog caught up to her and flowed past.

Well, no time like the present. She had things to do while the light lasted.

In the kitchen she took the pot of beans off the stove and dumped them into the slop bucket. Pity to waste them, but better than leaving them to fester. She damped the fire with water and left the firebox door open. She collected the whalebone pastry cutter in her apron pocket.

In the parlor she pried up each whale-ivory organ key and popped out the whale-ivory stops as well. They went into her apron pocket with the pastry cutter. In Abishai's study she sat down at his desk and wrote a brief note to her sister, wishing her well. She dropped the key to the house in the envelope, sealed it, and laid it on the blotter where it would be seen. Probably by Joan and Reverend Slater, though maybe not. She doubted March and Burbank would come up the hill to inquire, though they might send their clerk. Well, he looked like a trustworthy enough young fellow. He'd had the decency to blush at least.

In the very last yellow beams of sunlight, she gathered up the pieces of scrimshaw Abishai had made or collected over the years. Teeth, pieces of whale rib mostly. She didn't forget the ruler or the small white chessmen that had been a gift when he was first made a captain. They too went into her apron pockets to be returned to their people.

The fog tide had come in, higher than the rooftop now. She hummed as she walked through the house, finding a piece of whale ivory here, a knickknack there. Her song started out as "Rock of Ages" but turned into "vast, unfettered, boundless, free…"

At the back door she paused, still singing, to unpin her hair, the whale-ivory combs merging into her hands. She had the melody now and the low tones too. She pressed her hands over her ribs, lungs swelling, whalebone and flesh merging, the once rigid cage of her corset expanding, opening wider and deeper. She waded out into the fog, swimming, growing heavier, more buoyant with every step.

She passed through the back garden, kelp waving across her face. The sea roses turned into a tangle of starfish and anemones. She swept the curve of the jawbone arch with her. The sailor had been right. She could hear the song all along her bones. Miles out in the ocean others sang in return. Her lower limbs shrinking into nothing, a vestige, a faint memory in the bone, she swam over the cliff edge.

Lagniappe

A Storm and Fury Adventure

Gail Z. Martin and Larry N. Martin

"I've got to catch that train!" Agent Jacob Drangosavich of the Department of Supernatural Investigations opened the throttle on his steam-powered experimental velocipede, pushing the steambike to its limits as he raced to catch up with the locomotive.

All of his attention was focused on the train, and he willed himself to go faster, closing the distance between himself and the speeding locomotive.

Mitch Storm, his partner, was aboard that train, and he was counting on Jacob to back him up. The sound of a gunshot in the train's sole passenger car doubled Jacob's resolve.

That's got to be Mitch, Jacob thought. *Question is, was Mitch doing the shooting or getting shot?*

Jacob coaxed a bit more speed from the velocipede, despite its straining engine. He was gaining on the locomotive, close enough now to see the automaton in the cab, a metal man taking the place of a human railroad engineer at the controls of the train. The *click-clack* of the train on the rails drowned out the roar of Jacob's steambike, and the clouds of smoke belched from the locomotive's stack drifted between him and his quarry, partially hiding him from view.

"Come on, come on," he muttered to himself, pushing the

velocipede for every bit of power its engine could muster.

Jacob had a Peacemaker in a shoulder holster and another, less conventional weapon holstered at his hip. The Department paid the best scientists in the country a premium to supply them with top-secret, often one-of-a-kind weapons, tools and gadgets that made the stories of Jules Verne pale by comparison.

"Just a little more," Jacob muttered, crouching low over the velocipede's handlebars to reduce the wind resistance. The steambike edged nearer to the train, and Jacob grabbed his second gun, an odd contraption with a bulbous grip and a metal tube in the center of a coil of wires. Jacob veered his bike a few crucial inches closer, leveled his weapon at the copper-faced *werkman* at the train's controls, and fired.

The gun emitted an earsplitting whine, growing high-pitched and louder in a matter of seconds. Just at the moment when Jacob was sure his ears were about to bleed, the weapon fired and an invisible blast of force hit the automaton through the open window of the locomotive cab, putting a large dent in his metal head and slamming the mechanical man forward with enough impact to twist his frame.

"Damn!" Jacob gunned the velocipede one more time and gave a mighty leap, grabbing one of the handholds on the side of the engine and swinging up to the platform between cars. The riderless steambike veered off into a gully, sending up a puff of steam and a dark belch of smoke.

The downed automaton had fallen forward, keeping the train's deadman switch active while the train hurtled down the track. Except for his smooth, expressionless face and his mechanical body, the metal man resembled a real person in form and shape. "First things first," Jacob muttered to himself, keeping his gun in one hand as he approached the *werkman*. "Now, if this is one of

Farber's fantastic creations, the kill switch should be… here," he muttered to himself, opening a plate on the automaton's neck.

"Uh oh." Just as Jacob spoke, the metal man shuddered, and the boxy metal head turned to fix Jacob with a glassy stare.

The automaton stood a foot taller than Jacob and wider by half. It would have been a giant of a man, ham-fisted, like Casey Jones or Joe Magarac, the workingmen of legend. The metal man towered over Jacob as it regained its sense of purpose and glowered at him with red-lit eyes.

Whoosh. One huge metal fist swung and missed. Jacob dodged, fast as a first-night boxer. He felt the breeze through his hair and cringed at the sound of metal groaning with the impact.

Whoosh. Strike two from the other side grazed Jacob's face and sent him reeling, his head ringing and his left eye beginning to swell.

Metal Man was on his feet now, fiery gaze focused on Jacob, winding up for another try. *I won't survive another hit,* Jacob thought, desperately working to clear his thoughts as the *werkman* took a menacing step forward.

Jacob still clutched the force gun. He had no idea what discharging it at such close range would do since the gun hadn't been fully tested in the field. Yet, as he watched the hulking metallic creature begin to rise and took a second look at the powerful metal hands the size of melons, Jacob decided to take his chances on the gun.

"Nothing personal," he muttered, pulling the trigger.

The ear-splitting whine sounded again, right before a ripple of energy surged from the gun. The energy blast threw the automaton into the steel wall of the cab and out the other side, hurling him off the train to bounce along the rocky ground beside the rails until the metal man clanged to a stop in a dented heap.

Jacob flew in the other direction, thrown against the opposite side of the cab so hard that his vision swam and the breath was knocked out of him. He sank to the floor, winded, ribs aching. *That's going to bruise*, he thought ruefully.

Jacob climbed to his feet, moving over to the engineer's position, careful to stay clear of the ragged-edged hole where the *werkman* had been thrown clear. He peered down the track ahead of them, looked at the map of the rail route tucked into a corner of the engineer's cab, and nodded to himself. "Going in the right direction," he muttered.

"On second thought, maybe I won't drive," he said to himself, unfastening his suspenders and using them to keep the lever pushed forward so that the dead man's switch did not bring the train to a halt. "Carry on," he said, patting his rigged contraption before he prepared to make his way back to the passenger car. He made sure his guns were secure and began the climb over the coal car. As he reached the roof, he drew the Peacemaker and swung the door open to the passenger car.

Two shots rang out, one zipping so close to Jacob's ear that he let out a yelp and dropped to the floor. Before anyone could fire again, he dove into the nearest row of velvet-flocked seats for cover.

"Mitch?" he shouted, daring to peer above the seat long enough to see who was shooting. His partner, Mitch Storm, was hunkered down, crouched in the aisle of the passenger car where he could dodge behind the seats for cover. A man in a dark coat with a scarf wrapped around his face was standing near the back of the car. The man saw Jacob's head rise above the seat and shot. Jacob threw himself onto the floor, hearing the bullet hit where his head had been a second before.

"Took you long enough!" Mitch retorted.

"One-two?" Jacob yelled back.

"Gotcha!"

With that, Jacob stood up and began to shoot as fast as his Peacemaker could chamber the rounds, pinning down their assailant with steady fire. As he shot, Mitch dove over two rows of seats and hurtled down the aisle toward the dark-clad man who had to choose between returning Jacob's relentless fire or defending himself against the madman charging at him with a gun.

At the last second, the man turned as Mitch dove toward him, squeezing off a bullet that nearly parted Mitch's hair. Mitch leaped for the assailant and missed as the man stepped back through the door onto the open platform and touched the lapel on his coat.

With a muffled snap, a white parachute bloomed behind their attacker, jerking him back and upward as the chute caught the air. The gunman waved an ironic good-bye as he was snatched away and out of reach.

Mitch scrambled to his feet and ran onto the platform, spreading his feet wide and bracing his gun arm to shoot at their assailant, although the man was too far away to see whether the shots hit or not.

"I'm losing my touch," Mitch said in disgust, watching as the man's figure receded against the light blue sky.

"Did your training include having to shoot at parachute targets from moving trains?" Jacob asked, raising an eyebrow.

"No," Mitch snapped, holstering his gun impatiently.

"Well then," Jacob replied with a shrug. "There you have it. Exceptional circumstances. Even so, you winged him."

"Yeah, well," Mitch grumbled, then looked at Jacob. "If you're here, who's driving the train?"

"Shit! My suspenders…" Jacob ran back toward the cab and over the coal car. The firefight had temporarily taken his attention away from the fact that the train was still rumbling at full speed down the track without an engineer. Mitch joined Jacob in the cab just as Jacob ripped away his makeshift tether on the dead man's switch.

"Suspenders?" Mitch asked incredulously. His hair, usually meticulously plastered with Macassar oil, was awry from the fight and climb over the coal car. There was also a rip where a bullet had torn through the outer edge of his coat's shoulder. "We've trusted our lives to a train run by a pair of suspenders?" He turned to look at Jacob and frowned. For the first time, he noticed Jacob's injuries.

"What the hell happened to you?"

"Just a little disagreement with the engineer," Jacob said, and pulled on the lever with all his might. "You should have seen the other guy," he said with a nod toward the gaping hole in the side of the engineer's cab.

The engine slowed, grinding to a halt. Jacob let out a long breath and drew his sleeve across his brow to mop the sweat. Mitch bent over to examine the twisted steel where the automaton had torn through. "One of Adam Farber's creations?" he asked.

Jacob shrugged. "A poor copy, more likely. You know what they say. Imitation is the sincerest form of flattery."

Mitch gave him a level glare. "Unless someone is imitating a *wunderkind* boy genius and his mechanical marvels," he replied. "Then imitation is the shortest route to the nearest cemetery."

Jacob slapped Mitch on the shoulder. "Lighten up. We made it this far, didn't we?"

Mitch and Jacob had been friends since their Army days back during the Johnson County rancher wars. They could not have been more different. Mitch Storm was a few inches shorter than Jacob with a compact, athlete's build and a five o'clock shadow that started at three. An Army sharpshooter, Mitch's cockiness was rivaled only by his ability, and his uncanny talent at annoying authority figures.

Jacob Drangosavich was tall and blond, with a long face and hound dog eyes. He spoke most of the languages of Eastern Europe fluently and had a talent for blending in that made him a perfect choice for undercover work. After a stint in the Army, both men had been recruited by the Department of Supernatural Investigation, a secret branch of the intelligence community dedicated to investigating the threats and unusual occurrences that defied rational explanation.

"Did you get what we came for?" Jacob asked, turning to Mitch.

"Didn't really have a chance to look—getting shot at and all," Mitch replied drolly.

"Someone's bound to show up sooner or later, and we'd better be gone when they do," Jacob replied. "Let's get going."

Mitch swung the door open to the passenger car, noting the bullet holes with a grimace. "There wasn't anyone else on the train," he said. "Just the engineer and Mr. Personality," he added, referring to his adversary.

"Was it Dallinger?" Jacob asked.

Mitch shook his head. "No. I got a good look at the shooter's face. Too young, wrong build—not the kind of thing you could fake, even with talent." He looked around the empty, damaged passenger compartment. The Pullman car was opulent, with burgundy velvet upholstery, brass fittings and flourishes, and rich wooden inlaid panels on the sides of the car. It was the type of accommodation only the very wealthy could afford, men like

Horace Dallinger, who made his fortune in patent medicines and a series of risky, questionable, and borderline illegal business schemes.

"Do you even know what we're looking for?" Jacob asked as Mitch led the way into the ruined passenger car.

"Not exactly," Mitch admitted, though the admission did not signal a lack of confidence. "It's here. Dallinger sent his personal train to pick up the Morrigan treasure."

Bart 'Blackflag' Morrigan had been the most successful blockade runner of the Civil War. His mad risk-taking, close scrapes, and fearless defiance of the Union Navy running illegal cargo into and out of the Confederate states were legendary, and grew with the telling.

"Ah ha!" Mitch spotted a small wooden crate on the rearmost row of seats.

Jacob frowned. "That's it? Looks rather small, don't you think?"

Mitch grinned. "If it's filled with gold, it doesn't have to be large." He went to see how heavy the crate was and looked utterly flabbergasted when he lifted the box easily.

"Not gold," Jacob observed. "Or else someone already stole what we came for."

Mitch set the box down and shook his head. "I don't get it. Our intelligence was dead certain that Dallinger was moving the treasure." He sighed. "Let's open it up and see what we've got, since we wrecked a train—"

"—and another velocipede—" Jacob supplied.

"—and another velocipede," Mitch repeated, "to get it." He went back to the cab and returned in a minute with a small crowbar, prying the wooden lid open. Inside was an oak chest battered with time and darkened from exposure to the elements.

He and Jacob peered at the chest.

"Looks old enough to be the real thing," Jacob said.

Mitch nodded. "Let's see what's inside." He lifted the chest out of the crate and picked up the crowbar to break the lock, but the lid opened easily and fell back to reveal a tattered satin lining.

"No doubloons," Jacob observed.

Mitch frowned, reaching into the box and removing the items one at a time. "One stack of old letters, tied with a ribbon," Mitch reported. "A nice opal necklace, ring, and set of earrings, a fancy corset, and a steamboat ticket," he said, staring at the chest in disappointment as if it were coal in a Christmas stocking.

"What if that's not the treasure?" Jacob mused.

Mitch glared at him. "Of course it's not the treasure! It's a bunch of junk! We are going to be in so much trouble with Headquarters—"

"You didn't let me finish," Jacob replied laconically, used to Mitch's outbursts. "What if it's a clue to find the treasure? What if Morrigan wanted to hide his map in plain sight, and we have to figure out a puzzle of some sort, with these objects, to get to his money?"

Mitch took a deep breath and slowly nodded. "Could be. Maybe. Everyone said Morrigan was a crafty bastard, and more than a few stories say he learned black magic down in the Caribbean."

"I heard that too," Jacob said, eyeing the objects as if they might bite. "Folks said black magic gave him his good luck— until his final run."

Blackflag Morrigan ran his own version of the "triangle trade" during the war and charged exorbitant prices to compensate for the insane risks he took. A desperate Confederacy gathered jewelry and silver place settings plus all the cotton it could spare to raise money and entrusted the cargo to blockade runners. Morrigan and the others like him ran small, fast ships past the Union naval blockade to sympathizers in Nassau, Bermuda, and Havana. On the return trip, the blockade runners brought the guns, coal, cloth, gunpowder, blasting caps, sugar, and rum that were in short supply in the Confederacy. It was a lucrative business, but fraught with dangers, and most blockade runners ended up in prison or at the bottom of the Atlantic.

Gather it up and let's get out of here. Kennedy's going to be here any minute," Jacob said.

Mitch grabbed the chest, leaving the larger crate behind, and the two men made their way to the rear of the car. Jacob poked his head out, gun drawn, in case Mr. Personality had doubled back, but he saw nothing but Louisiana scrubland, stretching to the horizon. "Clear," he reported, as Mitch emerged with the chest.

Right on time, a small airship was heading their way, gliding above the ground, casting a cigar-shaped shadow like a steampowered ghost. The name *Bienville* was clear on her rudder. Jacob waved his arm, the all-clear signal, and the airship gradually descended until it was about thirty feet off the ground. A rope ladder dropped out of the cargo bay, along with another rope and a net bag for the chest. Jacob and Mitch secured the chest and then climbed up, and the airship began to rise as soon as they and their prize were onboard, with the cargo hatch closing automatically.

"Nothing blew up. You boys are slacking." Agent Della Kennedy strode back to the bay to meet them.

"Who's flying the airship?" Jacob asked, skeptical after their run-in with the automaton on the train.

"At the moment, that difference engine your *wunderkind* inventor gave us," Della said off-handedly.

"You mean there's no one on the bridge?" Mitch said.

Della shrugged. "I wasn't planning on staying for a round of poker. Just making sure you made it in without bleeding all over my ship." Della Kennedy was just an inch or two shorter than Mitch, with the piercing blue eyes and dark hair of her Black Irish heritage. The daughter of a general and the only girl in a family with nine boys, Della did not take guff from anyone. Since she could out-shoot almost everyone on the force, and out-fly them as well, most of the agents had made their peace with her presence, and those who harbored any resentment knew better than to say anything, especially if Mitch and Jacob were around.

"Get us out of here," Mitch said. "We can figure this out once we're back on solid ground."

Della gave him a devil-may-care grin. "Next stop, New Orleans," she said, heading back toward the bridge.

The triumph was short-lived. "We've got company, boys," Della shouted back to them a few minutes later. "Either of you feel like riding shotgun?"

Mitch and Jacob scrambled up to the airship cockpit. The *Bienville* was small and fast, not unlike the blockade runner ships Morrigan and his privateer friends had favored, and the Cutter-class airships like the Bienv*ille were* put to much the same uses as Morrigan's ship, the *Siren,* a generation before. DSI used the quick, less noticeable Cutters for reconnaissance, night raids, limited pursuit, and picking up or dropping off agents to hot-spot locations.

"I thought these ships had a crew," Jacob said as they reached the bridge.

"We do," Della snapped. "Oscar is down in the engine room. Clyde's my First Mate, and he's normally up here with me, but the boilers have been persnickety lately, and he's down helping

Oscar."

"I'll do the shooting," Mitch volunteered, opening a hatch and dropping down into a glass-and-steel gunner's bubble. He strapped in to the swivel-mounted seat and grasped the handles to the modified Gatling gun.

"Jacob—I need extra eyes," Della ordered. "There are two air sloops dodging in and out of the clouds, and I'd bet a month's pay they're after us."

Jacob nodded and grabbed the spyglass from the First Mate's station. "I'm on it," he said, going to his post.

The air sloops were even smaller than the *Bienville*, designed for one- or two-person crews, often launched from a larger ship for patrols. The sloops had limited range, but they were wickedly good at short pursuit and carried plenty of firepower. "Hang on," Della warned. "This isn't going to be the smoothest flight."

"You've got one coming in at ten o'clock," Jacob reported, working at keeping his voice impassive even though sweat beaded on his forehead. He had never gotten used to these new-fangled airships and preferred to have his feet firmly on the ground, or at least, in a good set of stirrups on a fast horse. "And another at three o'clock."

"Do not engage unless fired upon," Della snapped. "That's an order, Storm." She set her jaw. "I'd like to try to get out of here with my ship intact for once, if I can."

Della changed course, giving the sloops the opportunity to pass by without incident. When the two ships shifted their course to pursue, the game was on. "All right, Storm," she said. "Give 'em hell."

Jacob muttered a curse in Croatian under his breath, grabbing belatedly for a handrail as Della slewed the ship around to face their attackers, making their pursuers the pursued. "Are you crazy?" he yelped, nearly losing his balance as the airship rocked.

"Probably," Della agreed. "But I am not running from gnats. Storm—take them out!"

Mitch opened fire, raking the air with the sharp *rat-tat-tat-tat* of Gatling fire. The sloops shot back, and Della put the *Bienville* through a series of tight turns and altitude changes that left Jacob struggling not to lose his lunch.

"Shoot the ships, not the clouds!" Della shouted. Mitch muttered something in reply that Jacob did not quite catch, probably for the best. A stray bullet from the attackers cracked one of the bullet-proof glass panels in the airship bridge, and Jacob gave a startled yelp.

"Sloop One is going high," Jacob reported. "Sloop Two is going low."

Della pulled back hard on the controls, so that the Bienville's tail sluiced around to set the airship on a perpendicular course away from the pursuing sloops. "I don't have to play the game by your rules, buster," she said addressing their pursuers, a look of fierce determination on her face. Mitch swiveled so that he kept Sloop Two in his sights, and bursts of gunfire vied with the whine of the *Bienville's* straining engines.

"What in the Sam Hill are you doing up there?" Oscar's voice carried through the speaking tube from the engine room. "Are you trying to kill us all?"

"Just keep those boilers boiling," Della called back. "Give me all you've got."

"The *Bienville* wasn't really built—"

"I don't care what she's built for. You've got to get us a little more speed."

"This is as fast as she'll go," Oscar argued.

"Then get out and push," Della said, hunching over the

controls determinedly. Once again, the pursuing craft had to make a last-minute adjustment to keep up with Della's changing course, and it brought the sloops perilously close to each other, nearly causing a collision.

"Yes!" Mitch exulted, as a burst of Gatling fire tore through the tail of the lower sloop, sending it veering away and out of control. Beneath them stretched swamps and the bayou, with its Cypress trees and black water. The enemy sloop dove for the ground, and Jacob lost sight of the craft as it crashed through the canopy below.

Mitch's triumph vanished as more gunfire sounded, zinging close to the *Bienville's* bridge and the underslung gunner's mount where Mitch hung suspended in mid-air. "Sloop Two is gaining on us," Jacob reported.

"Take us up—now!" Mitch shouted. Della pulled back on the controls with all her might, and the *Bienville* nosed upward, giving Mitch a perfect shot at Sloop Two's hydrogen-inflated main balloon envelope.

The explosion rattled the glass in the *Bienville* as Sloop Two became a fireball. The outer skin peeled back from the melting steel skeleton, raining flaming debris into the swampland below. "Got them!" Mitch yelled, as if anyone could have missed the conflagration.

"HQ is going to have my guts for garters," Della muttered. "We were not supposed to do anything high profile on this run."

Jacob sighed. "Seriously? Did they know Mitch was assigned? It's been relatively quiet, compared to the last time we went on a job."

Della raised an eyebrow. "The Department is still cleaning up the debris from that, and paying off witnesses," she replied archly. "I've been told that incident is going into the training manuals as a cautionary tale."

"And yet, here we are," Mitch said, climbing out of the gunner's mount. "So for all the gnashing of teeth back at HQ, they keep sending us out because we get the job done."

"Just get one thing straight," Della said, pulling herself up to her full height and looking Mitch in the eyes. "My airship is not expendable."

"Of course not," Mitch said with a smile that sank a thousand ships. "Who else would rescue us?"

Della turned away, muttering something highly un-ladylike under her breath, and Jacob rubbed his eyes. Mitch was smart, talented, and aggravating, not necessarily in that order, and Jacob had grown accustomed to the headaches—literal and metaphorical—his partner caused on a daily basis. He only hoped that the success of their mission would be spectacular enough to win them a pass—again—on disciplinary measures.

Della docked the *Bienville* at a field just outside of New Orleans, leaving Oscar and Clyde to see to the ship's maintenance. She joined Mitch and Jacob in the ship's small passenger area to have a look at the chest that had caused them so much trouble.

"That's it?" she asked, clearly skeptical that the item was worth the gunfight it had taken to get it.

"We think it might be a series of clues," Mitch replied defensively.

Jacob rolled his eyes. "Maybe. We're not sure. But that's more hopeful than assuming we've been snookered."

Della peered into the chest and examined the contents. "We'll have to have a look at these letters, and see if there's a connection to the ticket," she mused. Jacob knew Della would be champing at the bit to dig in, since she was a fiend for puzzles and often liked to have a try at working ciphers. She looked at the opal jewelry and frowned. "Pretty opals, but the settings aren't remarkable," she said, holding them up to the light. "Not the best gift, considering some folks think opals bring bad luck. Curious."

Della lifted the corset and let out a whistle. "Someone spent a pretty penny on this," she said, examining the fabric. "Whale bone stays, French lace, Chinese silk." She chewed on her lip as she thought. "Funny—why would someone spend a lot on a corset, which no one sees—except perhaps for Morrigan and his lover—and so little on the jewelry? Usually, people like to show off their money with their gems, not their underwear."

"You'd better hope that Jacob's right about all of this having something to do with Morrigan's treasure, because I don't want to explain a firefight over a corset to HQ," Mitch grumbled.

"Captain Kennedy, the ship checks out," Oscar's voice filtered through the speaker tube. "We're cleared to go ashore. Clyde and I will run the pre-flight maintenance, restock the boilers, and be ready to shove off anytime you want."

"Acknowledged," Della replied. She put her hands on her hips. "Well boys? What say we have a stroll down Bourbon Street and figure this out?"

While onboard the *Bienville,* Della had favored practical attire like modified bicycle bloomers and a jacket, but a more conventional traveling suit was required in public, even with New Orleans' *laissez bon temps rouler* attitude and even on the infamous Bourbon Street. It did not take much for Mitch to slip into his cover as a riverboat gambler, or for Jacob to assume the persona of an Eastern European gentleman. But, as usual, Della was vocal about her guise.

"Why do I always have to be the whore?" she groused as the three of them sashayed down Bourbon Street's crowded sidewalks. "Why can't Mitch take a turn? He's pretty."

Mitch choked and Jacob chuckled. "I'd rather not see Mitch in a dress, if it's all the same to you," he replied.

Della snorted. "There are all kinds of whores," she replied, and managed to bring a flush to Mitch's cheeks. "Personally, I think I could pull off the riverboat gambler look in a trice." Slim and athletic, with dark hair a bit shorter than fashion dictated, Della could probably pass for a young man, given the right suit of clothes, Jacob allowed. He avoided looking in Mitch's direction, unable to keep from laughing.

"First of all, our lodging is above a brothel," Mitch retorted, straightening his tie in an attempt to reclaim his dignity. "Since it's the one place that would permit us all to be alone together without raising eyebrows. And secondly, even here, it's the only cover that lets you have more freedom of movement than the 'respectable' ladies."

Della was about to reply when an inebriated well-heeled wastrel made a lewd comment as he passed by. Before either Jacob or Mitch could react, Della had grabbed the drunk, wheeled him up against the nearest storefront, and pressed a hidden dagger against his groin. "Say it again, and you'll be singing with the girls' choir," she hissed.

"Beggin' your pardon, miss," the man slurred. "No harm intended. Just don't rob me of my family jewels."

"Ix-nay on the iolence-vay," Mitch murmured as he and Jacob formed a human screen between Della, her victim and the passers-by.

Della turned the man loose with a shove that was a little more forceful than flirtatious, sending him reeling into the street. "Just having a little *tête-à-tête*," she replied. She glowered at Mitch. "It's what 'us' whore-types do."

The Department's idea of "hiding in plain sight" was to keep a room in Mahogany Hall, the well-known brothel in New Orleans's Storyville, run by the famed madam, Lulu White. The women of Mahogany Hall were famous for their beauty, and Jacob had to admit that the tales did not do them justice. Tall and short, light, dark, and in-between, White, Asian, Creole, African and Islander, the working women of Storyville's most prestigious brothel even included two curvaceous automaton prostitutes, for the adventurous.

Mitch was playing his role to the hilt, and a disconcerting number of Miss Lulu's girls greeted him by name as they entered. Jacob had the good graces to blush, just a little, and Della increased her swagger, lifting her head high as if in challenge.

Miss Lulu herself met them inside the parlor, a handsome mocha-skinned woman with dark hair and blue eyes. She wore a glittering necklace of sapphires and diamonds, and diamond teardrops dangled from her ears. "Oh my lands! Look at you. You look so good, I could just eat you up!" she said loudly, taking Mitch's arm and leading them out of the public parlor into her private office in the back of the house.

Once the door was closed, she dropped Mitch's arm and sat on the corner of her desk. "Well if it's not Storm and Fury, the *Sturm und Drang* boys," she said, making a play on their last names. "Tell DSI they're late with their rent," she snapped. "I could sell that room of theirs several times a night."

"My apologies," Mitch replied, still charming although he had eased back on the riverboat rogue act. "I assume we were on time with your pay?"

Miss Lulu's eyes narrowed. Jacob and Della knew the madam

had been on the DSI payroll as an informant for years, with ready access to some of the wealthiest, most powerful men in Louisiana. "Yes, my pay was on time," she growled.

"Then our credit should still be good," Mitch said with a smile. "Now, what do you know about Blackflag Morrigan?"

Miss Lulu raised an eyebrow. "Now there's a name. Bart Morrigan was trouble with a capital 'T'," Miss Lulu replied. "But he was also quite a gentleman, and he treated me and my girls like royalty."

"He was a patron?" Mitch asked.

Miss Lulu gave a throaty laugh. "Can't tell all my secrets; you know that. But I did know Bart—how don't matter none. Why do you ask?"

The last thing they needed was a massive hunt for whatever treasure Morrigan left behind. "The Department thinks he stole some of their equipment, and they want it back," Mitch replied.

That was true, to a point. Morrigan did a little piracy around the edges of his blockade running business, and one of the ships he boarded had belonged to a Department operative. The Department figured Morrigan either died with the plans he stole, or that he had sold the plans and so they deserved a chunk of his treasure in compensation.

Miss Lulu gave a knowing chuckle that sounded like whiskey and wet dreams. "You want his treasure? You'll have to get in line, boys. Everyone went looking for Blackflag's Booty when he died. So far as I know, he put one over on everyone. That was just like him. He probably started the rumor just to have everyone looking for something that didn't exist."

Jacob leaned toward Miss Lulu's views, but Mitch believed there was something to the treasure rumors. "We'll stay out of your hair," Mitch promised. "Just send up our meals and a little whiskey to wash it down with, and you won't know we're here."

"Humph," Miss Lulu replied giving him a gimlet-eyed stare. "You're full of promises, Mitch Storm. I had to have the whole room redone after your last visit, and we still haven't gotten the smell of smoke out completely." She wagged a finger at him. "It costs me business when we have to evacuate in the middle of the night. Some of those men can't go back to what they were doing when they get interrupted, if you know what I mean."

Della snickered. Mitch rolled his eyes. "I've got no intentions of blowing anything up this time," he said.

"You never do," Jacob muttered, just low enough for Mitch to hear. Mitch glared at him, then returned his attention to their hostess. "And when we get back to HQ, I'll get my friend in the office to speed up your paperwork."

Miss Lulu gave a nod. "All right then. Your room is ready, and I'll send up dinner when it's done." She paused. "One more thing—Old Blackflag Bart had a Creole woman he kept company with, don't know whether they were married or not, but she was his lady. She died when he was out on one of his runs, and he never got over it. Folks said they would see him, out at St. Louis Cemetery Number One, talkin' to her grave at all hours of the night."

"Thank you," Jacob said. "Do you happen to know her name?"

"Marie Doucet," Miss Lulu replied. "Her father had cane plantations down in the islands, and everyone said he bankrolled old Blackflag to do his blockade runnin', back during the War."

They thanked Miss Lulu again and headed for their room. Like the rest of Mahogany Hall, the room was lavishly appointed, as opulent as Hotel Monteleone in the French Quarter. True to its name, the mansion had mahogany wainscoting around the lower part of the walls, and watermarked green silk above, with molded plaster ceilings and a disturbing number of large mirrors. A four-poster bed—also mahogany—commanded much of the room, but there was also a sitting area with a red velvet couch, two brocade-upholstered wing chairs, and a small table for taking private meals. A crystal chandelier glistened with gaslight, as did two light sconces that dripped with faceted glass teardrops.

"Nothing but the best!" Mitch said, pouring them each a finger of Four Roses bourbon in Baccarat crystal glasses before dropping into one of the chairs. Della set the contents of Morrigan's chest on the table and accepted the drink, pulling up the other chair so she could study the items. Jacob sat on the straight-backed couch and joined Della in handling the items.

"Hand me the letters," Della said, and leaned back, sipping her bourbon, as she perused the stack of yellowed papers. She scanned one after another of the old letters, muttering under her breath, then rose and walked over to the ornate inlaid desk, spreading the letters out beneath the glow of the gas lamp. She plucked a pen from the inkwell and a piece of the scented stationary from the blotter, talking to herself in a whisper as she worked.

"Do you know what she's doing?" Mitch asked.

Jacob shrugged. "Code stuff," he replied, and sipped his bourbon. "I figure she'll tell us something when she's figured it out."

After an hour, Della set the papers aside with a triumphant smile. "Got it!"

Mitch raised an eyebrow. "You figured out the letters?"

Della shook her head. "No, but I figured out the codes. It's a Caesar shift cypher with steganography to make it more complicated. The steganography key is in the oldest letter by postmark," she said with a grin. "Tiny little dots that look like pinpricks of ink are under twenty-six letters. Their order gives us the outer ring on the Caesar shift cypher key. Plug in the regular letters they correspond to, and we get the message."

"Which is?" Jacob prompted.

"Opals and bay leaf, dress to kill, coins in the basement. Strong spirits open door."

Mitch gave her a skeptical look. "Are you sure that's what the code says? Sounds like gibberish to me."

"I'm sure," Della replied with a tone that said she was willing to fight about it. She riffled through the box to find the opal jewelry and the corset. "Now if you'll excuse me, I'm going to try these on, just because."

She shrugged out of the jacket to her traveling suit and sauntered over to one of the large mirrors that was nearly the size of the room's door. Della slipped on the opal necklace, adding the pendant earrings and the silver and opal ring. Then she held the corset up, turning to admire it from one side and another, then laced it loosely up the back and pulled it closed, tugging to fasten the hooks.

Della looked into the mirror and gasped. "Oh my God," she murmured. "Mitch, Jacob—do you see what I'm seeing?"

Mitch started to make a smart comment until he saw the stranger looking at them through the glass. "I see it," he said slowly. "Not sure I believe it."

Jacob crossed himself and touched the silver medallion that hung from a chain around his neck. "I see it," he said in a low voice. "Do you think that's Marie Doucet?"

"Strong spirits open the door," Della quoted. "Maybe Morrigan didn't mean liquor. Maybe he meant ghosts."

"Now you're talking crazy," Mitch said, but his voice lacked certainty.

Jacob stared at the woman in the mirror. She wore a dress that was at least twenty years out of date, and her center-parted dark hair was pinned up in the back with ringlet curls around her face, a style from a past era. She regarded Della quizzically, then turned to look at Mitch and Jacob, all the while giving Jacob the sense that the ghost was truly interacting and not merely a bit of stray memory, trapped in the aether. Before Della could react, the ghost reached out of the looking glass and her fingers touched the corset. The fabric ripped between the stays like a thin sheet of paper. With that, the ghost vanished.

Della was shaking. She went to the desk, downed the last of her bourbon, and sat staring at the mirror in shock. Her hands trembled as she unhooked the antique corset. The thin silk was shredded, revealing the whalebone stays that provided its structure. One of the stays fell out of the cloth into Della's hand, and her eyes widened.

"Scrimshaw," she said, staring at the narrow, yellowed piece of whalebone.

"What?" Jacob asked, moving quickly to stand beside her.

Della was already recovering from her shock. She had turned back to the desk and was tearing the old corset apart to pull its narrow, ivory-colored stays from their places. "Look," she said, pointing to the stays laid out on the desk.

Dark India ink stained scratches in the stays making scrimshaw, the artwork of seagoing men for hundreds of years. Etched into the whalebone were scratches that on each individual piece were unintelligible, but when the pieces were placed together, looked wholly different. "It's a map," Mitch said with surprise.

Just then, one of the servants arrived with their dinner. Bowls of fragrant étouffée in a dark brown roux, rich with fresh-caught crab and shrimp over rice, a bottle of red wine, and a pile of fresh, hot beignets covered with powdered sugar along with a pot of strong coffee with chicory made for a mouthwatering meal. As they ate, Della noticed a bay leaf in her étouffée and pulled it out with her spoon, dabbing it dry with her napkin.

"I wonder," she said, folding the bay leaf around the opal ring she still wore from the chest.

"Holy shit!" Mitch sounded shaken. "What the hell just happened?"

"Della?" Jacob called. "Della?"

Della looked at them as if they had both lost their minds. "What is wrong with you?" she asked. "I'm right here."

Mitch paled. "Are you? Because we can't see you."

Della unwrapped the leaf from around the ring. Just as suddenly, she reappeared exactly where she had been sitting before she vanished. "Okay," she said, drawing the syllables out and staring at the ring as if it might bite. "That was freaky."

"Black magic from the islands," Mitch murmured. "Maybe it was truer than people thought."

"The code!" Della said, and ran to the desk to grab the piece of paper where she had written the cryptic words. "Opals and bay leaf, dress to kill, coins in the basement. Strong spirits open door," she repeated. "Well, we know what happens with the first two," she said, giving a side-long glare at the bay leaf by her plate.

"Dress to kill," Mitch mused. "I've heard of women hiding a shiv in their corset, even a Derringer. And the whales are killed for their bone. The corset?"

Jacob nodded. "Strong spirits open door," he said thoughtfully. "Well, we've met a spirit, maybe of Marie Doucet. But what door does she open?"

"She ripped the corset to show us the scrimshaw stays," Della replied, more curious now than concerned. "Maybe if we find out where the map on the stays leads, we'll know more about the rest of the coded message—and what the number on the ticket means."

Together, they hunched over the desk as Della moved the scrimshaw stays around to recreate the map she had formed earlier, though the streets were not any Mitch recognized from New Orleans-proper. "Alley Number 24" he said, perplexed, searching a map of the city. "It doesn't exist."

"Here's another one: Alley Number 11," Jacob pointed out.

"Hold your horses!" Della said, pointing to another section of the inked stays. "Here's one at the bottom that says Conti Alley, and one at the top that's St. Louis Alley." Her eyes widened with excitement. "You're looking in the wrong place, Mitch. This isn't a map of the city of New Orleans. It's a map of a city of the dead—and I'll bet you all the beignets at Café Du Monde that it's Saint Louis Number One."

"So the number on the ticket, it's not a house number," Jacob said, not liking the direction the revelations were taking.

"Want to bet it's Marie Doucet's tomb?" Mitch's voice held a mixture of curiosity and horror.

"Coins in the basement," Jacob said, meeting their gaze. "There's only one kind of basement in a New Orleans cemetery, and that's a *caveau*."

The thought made Jacob shudder, and by the look of it, Mitch and Della were squeamish as well. New Orleans was famed for its above-ground family tombs. Most resembled small mausoleums, one drawer wide and two drawers high. A family would inter a loved one, allow the body to naturally cremate in the stifling heat, and when another family member died, the first body, now mostly dust and bone bits, would be pushed to the back, where it would fall down below the drawers into a small cave-like holding area—the *caveau*.

Della fixed him with a deadly glare. "You're telling me that we have to go to a cemetery and look for a treasure inside an old tomb?" she asked incredulously.

"With a ghost," Jacob added. "Remember—strong spirits open the door."

Della threw her hands into the air. "Seriously? You're really going to go through with this?"

Mitch shrugged, recovering some of his bravado. "The Department wants Morrigan's treasure, since it was earned by ill-gotten gains. And they'll forgive us our little dust-up on the way here if we deliver what we were sent to get."

Della sighed, knowing when to give up a lost cause. "All right," she said. "Let's make a plan."

"This is your idea of a plan?" Della said as she struggled to keep up with Mitch and Jacob along the deserted sidewalk. The items from Morrigan's chest were tucked in a small bag she carried beneath her arm. There was no fixing the corset, but they brought all the pieces, especially the scrimshaw-covered stays, which Mitch had managed to affix to a piece of paper with flour-and-water glue. The opal jewelry was in the bag as well, no doubt intended by Morrigan as a gift for his Marie, a gift she did not live long enough to receive.

"Yep," Mitch replied, now firmly back in charge despite any misgivings he might have felt. Jacob listened to the two of them argue, but he watched the night, concerned that the darkness might not be as empty as it seemed.

Mitch and Jacob both carried Peacemakers and Adam Farber's

experimental force guns. Della carried a Winchester rifle and what Mitch called a "Swedenborg Meter," a gadget that detected fluctuations in the aether common to ghostly sightings, named for the famed spiritualist. The contraption looked like a combination Edison cylinder and zoopraxiscope, and had a thick wire that led to a headset much like that of a telegraph operator, through which Della could hear the variations in pitch that supposedly indicated spectral activity.

Mitch picked the gate lock and gestured for them to hurry. "The Archdiocese is not going to be happy with that," Jacob observed, slipping through the iron gate.

"You never know. They've done business with the Department. We're all in this together," Mitch replied off-handedly, closing but not locking the gate behind them. Earlier that night, they had retrieved the velocipede Mitch left hidden beneath tarpaulins in the shed behind Mahogany Hall, and they had squeezed onto it for the short ride to Saint Louis Cemetery Number One.

"We're not alone." Jacob nodded toward where gaslights burned on one side of the cemetery, not far from where the scrimshaw map directed them.

"Let's see who's here," Mitch murmured. They made their way through the shadows, moving along the narrow gravel paths between the tombs. Some had elaborate wrought iron fences or were adorned with vases of fresh flowers, while other tombs were crumbling from neglect. Yellow Fever, Cholera, Malaria, they all left their mark, filling the tombs of New Orleans's cemeteries.

"Well, well," Jacob said quietly, inclining his head toward the group crowded around one of the tombs farther up the pathway. Banks of lit candles flickered in the darkness, and flowers, single and in bunches, were strewn in front of the tomb, which had been marked over and over again with the letter X. Even at a distance,

Jacob could see that gifts littered the edges of the tomb, and the small crowd of people who sang, chanted and danced ecstatically to the beat of drums were less like revelers and more like devout worshippers.

"Marie Laveau, the Voodoo Queen," Mitch said quietly. "Still has quite a following it appears." He gestured for them to slip down a parallel pathway, counting the tombs until they reached tomb number three hundred, fifty-eight.

"Here we are," Della said in a whisper, nervously rocking back and forth onto her toes. "Marie Doucet's resting place." She adjusted the dials on the Swedenborg Meter. Listening intently, she nodded. "According to this, the place is lousy with ghosts."

"We only need one spirit," Mitch said. "Let's do this and get out of here."

Della nodded and took the jewelry from the bag she carried, handing the Meter over to Jacob, who held it in his left hand so he could keep a gun in his right. She clasped the opal necklace around her throat, clipped on the earrings and put the ring on her finger. She gasped, and Jacob looked to her with alarm.

"There's something about the opals," Della said. "A connection with Marie Doucet's spirit. Like she knows the jewelry was for her."

"Can you see her?" Jacob asked. "Because this meter is going totally nuts."

"Yes," Della said, moving toward the tomb. "But how do we get her to open the door?"

Della had no sooner spoken than a gray shape appeared in front of the tomb, growing more and more solid into the shape of a woman. Before anyone could move, the woman grabbed at Della's jewelry, and the bricked-up and stucco-covered door to the lower tomb drawer shattered, revealing an empty niche.

Mitch dove for the niche, digging frantically in the gray dust and unnamed hard bits. The gray ghost's fingers tore at Della's necklace, snapping the chain, and an instant later, yanked the earrings from her lobes with enough force that Della cried out in pain. Jacob dropped the meter, since the ghost was clear to the naked eye, and leveled his force gun at the revenant.

"Leave her alone!" he commanded.

Mitch sat up, emerging from the tomb streaked with dirt but victorious, holding a small metal casket that was much heavier than its size suggested. "Got it!"

"I'll take that." The man's voice sounded behind Jacob. "Drop the gun," he ordered, poking the barrel of his six-gun between Jacob's shoulders. "You, too," he said to Mitch.

"Mr. Personality returns," Mitch said acidly. "Who do you work for? Dallinger?"

"None of your business," the stranger snapped. "I just came for the box. No one has to die."

Della vanished into thin air. Marie Doucet's ghost shrieked like a nightmare come true, speeding toward the attacker, hands outstretched. Jacob's gun rose by itself, hovering without visible means of support, and squeezed off a shot that caught Mr. Personality in the right elbow, forcing him to drop his weapon.

Marie Doucet's spirit was in a frenzy, attacking the newcomer with fury. Ghostly hands tore at his hair and clothing, opening long scratches on his face and neck. Mitch grabbed his force gun, but he had no idea whether it would temper the wild ghost's rage, or whether once Marie Doucet was done with Mr. Personality, she would avenge herself on them.

"Be still, my child." The voice came from behind Mitch this time, and Jacob looked up to see a dark-skinned woman standing just behind his partner. She wore her hair wrapped in block-printed cloth after the African fashion, a shawl around her shoulders and large gold hoops in her earlobes. A sense of power and peacefulness radiated from the figure, and as Mr. Personality dropped to the ground in a terrified, bloodied heap, the ghost slowly withdrew her vengeful attention from her victim and turned to look at the woman in the shawl.

"Your lover brought you a final gift," the dark-skinned woman said. "It's time for you to go to the gods child, and rest."

Marie Doucet's ghost nodded, and Jacob saw that somehow, the ghost now wore the opal necklace and earrings it had ripped from Della. Della was still invisible, using her bay leaf and the opal ring to hide herself, in case their new savior turned out to have ulterior motives.

"Take your treasure," the woman in the shawl said, her voice contemptuous, addressing Mitch. "It has troubled this place for too long. Take it and leave us in peace." She turned to the empty air next to Jacob. "Do not become fond of that bit of magic, girl-child," she said to Della. "It is dark power, and it cursed the one who wrought it. Leave it here, and be free of it."

Jacob blinked, and Della was visible once more. Moving slowly, she walked over to Marie Doucet's tomb and placed the ring just inside the open doorway. Jacob had already moved to secure Mr. Personality, in case fear of capture won over fear of the dead. Mitch rose to his feet, keeping a watchful eye on the woman with the shawl.

"Thank you," he said. "*Merci.*"

The woman inclined her head, and then turned and walked back toward the dancing crowd near the candle-lit tomb. The crowd, intent on their revelry, paid them no mind. As Jacob watched, the woman's shape grew indistinct, and then faded altogether before she reached the row of candles.

"You don't think—" he stammered.

"Was that who I think it was?" Mitch asked.

"We've got an airship waiting," Della said, glancing overhead as a dark shadow glided past the moonlit clouds. "We got what we came for, and captured a prisoner—a bonus. Consider that a *lagniappe*, a little something extra. Let's go home."

About the Editor

John G. Hartness sometimes finds himself at dinner with wonderful and creative people, and projects happen. This is one of those. John is also the author of the Black Knight Chronicles from Bell Bridge Books, the creator and co-editor of The Big Bad anthology series, the author of the Bubba the Monster Hunter stories, the Quincy Harker, Demon Hunter novellas, and the publisher of Falstaff Media. Because he hates sleep.

For more information, check out www.falstaffbooks.com.